Tenement of Clay

A novel by

PAUL WEST

Afterword by Bill Marx

McPherson & Company

This edition published by McPherson & Company, Post Office Box 1126, Kingston, New York 12401. [Originally published by Hutchinson & Co., Ltd., London, 1965.] Manufactured in the United States of America. Publication of this novel has been assisted by grants from the literature programs of the New York State Council on the Arts and the National Endowment for the Arts, a federal agency.

Library of Congress Cataloging-in-Publication Data

West, Paul, 1930-
Tenement of Clay : a novel / by Paul West.
p.   cm.
ISBN 0-929701-27-5 (alk. paper) : $20.00
ISBN 0-929701-28-3 (pbk. : alk. paper) : $12.00
I. Title.
PR6073.E766T4   1992
813'.54—dc20   92-16449 CIP

FIRST AMERICAN EDITION

1 3 5 7 9 10 8 6 4 2

1993   1994   1995

For
Sheila and Bill Forster

A fiery soul, which, working out its way,
Fretted the pigmy body to decay,
And o'er-inform'd the tenement of clay.

DRYDEN, *Absalom and Achitophel*, i, 156-8

If there were only darkness, all would be
clear. It is because there is not only darkness
but also light that our situation becomes
inexplicable.

SAMUEL BECKETT

Contents

LAZARUS

11

PAPA NICK

47

LAZARUS

203

Lazarus

———————

PARDON ME for interrupting whatever it is that you might
better be doing just now. Having got this far, I hope to grow
on you. The first fact, which you must not overestimate, is
that I am three feet five inches high. Such a height has advantages and, because I talk with no kind of an accent but recog-
nizably in an English sort of language, lets me pass among men
like a radio tube walking on its needle plugs. And, believe me,
I talk back. Even when I'm telling a story I talk back, quick,
just in time to knock the echoes back. It's all a matter of perspective: for toilet basins and washbowls I am lower, and to
whatever they contain or diffuse; I have it both ways because
I flatter high shelves by getting a ladder to them. Call me
navel-high if you like, or buttock-low: it's true. In baths I am
short, but when I play the slide game I can go right up the
back and slide quite a way until my feet hit the far end. I soap
my back hard as well as the slope of the bath back. And then
I go, like a wad of pulp shot from a potato gun.

At you, now, with this story which I tell because I cannot
quite understand it myself. My perspective, as I said, is wrong.
But every time I think about it I organize myself in readiness
for an understanding. First there is my three-part billiard-cue
which, unscrewed, disappears into itself and becomes a two-
and-a-half-foot-long baton of shiny black. This I put at my
left hand, having first carefully pushed it deep into the felt
cloth; otherwise it would roll. Then I put on my hat which has
an Eagle label inside; in this way, as I see it, I keep all the
blood in the lower part of my head. After this the ear-plugs

and the cigarette I never pull at after lighting it; it burns, balanced and re-balanced on the ashtray. I just wish I could plug up my mind too, because I don't want this story to give you the wrong impression of me. I'm no saint of any sort, but as you can tell I started with no advantages and at the age of nine had already lost upward dimension such as is free to any boy until twenty-one, they say. I mean of the anticipation of getting high.

So I should really first of all put you wise to the shocks so that you can give up now. It is not the nicest person who is telling all this. Now I was going to tell you how I have been a stoolie: people talk above me as if I am not there, but they see me climbing up to the phones. A good way I learned from a movie was this. Some guy had fallen into this pit, but he worked his way up and out by bracing his back and feet against the walls. Now speaking for myself, I am strong, which is what counts. So now I brace across the booth with the dime in my teeth. When it is not an emergency I use the phone books if they have hard covers and are loose. Some monster: either spanning the booth like a thick shelf or perched like the kids who stand on the walls of stadiums—too poor to pay. When I shoot pool or some other game on those lawny tables I perambulate by trolley. Once the wheels squeaked so much I had to leave the game to find oil; and believe me they shifted the balls around while I was away. But that is only because they cannot do it while you are there. I notice a great deal of ball-shifting from where I stand, such as other people quite ignore.

But I have been more than a stoolie. I have wrestled, which was very profitable until I cracked a rib through a miscalculated fall on to the concrete outside the ring. Or maybe it was ice at the Fig-Leaf Gardens. When you wrestle, the women pester you in your hotel. Some of them ask you to wear their snow-shoes—the elegant ones with the high thin heels. I once caught sight of myself in a mirror, stark naked and swollen with the black suède boots half-way up my legs. Before the session began, that is. I looked like Tom Thumb with a cloven hoof. My wrestling name was Pee Wee Lazarus, and my favourite partner, with whom I worked out some astounding fall routines, was called Elroy Kitchener. I don't know why, but there was some joke behind that name: his real name was Roger Briggs. Anyhow, what with being a stoolie and a sawn-off stallion and Pee Wee Lazarus as well, I made out and never needed to try this fairground stuff. You get enough insults, anyway. The injuries too are rough: dames swinging heavy purses into your diaphragm and guys with pockets full of keys and cash, both hard, belting you on the side of the head as they race for the subway. Sooner or later, then, you learn to retaliate. You carry a long pin in the big stores and puncture them in the convex. You learn how to mix a very bad spittle, cache it in the side of your mouth and then launch it hard at the backsides. One of my best tricks is to wear a very old jacket with shoe-whitener smeared specially on the shoulder. You then pick on some guy in a dark suit and contrive to rub your shoulder against his fly. That mess you leave behind is very suggestive. But I don't really like to get my own back and all that. As you will have noticed, I think, I am educated beyond my stature, which I have managed to do by reading and thought. Instead of over-using this revenge routine, I take things out in the bath. It is more civilized. I soap my belly, which is hairy as one of those black caterpillars you see on the sidewalk, until the sudding is really thick. Then I slap my palm down and the white curd flies while I yell. This not only releases me but keeps the paunch down. I have faced so many paunches, corseted rolls and wobbling cliffs of fat.

So you can see what I have been. What I am will come out as I go, because that is part of the idea. I am not supposed to know that I am exposing myself just as some guys in the Park on Sundays never know it. But I do and the pen is dipped in shame. So all the drink, graffiti-writing, dandruff-collecting, toenail-clipping saving, ear-picking, food-fouling and God-affronting cheating will come later. You can guess how bad I have been as well as how bad I think I have been when, in fact, I have only been having fun. When a man goes to all the trouble of emptying a can of minestrone (mynestroan, some of them call it) and filling it up again with dead mice before having it re-sealed by a friend at a canning plant and then planting it back in the supermarket after first buying the one he replaces—well, there is more to be said. And I have made a few speeches too: all stopped before I could finish. Have you ever talked to yourself with your head at table-level? Well, don't. Every time you shout, the noise seems to bounce back at you from the table-edge.

This city, then, that you all know—where you must curb your dog and walk now and not turn left here and certainly not expectorate—well, I am calling it New Babylon. Take that or leave it. Fill in or give up. Signs everywhere are rude; except in England, they say, where 'please' is written. In trains in Europe they have a sign forbidding smoke; after some guy told me this, I tried it out. Walked down the New-Craven Failroad's trains when I commuted, shouting NICHROWK at all the commuters' faces. Boy, did they stare, and the educated ones stubbed out their smokes in case the boss was testing them for charity. Indulging the dwarf and all that crap. You never know who is not trying you out for charity to the undersized: like the big dogs who arch their backs so you can walk underneath. I personally always walked round the beasts. So, New Babylon, which is more city than one, but the same to me. Same sidewalks, currency, manners and rancid-smelling nether parts. I could tell some stories, but not during this one.

From all this you would think it is a city without beauty. Not so. I have followed women for miles; when they spot you they stand and laugh (always the most wounding response) or shout loud enough for God to stop his ears: 'Hey, you walked under a low bridge or sumpn?' 'Go buy a stilt and come back in two years!' And other things. But some of them take you home for a drink and a talk and sit you on piled cushions naked while they take those instant photographs with electric cameras. I tell you I am nowhere near half as stunted as some of them. It was worse when I had a beard because what they proposed I did with my beard for a few dollars is unspeakable; in fact I only just allow myself to remember it at all. One fat executive asked me to dance on his stomach, which I did; and it was like stomping on a mattress. You could feel the muscle-thongs resisting. But I was talking beauty. You will have noticed by now that I tend to say 'you' when I mean *I* have done something disgraceful. Well, that is my weakness but also my strategy because I want to involve you too. And you are all easy to involve, even at my level.

Back to beauty, and not that which you get on the surfaces.

I mean deep inside, like why God made us at all and why He made us as He did. I mean in particular this guy and what He did for this poor slob, this poor slobbering lump of person He found one day. It had been snowing and the stuff crept up on to your shoes like small flowers at the welt. I had just left the gymnasium after a two-hour workout with the weights. Those were my wrestling days. Usually I went down the main avenue and turned right at 119th where there was a house I was welcome in. That was Papa Nicko's place where all the bums gathered and slept and drank. Sure they made fun of me but they also listened to me talk. Anyway, I walked down there, making my toes crouch in my shoes from the cold and hardly daring to step on the new snow. The building was an old brownstone, now gone, and you approached it through a frenzy of neon—about men using versatile new resins in new ways, pushing this button rather than that, wearing this wrinkle-free shirt all day, discovering how this whisky tasted the way more people want their Scotch to taste, how that bug-killer annihilated, and plaid shirts for golf and reduction of brake-fade and sips of liquid gold of the fine Italian liqueur that conquered America. The cars crunched and they spewed sour gas. The other people—or should I say the people—zig-zagged so as to avoid snow. They always tried to step on the black, wet patches as if afraid of the new icing.

So, on past the colours, which were already blurring in the uptown fog and the mid-afternoon light, to the right turn. And you went right, into gloom. Past three brownstone houses and there was the phoney façade with the phoney-looking pillars on either side. It was not, as many people thought, any kind of whorehouse, although some had used it as that and were in fact using it like that even when the demolition had begun. It was not like those TV shows when they welcome three *interesting* guests in case you never realized; it was like the new coffee with the stars on top, but in the old pack, with the old brand inside. And the old brand was the men I cannot rightly name, any more than I can Papa Nicko rightly because we variously called him Nick, Papa, Nicko, Papanick and, because of his head, the Buzzard. The head I have to explain. It was long; it went a long way back after the bald front and the nose drooped, hooked suddenly almost as if it were aching to drop off. But the man was not what the dictionary of birds says. No great variation of plumage in him, except the hair disappearing and the skin yellowing. Sluggish and inactive: but only if you didn't know him well or watch him close. He never seized a victim; he never had a victim. But he certainly did, as the book says, ascend to a great height in the air not to swoop on mice, adders and so on, but to ponder. The nest, so the book says, is rough, and it was; and as many as thirty field-mice have been taken from the crop of just one bird. If we were the mice, then that is right and a little on the conservative side. He gathered men in. There was a girl too, a crazy Jewish girl who had come out of Buchenwald into a random marriage of surviving parents. She wandered in and out, combing her dirty hair while she walked. Another woman came there too—a wealthy woman with a noble curved nose and a black hat with two marionettes of porcelain pinned on. She was the other side of Papa's life, the mink unscarred by bums' binges but taking us all for granted. And by granted I mean as if we were a gift.

On the step, at that time, there was Brownie, an old rummie with a scarred face and a once silver necktie which he must have worn, I guess, since he was chasing girls as a young wolf. That necktie was polished bright with grease and sweat and tied in a fat knot that left an inch of collar showing. Now—not that you would see why—I hardly noticed Brownie; he was like some third pillar to the two stone ones, but lower, and crumpled up. I give him a Hi and he lowers his head an inch or two to return the greeting. He doesn't talk unless sober; and even then all he can talk about is how he hired some dentist to extract the gold from his teeth so he could pay for his son to have lessons in music. I needn't tell you I never set eyes on the son and the teeth have been done for years. The bums you meet. The full-sized, dumb bums you meet who think the world has fallen in on them when they are sitting on top of it still. I have always thought how the normal-sized guys must envy people like myself because there are so many things we never have to live up to.

Anyhow, I go past Brownie while he is hawking for a spit on to the street. The entrance hall is brown and shabby, full of the smell of garlic and rancid butter. The floor is marble but it looks more like cheap plastic fouled and scored by heels and spitting guys and centuries of wet mops. It hasn't been washed down in years, as you might guess. To find Papa Nicko I have to climb those steps which are too low and too wide so that your feet are always in the wrong position and at the wrong height. You grunt for air as you go. You reach the next floor with your heart thudding and pass the apartment where two Polish boys live with some foul-mouthed girl who studies Greek at the university. The bums you meet, and I am, as you know, no prude. You never go past their door without finding it open and this broad screeching at one of them or the both. One day the boys asked me in when I passed by. 'Come in and have a look at something,' they said. So I went in and had my look at something. There she was sitting up in bed with her book against her; then she lowers the book and I get an eyeful, from a downward angle you see, of her two notable jellies, while the boys howl with laughing and some crack about me wanted to be a mountaineer. You might guess. This is the sort of person you can't avoid, but you don't have to stay with them. And all this time she did not even blink. That is why I run past the door because it is always open. If I went in again I would be tempted to do something dangerous. So I run past.

A few more stairs, then, and you have reached this circus run by Papa. There too is a door never closed. There too is the same cooking-smell. But, once you have walked inside, there is a strange absence of walls. It is a long, bare room with low couches which serve as beds. These are scattered around like ships in some carelessly made-up convoy of ships, with human driftwood in between. Not that I hold it against these bums that they have drifted in here; but you have to know drifters from stickers if you know what I mean. And these drifted: in and out, up and down, jawing and hawking and hauling at their eye-slime in the early morning, by which you must understand any time before three in the afternoon. Papa Nicko was usually smoking his pipe and lounging on one of the beds. He insisted that they made their beds and arranged the top cover neat. But you could always smell the stale air that had been slept in; you can't ever use it again. But these guys did. It was as if they found it safe because it had been in and out of their lungs how many thousand times during the night. It had touched their blood and, because it had kept the life in them, they wouldn't let it go away from them. I used to feel that way about a pair of shoes, even when one of the shoes had a gash in the side which admitted the rain. You never know what a guy will fix on because there are too many things around him which are always moving.

Now, this particular day. I went right up to Papa and smiled my honest smile. This means that, because he was sitting, I was level with his face and could smile right into his eyes. I never could see how anyone could smile without trying to send it deep into the other person's head, through the eyes. Nick smiled back, but you could see he was thinking and, if asked, could not have said exactly who else besides myself was in the room. Actually there must have been half a dozen guys in various stages of undress, lying around, smoking, having a slow drink or reading at a piece of the paper. The one window, at the far end from the door, started above the height of my head, and the ceiling was very high indeed and painted, I guess, faint green. It was like walking into a canyon and there was even an echo. On one wall there was an oil-painting that Papa had done on the reverse side of a waterproof tablecloth; it was blue sea, white harbours, enormous green gulls and pink fish, like some stained-glass window in the room. Like some chapel. Some days—the worst days when I felt everyone was laughing at me because I had crawled from a hole to walk to some gook music which made me awkward and ridiculous, and when the room was crowded with bare mattresses that Papa had brought in for some extra transients—I used to look around me and wish it were really a chapel and the mattresses hassocks and the lounging bums kneeling and the painting pinned there was some kind of religious theme. But you know what you get in this life: just wanting and wishing and the facts like iron wool between you and your underwear.

Anyway, on the day in question I smiled at Papa: direct and tough. The trouble was that he was always halfway towards a smile that he never quite reached. You had to finish it for yourself. Plus the fact that you couldn't see his mouth for his walrus moustache which I guess he never combed or trimmed. It was like some kind of fog-bank hanging over his mouth and sometimes I wished I could have reached high and

lifted it up or shoved it aside, like that guy who spent twenty
years wishing he dared bite his boss's big flabby red ears. But
he was smiling behind his mouth anyway. He did not always
have socks on, so that is why his foot sweat had soaked into
the pile inside his slippers. When he was too warm, whether
or not he was wearing socks, his body heat drove the old pers-
piration back into circulation and hit my nose first as I was
closest. But he never threw away those slippers, which used to
be dove-grey but which had become coke-silver and used to
be soft, soft as a dove's armpit or wingpit, but were now hard
and dried-out. You could just make out the monogram on
them: EN for Edward Nicholas in hard cord that once was
red or gold. He slopped around in these and, I guess, pre-
served them for so long only by keeping his toenails short;
otherwise the thin bone would have scissored a slit into the
fronts. About the rest of his outfit I have to be as clear as I
can; it was so familiar that, day after day, the same sight just
about wore itself into and out the other side of your memory.
A green jacket from a combat suit with God knows how many
pockets and pleats; one of the lower patch pockets usually
knobbly with his favourite peanuts (unsalted) and one of the
higher ones on the left solid with pens lined up on their clips—
as many as seven or eight, of all kinds. Under that he wore a
dirty white shirt but the sleeves were linked by some very
expensive-looking ivory discs with animals' heads carved on
them. These, he said, had come from Africa. If he had said
they had come from Hades itself we would have believed him.
On his legs some cotton checks in black and white and narrow
round the ankles. When he went out he pulled a thick felt
scarf out of a shallow closet and wrapped it round his neck
with one piece before and one behind. It was broad black and
white stripes. Boy, did he look like some national flag at
international half-mast when he faced into the March winds
off the river and blinked away the tears from his eyes.

So I said my good morning and he nodded. You could tell
he had been reading again; one of those tough books he
warned us about: to be taken, he said, only with liquor or loud
music. Some days he would drive the bums crazy with long,
tuneless music he called great. That was a room, to be sure.
There was everything you might think of as crummy, and

there was all sorts of other stuff, mostly held off to the side in closets or boxes but from time to time slid out. Record-player, books, typewriter, stacks and stacks of newspapers and heavy, shiny monthlies. The only thing always on show was the rye and so on and, in the kitchen where the ants came up from behind the sink and you fell over the linoleum strip on the floor there were, I guestimate, three hundred cans of soup: all kinds, and the clever can-opener screwed into the wall. The range had four rings and Papa had four pans. That kitchen stank of soup. But whether they were soaked to the skin or weak with being hungry or just plain lying, he ushered them in and provided soup. They took it direct from the pan, with dessert spoons, cradling the pan on their groins, while he looked on, nodding and tugging at his moustache. Maybe now, because I have said something about him, you think you can see what a kind of guy he was. But wait: nothing of what I say can tell you enough of the kind of guy he was unless you know from your own life what kind of world this can be. He was of it, but it never soiled him. Some of those bums crapped all over the lavatory and used Papa's own tooth brush, but he never complained. I once saw him standing there taking in the mess like some guy who's been out and on his return finds a message from someone very close to him who has called. He just looked at the sick-making mess and nodded. That man could, can, nod away any disaster. Like he always knew and, because he knew, never needed to find out again.

'Long time no see,' he said. I think he said. I was just about hypnotized by that near-smile of his.

'Long time, short guy!' He flinched at that. He had once spent an hour trying to talk me out of being my witty self. I am witty *against* myself, so what is wrong with that?

'Long time,' he said. 'That means you must have been busy. Which suggests you found some work. Which suggests too that you have redeveloped the sense of mission. In other words, I guess, you have been spending over a week pleasing your ignoble self.'

Now how could you answer back to that? Before you spoke he had thought up what you were going to say and had three answers ready. I used to knock my knees together and waddle across the floor like some cripple, and pulling a hideous face.

That used to put him out. Or I would howl at him and crouch on the bare black-painted boards, telling him I was a bed-bug and would bite him. He laughed. Then I would put my finger right down my throat and hawk at him. That upset him a little; but no more than that. He would just pull at his pipe with both hands and wait for me to stop. So, after a time, I would ignore his insults and try to answer back.

'Pleasing myself, Papa,' I would say, and said that day, 'is something I can do.' That fixed him. He just looked. Then he started up again, and, on that particular day, stabbed his pipe at the air while he talked.

'You are lucky because you were born into affliction and didn't have to start learning it late.' At that I just sucked all the air I could into my mouth and made a crude noise by pushing my forefinger at my cheek. He didn't even notice. He could be so far away and so hard to follow. I guess he never did know our kind of talk, what with his being at Princeton and Oxford and being an officer in the army.

'But you sure used to sound off.' He was still talking: slowly, as he always did, and shaking his head sideways as if his blue eyes were loose. And he was right. 'I remember,' he went on, 'the days you came in here to rave about the spittle-kneed toads who offered you money to expose yourself as if you were some newly discovered, swiftly netted and carefully transported freak animal from the Manchurian hinterland. A human pod on short legs in whom they saw much of them-selves, but not quite enough to prevent them from hoping to use you as a trash-can of lust, a moral litter-bin, an anthropo-morphic sink. Exalting themselves while belittling you; but forgetting that to belittle you was simply effacing you and therefore leaving them all the more painfully alone with their own depravities.' It has cost me some pains to recall all this as he said it. But I soon got the habit of imitating his words and then going away to look them up. I had money those days, so I bought some books. And he would say a word, I would repeat it, he would say it again and then spell it out. This, I thought, would teach me about myself, but it mostly taught me about him. Being unhappy is the same in any words; but it is worst, I found, in simple language. So I guessed why he talked so high above me so much.

'Not to speak of those shabby, uncertain edifices, their phalluses, about which they thought most of the time because that kind of size is their criterion for virility despite the fact that all glandular contractions and vascular urges only serve to tie us together in repetitive misery, accumulating ordure like a cow's after a long season in the field with the olive pellets bound by a thousand coarse hairs. Don't interrupt. To look down on man, on any man, is to ape God. That is, in your terms, to make a monkey out of man, which he was and is, and to monkey with God's self-elected status. But not really to affect God at all except to give Him a lower opinion than ever of the minor monster, man.'

There was hours of that. Like you turned on the radio at the usual 457 which brings you WKXR, or should, and you get instead a horse whinnying or the sound of a tractor non-stop or the same guy just saying effthat under his breath right into your ear. You attend. 'Attend?' he shouted so that one bum rolled right off his mattress. 'Attend? Did you say that? Did I? What else do we ever do? Look around you. There is a man so tired he has actually prayed in a drunken outburst never to wake. There is a man who has spent a whole morning trying to squeeze a blackhead out of the crook between his thigh and calf. Imagine the attenuated maggot of soap which he has spent a lifetime accumulating. And the difference between those two men is that one is willing his death and the other is discovering his irrelevance. And you, you vast cynic in small physical shape, you stare at a man who talks and think he's some kind of pervert because he fills in the space between him and God with verbiage. Well, you are right to stare; I stared at you when you first came in here. You had no idea. You yourself took yourself for granted—as I do now. But at the time, I thought to myself, how blessed are these full-sized bums who suck me dry of soup and liquor. And now, I have to think twice before I can see you in your proper dimensions.' He talked on, and I listened. I'm sure I didn't understand but at least I was getting attention. And if you attend, well, you learn. Or you discover that you have no ability to learn. When this grand world runs out of screaming lunatics, as well as the quieter sort, we'll start a new race of the screaming sane.

'Sure,' he said, 'you can't forget the fact. You know all along that you, of all the people around, will get the extra half-look. You should be grateful; as grateful as I am sad that in this copperplate world it is only the distorted who merit the full attention that every human ought to have. You would be even better off if you had no legs and went around on a trolley. And their brutality to you is better for you than their pity, for their pity destroys and their brutality toughens you. I can't say I envy you; but you ought to know what you do have in the way of special privileges.'

He made sense with that. I guess he made the first sense he ever made to me with that. Once I stood on top of a snow-drift and shuffled my feet until they began to make a pair of holes. I thought I could just shuffle a hole big enough to hide me, so that I could go down to defeat while standing up like a man. But gradually the snow under my feet hardened and would not give; so I stood there like a badly planted tree, ugly trunk and all, and there was absolutely no chance of anyone coming along later in the thaw and saying, 'Poor little dwarf, he done froze here in the shallow snow that was made for taller creatures only.' So I guess I discovered I was part of the world like everyone else. That morning, anyway, I faced him with all he had ever said ringing in my head; so much so that I never could tell what it was he had just said or even just done. 'You see,' he would start as he shuffled towards the kitchen and there made the sounds of can-opening, 'we have to look at one another and we have to recognize'—he grunted as he slopped the congealed soup into the pan and stirred in the garlic salt, the butter and pepper—'how alike and how different we are.' Then he reappeared. 'Now don't let me let that boil dry,' which he said while looking down the long room towards the intended recipient of soup. Papa nodded, set his head on one side, and pushed his lips forward reassur-ingly to this latest of the hungry. No doubt just another one looking for a foundation for alcohol, which Papa would also give them free. The floor was always littered with pans, specks of soup crusted inside and heavy family-crested spoons angling out. I have seen one of these bums so excited that he spooned in soup while holding a cigarette and supping from a bottle. It was only to the weak and needy that Papa gave his vitamins

and iron-yeast pills: one multi-vitamin and nine iron-yeast a
day while he watched with a kind of patience and absentminded kindness. He could spot the phoneys at once, but he
fed them all the same. He once bought up a second-hand
supply of bath-towels but they were never used. 'You know,'
he would say, 'I had the chance to ruin myself with high living
and being priggish with money. And you know what I did?
I ruined myself; yes sir, I did. And then I knew what I had
done and that I wouldn't need to argue with myself any
more.' Many a time I heard about his night-clubbing and the
Bahamas. He never used any names but you could tell he was
on the level. To me it was like reading *The New Yorker* and
suddenly finding the women in the advertisements walking
out to hold your hand, speaking to you. The silks were floating
around your head, the perfumes were real, the gold links were
golden and the tweeds were rough. But he would never linger
for long without wrecking the illusion. If it was a honey of a
woman, she was a mental canary. If it was some great club,
it was for stupids. If it was a perfect meal, there was some
waiter starving in the back. And if it was great to be high and
drunk, it was lousy to wake up. Private planes took them for
week-ends among the talcum-soft, pink sands and brought
them back for rainy days and stockholders' meetings. He was
not very wise, he said: he sold stock at the wrong time and
believed all he was told. His mother had known, but she had
studied the market whereas he played hunches all the time
and found it only worked with ponies.

Anyway, that morning, as by now you can see, is like the
stretch of sand the tide never quite reaches. I keep coming in
and we never quite make it. Well, he talked at me for about
an hour, by which time the toenail smell in the room was bad
and the cigarette smoke was blotting out the window. It must
have been about eleven-thirty when Papa yawned and reached
round to the back of his neck where he made the muscles
crack like tough rubber cords. Then he washed his face with
his hands, massaging and gently slapping himself. After a long
stretch he suggested we take a stroll, the six-foot man and the
half-sized me. All the time he walked he spoke, so he had to
shout downwards and quite often I had to save him from
traffic. He just didn't look. Our mission was to be cheeses and

beers; more cheeses than beers. We took it easy, taking care not to slip on the stairs. It was interesting to note that, after he left, the bums began to talk and holler as they never did when he was there. I told him this and he smiled, muttering something about penguins and parrots. I never knew what. There was no mail; or rather there were some circulars we had left there the day before, where the mailman had left them. 'Expensive economies,' he said as we passed the wooden shelf inside the heavy glass door. Then we were out on the street in a whipping cold that hit him at once and sent him back for that black-and-white scarf. I was always glad of him because he got between me and the two Polish boys who had the wild woman in with them.

You know how people in a crowd on a street usually don't stare at you. Well, hardly anyone stared that day. Most of the people knew us anyway. Officer Rooney gave us a wave and Mazzini shouted something in greeting as he bent over a heap of trash. That guy just lived for cleaning up the streets and the trenches of the basement apartments. Every negro I met gave me a big, banana smile, as if I was Pee Wee the wrestler all over again, just having done a crotch-hold and slam on a notorious fouler. This morning, as we walked, Papa got to burping a lot into the cold air and, in between, describing the time he spent at Oxford, England. He had never, he said, met so many people so anxious to hide from each other; to give nothing of their real selves away. That was in the early twenties, he said, and it sure seemed constipated even after Princeton. He had shaken hands with people whose hands were not to be shaken. He had tried to make girls outside the college hours approved for the attempted making of girls. And he had kept on forgetting to wear his little black gown. He had also gone drinking and practical joking but, also, when he found time, had done some reading. Marcus Aurelius, which is how the books spell it, he said, and the Bible. By the time we got to Joy's store, the traffic was heavier and noisier but we were both a long way off in a world of green oaks, sluggish rivers and biscuit-coloured towers sprouting from behind college walls. I guess I would have been terrified in such a place. More than I ever was in the wrestling ring the first time out. Suddenly, then, we were into cream cheeses, Cheddar,

Budweiser, Schlitz, Camembert (this for him only) and Dutch cheese in red wax casing. He knew cheeses and he knew I wouldn't interrupt once he had started talking. I learned a lot that way.

So I watched Papa while he paid Mrs. Joy. You know how these Jewish women go from ripe to a kind of bloat. Well, she had gone that way but without ever looking wrong. Rosy cheeks and, fresh every day, a crisp white coat like a bridal cape clinging to her turnip hips. She wobbled when she laughed and Papa stood there, very grave and attentive, as if he had no sense of humour at all. From the side, his moustache looked untidy, like one of those feather dusters they use in the genteel stores. And it looked damp or greased against the morning pallor of his face. He never put a word wrong with Mrs. Joy but he was always having some kind of discussion with her husband, mostly about liquor and the price of salami. I used to keep myself to myself and wander round the shelves, looking at the prices and trying the cans for weight in my hand. For all the time we took we never went away with much; and the morning in question, we didn't even take away any beer. I guess Papa forgot or just decided he had enough.

So, Papa carrying the stiff brownpaper bag with the cheeses, we took off down the street, past the Union bar and the Wrigley gum advertisement, past the radio shop and all those delicatessens. Papa had stopped talking, and when he had stopped you couldn't start him again by asking him questions. I think he was humming something under his breath, but I couldn't make it out because, I suppose, of my poor education. Well, we walked on and while we scowled our mouths at the wind off the river I fell to thinking of all he had told me about the high life. Closed-circuit TV in the big hotels, telling you the stock prices, the store prices, the new movies and shows, the weather report and the ball games. Then the fire-works higher than I was, exploding higher than the daily jet's vapour-trails over the Bahama sands. Ju-Jube the model was there in her mink sheath and with her collection of Mozart discs. There was an orchestra for all these barons and dukes and Hollywood stars to dance to on that shiny terrace under the moon. That must have been some lousy envious moon, what with the senators and sirens beneath and the wasted food in the pewter trash-cans in the basement of that hundred-room luxury hotel with the fig-leaf statuary sprouting all over the grounds and the beds made up on private lawns between waterfalls and fountains of all colours. All the books of matches (which you didn't need anyway because they had perpetual flames from silver pots like the Olympic Games or whatever that is) had CHARM written on in embossed gold. When you had paid, he said, everything was free: the velvet horses so long as you had no whip, the tennis coaching of some famous pro out on the tinted gravel of the courts (you could book pink, gold or grey), the iced towels for which you rang a special bell conveniently placed, the underground tubs of sun-tan lotion covered by special heatproof lids which read USE ME and, when you lifted the lid, said U SMEAR ME. Some joint. A Coney Island paradise for the heeled. And all those negro waiters in silver uniforms, the bare tanned backs of the actresses and the crew-cuts of the arty boys who came along for the ride and in the search for inspiration. But, all the time, Papa told me, he gave the guests these things to occupy them so he could read a few books. I never got that. Why go there with them all? Why pay for them to go there by plane and then have to avoid them? He doesn't go there any more because he has sold the joint, and I guess he hasn't much of the money left. But I wouldn't swear to that because you never know with that guy. Why, once he told me he was rich in books and ideas, so what the hell about the money? You never can tell and in the other sense of tell you can't even start. I was thinking all this while we walked. I was thinking far out-side myself, and where I was, when he pulled at my shoulder and said I was to look. I looked, and there was a crowd around the green metal barrier of the subway steps. At first I thought some old woman had fallen, for those stairs are sharp. Then I thought maybe someone is being brought up from an accident with a train. And as we walked nearer I began to wonder because no one was coming away and no one was bending over anyone.

Papa shoved into the crowd, holding the bag of cheeses high so as not to crush them. I stood on the outside, mostly for the reasons I've already given you. You know, you never get a square deal in a crowd. And then the crowd spilled the

other way and I could see Papa was trying to talk to this
weird-looking guy with the long hair down to his shoulders.
It was like some of those pictures you get in *Life*, and this guy
looked like one of those Indian priests who leave their hair
long. He didn't seem to see Papa; he didn't see anything much.
He just looked right out and away. He was in a dark brown
suit and what looked like a very old plain shirt open at the
back because I could see the loop flapping gently in the wind.
On his feet he had something I never saw on feet before: black,
dirty button-up boots done up tight, so I guess his blood was
beating away inside those ankle-pieces. I guess this guy had
not shaved for days and I cannot even guess when last he had
spoken the English language. This is how it went, with Papa
putting an arm round him and then taking his elbow.

'Yeah, we just found him there, just standin'.'

'Can I help you in some way?'

'Don't waste your breath, bud; he can't talk.'

'What is your name? Who are you?' Papa waved his open
hand in front of the guy's eyes. But the guy just looked through
them all. One of the spectators was reading at some paper
they had found in the man's pocket.

'Say, I can't make this out, it's been in the rain or sumpn.
This could be "soldier" or "sold her"—I don't know. . . .'
Papa took the paper and I noticed several people nudging one
another when he did so, and smiling in a snide way. They
knew Papa. He frowned, and all the time he puzzled over the
paper they joked about him and the silent guy just shifted
from foot to foot. This guy had some trouble standing. Now
you would think he had had some kind of stroke or fit, but he
was very calm and breathing evenly. I watched, chewing at
my thumb.

'It says,' Papa announced after a while, ' "I have a need to
be a soldier in the calvary"—that's "cavalry" I guess, or
should be. "My folks want that for me!" ' By now they were
all having a laugh. In fact I laughed myself because it is not
every day you find some dumb, nameless guy leaning at the
top of the Rapid Transit with a letter in his pocket like he is
some dumped parcel, saying he wants to join the cavalry. But
Papa is not laughing; he is once more trying to get some sense
out of this guy, but the guy is motionless, wordless. Like some

old lump of wood they find on the sunken ships; but there were no barnacles.

'Who are you?' Papa was trying but you could tell he was getting nowhere. Just then a white slim dog ran across the road and disappeared into a store. So fast I wasn't sure if I saw it. And while I was wondering, this guy starts a kind of spittle-rumble deep in his throat and his face twitches while his cracked, skinned lips twist. 'Say that again,' says Papa, smiling anxiously. The guy did, but worse, and here came a cop walking up. It was Officer Rooney with his eyebrows like bristles pointing directly out in front of him. 'Yes,' says Papa. 'Land, is it? Lagald? Lagrand? Lackgland?' Then he stood aside and announced to the group who were now very quiet: 'He said his name is Lacland or something. Anybody here know him?' Nobody moved. So Papa tucked that letter into his patch pocket and spoke again to the guy Lacland, 'You come with me; you'll be O.K.' The man never stirred an inch, so Papa tugged at his arm and, slowly, like some animal preparing to get up and go, this guy starts into motion, and off we go back to the brownstone with him between us, Officer Rooney a yard behind to keep off the sightseers. And, sure enough, before long, here is the Press with the big ugly cameras and we are immortalized in print for one day. Walking down the avenue: Papa, tall eagle or buzzard; Lacland, as we came to call him, like a bum or scarecrow being blown along by the wind, and me, small as I am, supporting this guy on the inside of the sidewalk. The wind blew sharply and our eyes watered, especially Lacland's. But he didn't seem to notice because he was having so much trouble walking. It was as if he was trying to put both feet forward at the same time; and backwards too. Anyhow, we dragged him along and he just looked down, breathing hard and gasping. There was a queer smell off him —like senna, which is sour, or oilcloth, which is more sickly. Like those two together. When, finally, we arrived back at the brownstone we were pretty worn out because we had in fact carried this guy and he was only a few inches short of six feet and a few pounds short of two hundred.

Then a stranger thing happened. We shoved through the glass door and took a rest. As soon as we let go of this guy, Lacland, he crumpled up and settled to the marble floor like

one of those chemical snakes you buy for parties; it's a kind of
ash snake that comes out of a cone; it writhes around and
slowly sprawls across the tray. He didn't drop, but he sagged
down without a word. Papa put the bag of cheeses on the floor
and knelt by this crazy guy's head. I said we should get a
doctor but Papa said to wait. 'Can you walk?' he asked. The
guy began to cry, very gently, and Papa took out a red and
white handkerchief and wiped away the tears. No sooner has
he done that than the man takes in a mighty breath which
sounds like the sea drawing back, and then roars one word as
plain as green shamrock: 'NO!' So we knew. Papa seemed to
know what to do then. He unbuttoned Lacland's boots and
took them off. There were no socks and the feet were wealed
from the tight boots. White patterns with red networks covered
the top of the feet. But that didn't seem to ease him at all.
Then Papa opened his bag of cheeses and quickly unpeeled
the Dutch, tossing the red wax aside so that, in fact, I caught
the mould without trying. Papa then thrust the disc of cheese
in front of the man's eyes and asked him if he would eat.
Lacland just shut his eyes. Papa cursed softly at that and
looked at me, curling his mouth as he did. He was getting
nowhere. So then I did what I did, but without malice. I
opened my mouth wide and slotted the red wax behind my
lips so that I looked like a fiend from hell with a red blob
where my mouth should be: like looking down some animal's
screaming throat, except that the wax bulged forward. I then
went across the hall, into the unlit part and charged with my
arms waving, making what noises I could. I finished by
plunging my face at this guy, and he flinched, tried to fight
me off while I slipped my hands at his throat and made my
eyes pop. Suddenly he roars again and heaves round, trying
to roll away. But he had no power of motion. So we lifted him
up and dragged him to the stairs, sat him down while Papa
went to fetch the boys and I took that wax out of my mouth.
It tasted rotten and there was a grey fur on the inside. I tasted
that for days. Lacland just lolled where we had put him and
I began to hope that Papa wouldn't bring down that woman
with the jellies behind the book. He didn't; just the two boys,
who got very hearty and jolly as they lifted Lacland and
heaved him up the stairs, past the open door (but with no

woman visible) and up the next stairs to the door of Papa's place.

When we entered, the bums took not the slightest notice but continued lying or dozing or quietly talking behind their hands. We set Lacland down on a mattress and Papa hurried into the kitchen to make some coffee. In fact, during the next hour or two he tried coffee, whisky, tea and milk, but Lacland would touch only water. Soup too we tried, but to no purpose. He would only take bread, and the drier it was the better he liked it. Later in the day one of Papa's friends, a doctor, came round—Doc Rumboldt it was, with the limp and the brown 'spatclogs' on black shoes—and said Lacland was not sick but exhausted and undernourished as if he had been in jail or some captivity or exposed somewhere. We could check none of that. All we knew was that someone had set him up to be a cavalry soldier, that Lacland just couldn't stand the daylight —even the smoky daylight of Papa's place and wanted only bread and water.

Now we couldn't darken the whole place, not even the kitchen or the bathroom. So Papa wondered where to put this guy who, although hating the light, showed no urge to sleep. There were always, at any time of the day, a few bums snoring away in that big room. Eventually we took Lacland down the stairs again, almost breaking our necks at the turns, and into the basement which had a dark chamber where the washing-machine was. There was here an enormous crate in which some piece of the furnace had come. Now I am not kidding: when Lacland saw the gloom of that chamber and then, as his eyes got used to the dark, saw the crate, he smiled and held the smile for a full minute.

'It's obvious,' Papa said, 'he's been caged up somewhere and he doesn't feel safe in any other kind of place.' I could see that, but I could also see that you don't take a guy in and then stow him away in a crate in the cellar like he was some piece of rusted equipment. I think Papa saw that too for he tried to get the guy on his feet again and called to the two bums who had helped us down and were now waiting at the doorway. But Lacland mumbled and slavered again, wrenched his arm free and motioned at the crate. 'No,' said Papa, 'he can't. That's just crazy, he won't ever get well that way.' So we pulled again to get Lacland to his feet. But he got really wild this time and you could see that he had a sort of animal life anyway, if not human. The sound he made was like 'Urk, urk' and when he covered his eyes with his hands he said in a whistling sort of voice, 'Arra,' or something like that. He had me beat. Papa just stood there, considering.

Then something happened that settled it. Lacland was crouching like some scared puppy although in years I guess he must have been between twenty and twenty-five. Suddenly he reared up and fixed a look on us; and I tell you it was just about the most pathetic, hang-dog thing you ever saw, with the whites of his eyes appearing to expand and his mouth drooping slack. 'Wait,' Papa said and moved away into the other part of the basement to return with a piece of rag and a hand-brush. He dusted out the crate with a good housewife's hand, then tipped it on its side as if it were some display case. Then one of the bums appeared with a stack of blankets and soon, after all hell of a noise of dragging and struggling, two more came down hauling a mattress which they then shoved into the crate as far as it would go. The mattress was too broad for the crate and projected a foot and a half. Lacland had watched all this without a sound, but grinning sharply now and then like a child awaiting candies. When we helped him into the creosote-smelling crate he cried out in a kind of whoop; and, boy, was he glad about it. We had no sooner put him in there than he stretched out, made himself comfortable and began to talk: not easily or very fast, but in English anyway.

'Thank you, thank you,' he said slowly. Papa stared and exclaimed: 'That's it! I can lip-read him, I think!' And that is what he did, speaking after the weird, distorted sounds of the other man. It went like this, and I will try to recall how the Lacland guy sounded.

'Vrynd.'

'Very kind, I guess,' whispered Papa.

'Lontam ho-wal.'

'Long time, that's clear,' said Papa, 'in a hole.' Lacland nodded furiously at this.

'You know,' said Papa, 'he talks like some kid learning for the first time.' And he did, but with maybe a few more words than a child would have. They went on.

'Zhooze art.'

'I think he said the shoes hurt him. Did we take those upstairs with us when we came in?' I nodded; I had picked them up, but they were boots, not shoes.

'Lak bradwot-ah,' mumbled the man in the crate, and Papa said that meant he liked bread and water. Did he want some now? No, he shook his head and motioned at his belly. I guess that meant later and I told myself to remember. While I was telling myself to remember I began to daydream: you can take just so much of that kind of monkey-talk and your mind gets on to other things. It was as if I saw one of those flooded cathedrals, you know, with the coloured glass affecting the water and the water breaking up the lights of the glass. I don't know where I saw such a thing in reality. I was standing fairly high; or maybe I was floating; I could see a boat going down the aisle, or I guess I mean up. The boat was this crate, even to the rope handles on either end, and Papa was in there with this Lacland and they were presenting some kind of document to a guy in priest's robes who kept looking up at me as if he was sore at me. Well, the crate slowly floated up to the altar and I could read what was written right across the altar: the word 'Interborough' as if it was some kind of subway station. And then, suddenly, they had gone, as if the crate had sailed right through the purple velvet around the altar. And the priestly guy had gone too and I was alone up there, somehow higher, as it is in the nightmares I get when I grow and grow and they all try to squeeze me down again to my usual length. Then, just as quickly, I was falling, but not rapid; just swooning through the water down towards another crate, but too small like a jeweller's box, and with a square of black plush in its bottom. They were going to pin me in there to show me off in that cathedral window. So I began to scream, and the more I screamed the smaller the box became; but that, I realized, was because it was getting further and further away, and I felt happier although I was still howling. Next thing they had put me sideways and were pushing my face against the tree trunks, bruising them through my lips and chin. I clawed at the branches because the trunks were too solid and thick but could shift nothing. Then I kicked, with most of my howling inside me, and I heard a cry as I seemed to wake up. I had hold of Papa's moustache because he had his horny hand across my mouth; I had kicked him in the groin somewhere and this had made him let go. All I could hear was my own breath sobbing out and the bums muttering in the other part of the basement. Then Papa motioned for me to look at Lacland. His face was bulged up red, as if he was suffocating, and the cords on his neck were like tent-ropes. He was waving his head around like his neck was broken and trails of mucus were swinging from his nostrils as he flung his head. His mouth was wide open and he had long teeth: human teeth, though, with a long grey tongue flitting in and out. I guess I have never been so afraid in all my life: this guy looked as if he was going to burst and, when he did, spill acid all over us. I scrambled away, but Papa caught my arm and pulled me back.

'It's the noise he can't stand. Darn it, shut up! You're still yelling! What in God's name is wrong?' I stopped howling then, completely, and Lacland's colour became normal. You ask how I knew what colour his face was? Papa had a small battery lamp in his hand, so I guess that was why I thought of all those cathedral lights. 'Come on,' said Papa, 'let him be.' So we went upstairs again, and Papa carefully locked the basement door. I didn't know what to think. I just knew that we had big trouble on hand and I was certain of that when, later on, I heard Papa tell Doc Rumboldt that this Lacland had had some soup and coffee, some cheese and bread, and had gone his way into the raining afternoon. Down there, not far below the mattress room, there was something horrible and pitiful, which had only just started in its ways with us and which would give us all a bad time before very long. I said goodbye to Papa and went for ham and eggs at the drugstore. I was due to wrestle in two nights' time and I already felt that the fight had gone out of me for some time to come. That was a bad enough feeling a couple of nights before a match. But, as you will soon see, nothing compared with what was to follow.

I was in my chair reading the wrestling column in the evening paper and, as it were, overhearing the radio, a bad habit of mine. Sugar Samson was wrestling in Detroit and John Sheppy was gassing away on the radio with the jazz

music half blotting him out. I was listening to him and
thinking about Daddy Rogers' best holds, and yet I was on a
different wavelength altogether, thrown out by Lacland. He
had kind of knocked the comedy out of me, just as the guys
said I lost my zip when I gave up the stoolie game. I lit a
cigarette and blew smoke right into the radio speaker, but it
didn't stall that garrulous guy for one second. My landlady,
Mrs. Pomeroy, was reading in the chair opposite me at the
other side of the room. She read romances nonstop, was about
seventy-five and lived a peaceful, rosy-cheeked life from the
mid-morning when she bumped down the stairs with her bed-
pan in hand, the other hand concealing the contents, to her
long going-to-bed process: she usually made six or seven trips
up and down the stairs before she had readied herself for the
night. She never looked up when she was reading but she was
always ready to provide currant cake and cups of tea. I guess
she spoiled me. It was another old house, with the carpets
worn and the chairs floating a thread here and there. The hall
just outside the room was crowded with glass cases full of dead
birds, old umbrellas, walking-sticks and heavy, cast-iron
chairs. The furnace puffed quietly up through the grille and
the brass dishes hung against the wall shone like shields. It
was a highly respectable atmosphere and I never felt quite
right there. But I managed to keep up appearances. After all,
I never found a wife so I decided to live a respectable half
which I could think about when I was among bums; I had
that half, anyway, and you felt private. I had trained Mrs.
Pomeroy in my ways, even to the extent of persuading her to
let me leave my bottle of whisky on the living-room table or
the old, never-used harpsichord. In fact I think she once tried
a nip and that made up her mind for good; she did not drink,
except for the sherry in her geriatric potion. It was a room of
lamps: they had faded, brown parchment patterned with even
more faded roses and leaves. There were even some very low
chairs and tables which she had looked out from the attic. A
fire burned in the grate and reflected in the glass doors of the
bookcase. When Papa came there he settled in as if he had
known the room for years. Mrs. P. eyed him more than once,
but there are limits and Papa was too busy a guy to con-
template marriage.

So I sat there, a pair of cushions behind me and my feet on the worn hassock. The fire chirped. The furnace purred. The clock chimed. I guess I dozed a little and began to dream. You know how it is when you have almost fallen asleep, and suddenly you jump. Well, I jumped but I didn't jump out of sleep. I fell into something else—that crate in the basement. But this time it was fitted out with a chair and round the sides, on hooks, there were instruments. Lacland was there to show me round, explaining in dumb show what the things were for. First I saw a rubber collar for squeezing the neck; or so I gathered because Lacland motioned with his hands and pretended to lift his head right off. I felt sick, but even sicker when I saw the electric rod they used for shocking your parts. There were also small scissors, heavy little whips and pointed rubber hammers. Lacland then got the bums to fit me into the chair and, before I realized, they had buckled my legs to the front and strapped my arms to the sides. Then, from behind, they brought something that rested on my head and it was strapped round my neck. I could see white wires for a moment and then I saw God's universe in flashes and fragments, the night smoke falling and the dawn rising like darts. It was a world of inward needles, not pine needles but gramophone and surgical and I was racing crazily against the walls and the ceiling like some buzz-fly; and every contact was pain. Next, because I had closed my eyes, they stitched my eyelids to my eyebrows and then looked hard in at me. They were still turning the power switch on the chair and shining lights right into my eyes. I couldn't move and I couldn't shout because if I shouted I caught my mouth on some electrified rod they had arranged just in case. At that point I woke, or fell back into the right kind of sleep, from which I then sat upright. Mrs. P. was still calmly reading and there was a buzz-fly racing round the ceiling. I picked up the remainder of the evening paper and shaped to throw it at the fly; but then I checked my arm. Lacland was looking down at me with that contorted face of his, so I put the paper down and closed my eyes.

Next thing I had run out of the room. Those who might have seen me would have said I scuttled—a small guy scuttling out sounds right. Down the steps with a hot wind chasing me

and into the subway. I took a local, brilliant with harsh light
and almost empty save for a few drunks and a mailman. By
the time I reached Papa's I was in a sweat and hardly able to
explain myself.

'You have been drinking,' he said without surprise.

I stared at him, then babbled something about Lacland and
the crate. Papa stared, then said: 'Sure, he's fed. He took a
slice of bread and a perfunctory toothglass of water, which is
all we can expect of him. Sleep? Sure, he sleeps. But who
knows when? He has his dark down there and his legs
stretched out and I guess all the company he needs, which
amounts to not a soul. Satisfied?'

I sat trembling on a mattress. From down the room there
came a grumbling noise and a heaving of bodies. Only Papa
was awake there. I had disturbed him at his reading. 'Listen
here,' he said, reaching from behind him for something—a
book. 'Listen to this. It's Shakespeare, from a play called
Troilus and Cressida. "Heavens what a man is there! a very
horse"; (he doesn't mean a horse really). "That has he knows
not what." (We can say that again, can't we!) "Nature, what
things there are, Most abject in regard, and dear in use."
(That's both you and Lacland; nothing to choose between
you.) "What things, again, most dear in the esteem" (I am
being sincere.) "And poor in worth!" (Don't let that apply to
you.) "Now shall we see tomorrow"—(And so we shall. So
what are you worrying about?)' That was how he read it out,
with his own comments, trying to cheer me up. And I guess
he succeeded; in part. I was still shaking and shiny with
sweat. So he crossed the room and picked up a bottle of
whisky; I noticed that he poured the drink into a used glass,
but I didn't care. It fired my tongue and did me no good. I
still felt overcome with something like a disaster to come but
I couldn't put a name to it. I didn't take the second drink he
offered, so he took it himself, from the same glass. I now had
a fairly precise idea of what was likely to happen; it had
happened before. Papa would slap me on the back and suggest
going on the town: you can imagine what kind of a pair we
made, the tall gaunt buzzard or eagle and the stumbling
midget. We were always being given free drinks because
people would come into bars just to have a look at us, the

women especially. Papa never worried about being stared at but I did, although I have been stared at now for over thirty years. The usual course of events was to call first at the Union bar where we took a booth and had several beers; then we would switch over to the other side of the bar and have French fries and a steak. While we had our food we could watch TV; but Papa talked all the time, even while he was looking at the screen, so I could never follow the shows except the boxing and so on. He ate slowly but I ate fast. He ate English fashion with knife and fork; I scooped up and cut with my fork. But there were many times when I missed my mouth altogether from being embarrassed by people staring at us. They always gave you that knowing look as if they had summed you up in a second as a couple of perverts taking in calory for a tougher orgy than usual. Sid the barman at the Union was fat and bald, with a wax face, but he always cracked a smile for me. That was one of few smiles of the right kind that I saw. So, as I said, I would smear my face with grease from the fries or the meat, or even accidentally plant a lettuce-flake on my cheek, because I kept moving my head to see who was watching us. It was even worse when we got up to go; you could feel all those eyes boring into your back and feel the eyes in front of you sucking your whole personality right out of you. But this time Papa said something different: he suggested a movie; and he must have known that I would like nothing better than to be in the dark with someone I knew was safe.

So we went. It was late but we caught the beginning of the main feature, stumbling to our seats over the legs of sleeping negroes, who had been there since the afternoon, and skidding on Coke bottles and orange peel. Down there they gave you violent, colourful movies two at a time and those negroes yelled like children at the carousel. I personally never made much noise at the show, liking to keep myself to myself and sneak looks through the darkness. The feature we caught was a war movie and all the time it was showing I could see Papa's mouth moving and hear him muttering. It was always a mistake to take him to a war movie because he got so worked up and, this time, before the evening was over (and *that* went until three in the morning, whatever Mrs. Pomeroy said) he was in worse shape than I had been. Papa had a queer habit. In the daytime he could talk to himself without getting upset: if you went into his mattress parlour it looked as if he was talking to the bums, but they hardly ever listened and would not have understood anyway, being for the most part poor trash and dazed with liquor. But at night he was a different man; he always tried to read, and if he could he was fine. Sometimes, though, reading helped him not at all, and he had to have an audience to attend to him; and I was always it. But, I tell you, not usually so late as this. All I could tell myself was that I had started this and would have to see him through.

After the movie we went for a beer in one of those cold, light green bars near the El or where the El was. My own head was still full of Audie Murphy bravery, black earth from shell-bursts, red blood on khaki suits, chattering machine guns, dive-bombers knifing down and the scared faces of young conscripts. Papa had seen the movie but it had just triggered him off into his own war which he re-fought on average once a month. He sat there with his tall glass of beer as if it was the barrel of some mortar, and he was waiting for orders to fire. And when he fired it was all words, like the times he fired off about his sex-life and his villa and his paradise island and his days at Princeton. Somehow his life was more real to him when he looked back on it than when he had lived it. I guess he had forgotten about Lacland in that crate in the cellar, but I was pretty sure he still had the key. And I still had that feeling that something was wrong.

Suddenly he said, 'Now, for example, that poor unfortunate we have back at the apartment in that crate,' just as if I had turned on the radio and this guy had been talking for ten minutes already, 'he's not unfortunate at all or poor: he is lucky and rich. Lucky and rich as we shall never, never be.' We were off; you could tell it was going to be a long night, and I must admit I thought about the wrestling bout—a tag-team match I was supposed to be in only a night from now. Some preparation. But then I knew Papa would probably come and watch and I also recalled, once again, that I had started this myself. Papa had continued talking:

'We were fighting through thickly wooded country, and for

two days past there had been warm sunshine and sudden storms. You never knew what was coming next. There had been one skirmish in which we had lost four men, and one of those had been taken prisoner, I guess, and then bayoneted in the neck. Not a pretty sight. I mean that the bayonet was still there and the man who shoved it was still attached to the rifle because someone, somehow, had shot him. So I guess this man who had been taken prisoner had snatched a gun or something. We were awaiting orders—you always are—on the edge of a wood, and it was a nerve-racking time. At dusk the mist rose from the river which was about a mile away. You see, we were fighting parallel to this river, and no one knew exactly how far the Germans had gone back. They held Carrigione, which was a town about ten miles away. We had shelled the woods between ourselves and the town and the patrols had found nothing. So the advance had begun and so far the Germans had not shelled us or anything. It was all too easy, if anything in that sort of life is easy. There was a heavy silence, packed with cicadas: you know the sort of noise *they* make; well, that filled the silence and the noise somehow got lost. The rain slithered down the leaves. The day before you could hear the ground sucking in the wet but on that day the ground was saturated, drenched. So were we. And there were pools of water on top. We had scooped holes out of the banks and we just crouched there like worms or dead birds, with our knees pressed against our chests and the stink of wet clothes all round us. I think it was a Tuesday. The radio was working so we were still in touch; our last orders had been to wait and keep alert. It wasn't easy to keep alert and it was hard to realize that we were in Italy. A beautiful, squalid country which you ought to see, but I suspect you never will.' He paused and drank deeply at his beer. Some well-dressed people had come into the bar and their faces were pink with the heat and what looked like a good evening's drink-up. I knew what I had to say now. 'No, I guess I never will; but what happened next?'

He frowned and ruffled his moustache with both hands. 'During combat I acted on a kind of instinct; but waiting poisoned me because I was afraid. You never knew how long you had left and waiting like that seemed a lousy way to spend what might be some of your last minutes or hours. Minutes, hours, it made no difference; they just went by. You dreamed, you studied the ants. You tried to look forward to your next K ration. Well, the mist drew denser and whiter; the spaces where there was no mist looked black and foul—almost as if there were some horrible thing waiting in them. I remember feeling very small and alone.' He looked at me suddenly, paused, and nodded. Then he scratched his ear. 'I was watching one man who had suddenly had a kind of hysteria some days back. He was calm now. Battle-fatigue I mean; that sort of thing. And now he seemed the only one of us immune to the drizzle and the mud and mist. His eyes were closed, his fingers tight round his carbine. There was a cut on his cheek and he looked like some man in a small room, in a city like this, watching the snow form in the sky and then begin to fall. And I suddenly felt that I would give anything to see a snow-sky forming over Manhattan, just poised there over the smoke. Strange what a man finds comforting; he feels wrong if his billfold is in the wrong inside pocket or he has his cigarette lighter in the bottom of his pocket when he's been in the habit of carrying it in the special small pocket provided. Well, when we finally advanced into the wood we just squelched and slipped. A hell of a noise we made, I tell you. It was a whole world made of mud and slimy leaves. It grew darker and we all began to cough. I kept trying to shift my toes around inside my boots, but the toes were numb, not with cold. I guess I don't know *what* they were numb with. But numb they were; it was just bad circulation, I think. Then someone called out that he had found a dead German, so I went splashing across to the voice. You had to feel. The face had been deep in the mud and there were smashed branches all round. His chin had gone, and when we put the body down again it sank down into the mud as if the mud was glad to have it back. You could always say that the springy ground never welcomed a corpse; but the mud did. (And it was from mud that our ancestors dragged themselves on those fins we now have as legs.) So we went on, for a good hour. You could just make out the shapes of the other men scattered about you, skidding forward and cursing very quietly. But cursing all the time. I never did rightly know what happened next. It was an orange flash to

my right and a bang that seemed to follow much later. I
couldn't be sure about that. Everyone dived flat and it
sounded like wet fish being slapped on a metal counter. It
sure didn't sound like men diving for their lives. Any more
than a bullet over your head sounds like a reprieve. Then
there was another bang and another flash. It was a minefield.
I had never been in a minefield before and I haven't been in
one since. We lay there, you know, gibbering a little and
shaking. You had to think about the ground in front of you,
and behind, and at your side. So everyone was very still. You
could hear a lot of gasping and a wounded man moaning. I
remember thinking how some men live as still as that all their
lives, in their office chairs, panting and darting their eyes
about, just wondering where death will come from. By sitting
tight there, in the mud, you could be a success in life; you
could keep your life so long as you sat still. And keep a life to
have your life in. Was the way out round the back? Could you
test the ground in front with your foot? Dare you even move
your hand or even press your finger deeper into the mud? All
you could safely do was ask questions. So you could walk a
zig-zag could you? A straight line might save you and a zig-
zag take you on to a mine. Had they allowed for every move?
Had they already read our minds? We needed some kind of
water-diviner with a crooked stick. And I remember feeling:
right now I just want to retire, phone a cab and go home in
style, leaning back deep in the cushions and flicking ash on
the floor. I guess I had a somewhat elevated notion of a taxi.
But I just wanted to go home, without disturbing anyone or
anything, not even skimming the ground as I went—like
people who are supposed to be happy. Or Christ walking on
the water. Then I came to. Panic is a taste like brass, like
chewing a dirty quarter or a key. I recall shouting, "Who's
there?" And someone answered. They were sitting still; you
know how they sometimes stop a movie. That. It was hard to
tell, then, how far we had gone into the minefield. Not far;
or were we in deep and had we just been very lucky? We
couldn't even be sure what would happen if we walked back.
Slowly, then, slowly as slowly can be, we got up, staring down
at the ground—that decent bit of land that had saved some
of us so far.

'Then we began to walk back, with one wounded man: how
we dared to go and find him I shall never know, and how we
got to him safely God only knows. His arm was torn apart.
No man there really wanted to trouble about a wounded man,
but we were too ashamed to admit it. We did a tourniquet
anyhow, and hauled him along. His stumbling feet would sure
as goodness hit a mine; but the end would be quick. The man
who had been next him was dead and in several pieces. You
know, we were intended to be dismembered like that, just to
prove how fragile we are. Well, you put down the first foot,
settled your weight on it firmly and then fished out gently
with your other foot. You can guess how delicately we did that
while we were holding up a fainting man. Heaven had to
protect us then. No noise. Like cats. Yet not seeing anywhere
near as well as cats. The mist kept reaching at us and I
thought of the ghosts I used to believe in. I had begun to
believe in them all over again. Shapes formed and melted
away again. One man would make a sudden detour because
he had a hunch; maybe his face had suddenly itched on the
left, so he turned right. Another would veer if the rain ran
into his eye. A good omen for one was a warning to his neighbour. And I, well I just walked straight on, forcing myself to
walk straight. Lord knew, if we had all followed our hunches
we would have ended up miles apart. It was all madness. The
men were beginning to talk now, making little jokes. We had
gone about a hundred yards so we were getting confident.
Too confident, perhaps? I asked myself what I would do if I
were setting a minefield. I had never set a minefield, though I
had marked out a football field. I called a halt. Told them we
were going back; don't ask me why. They murmured; they
didn't like it. But one man close to me turned without hesi-
tating. Back we all went, silent again. Walking at first; and
then, suddenly, when I whispered, running like mad, sprinting
on like ghosts trying not to touch the damned ground. We ran
on and away for fifteen minutes, and nothing happened.
Nothing exploded. A slight wind had come up, blowing the
rain and mist sideways. There was no moon. I felt chilled and
then I heard someone laughing over on the left. That was a
good laugh to hear, and everyone seemed to echo it. Then,
suddenly, the wind stopped. The undergrowth was thick and

tough and we were going slightly downhill, relaxing just a little. It was then that the worst possible thing happened. Several guns began to fire on us, from all angles: violet and yellow flashes in the dark. Down into the mud again, sliding and praying. I fired at a flash, heard a rustle, thought about it, fired at it; no reply. Then the rain whispering at us. A groan and some sobbing. Then more firing and scuffling; someone began to scream and then everyone must have begun to fire and shout and run. I blasted away into the trees because I thought that was where the flashes were coming from. Something came crashing down. There was an awful commotion then; I guess it was a hand-grenade. Then more firing and I felt the slug-suck noises coming nearer. "Oh, leave us alone," I said aloud, "give us a break." I rolled over and then sideways. Then a blinding flash and then another and something burned right through my leg. I fired as best I could and then collapsed into the mud. I don't remember any more for a while; and then I woke up and I thought I was dead. My lungs felt full of mist; I was choking. Then I felt what I thought had been my life swilling out below the waist, very fast and thick, and I was trying to scoop it all back, blood and mud, any fluid, into the hole wherever that was. There was no clear pain, you see. Then, I don't know why, I relaxed, all of a sudden. I guess that was the surrender-point.'

The mist was still with him, he said, but the flow had stopped. He was still in the wood and he would found a colony there, of men who hated sunlight. They would always be groping through the mist calling and whispering, with their eyes on the ground and their arms in front of them like blind men, knocking on the tree-trunks as if they were doors, offering name, rank and number and number of children. Their whispers died. There men fired at a call, at a commotion in the brush. The mist tangled them, prevented them from greeting one another. Their feet rotted and fell off, so that they couldn't walk nobly or even awkwardly down the corridors of trees home to their wives. And no one knew how to shift mist, how to kill spiders, break webs, just to improve the situation for its own sake, like giving a magazine subscription to a dying man. They have to feel. The man is churning the mud with his elbows, slapping it with his palms, spitting. He feels

monstrous. He is raving. They grope for his legs. His legs feel
at the wrong angle to his trunk, and it is not quite a man they
are touching. It is nothing new; just flesh-débris which
emerges sooner or later from man's cleverest experiments—
raging and resigned or just a few tatters, cheap at the price,
and needing only the price of a bandage-kit. There is no firing
now. Only the rain sucking them down. Tourniquets. Muddy
fingers dabbling in the slush round the wound and, as Papa
says, a brutal kindness which has to be and goes probing the
secret areas of torn flesh, deep under his skin, making the
tamed body convulse with a slavering cry which has no re-
lation to any man distinct from mud.

'Stop shaking!' I stared at Papa.

'Stop! Stop! Here—' He thrust my beer into my hand.
'Now close your mouth and sit back.' I did; I had been standing up and must have looked like a very tall man sitting
down. Then Papa stopped talking for a long time, and just
drank beer after beer, never once getting up to visit the men's
room. And I just sat quietly, making circles in the spilled beer
on the booth table, and quietly speeding up as if I were
writing a long letter of letter O's to someone who would never
read it. I rubbed my finger faster and faster until I was
making the beer squeak; faster and faster like a whirlpool
right through the table and into that knee of mine beneath,
like an auger. 'A good movie, that,' Papa muttered as he
stared into the middle distance. 'I wouldn't mind seeing that
again. No, I wouldn't mind seeing that again.' I kept rubbing
and my finger was getting warm. 'No, I wouldn't mind seeing
that again,' he said. 'No, no, I wouldn't mind.' And I saw that
his eyes were wide open, bulging; and he was crying with his
mouth very tight and his hands still round the glass as if he
could will it to come to life and escort him back to the movie-
house. I said nothing but took out my handkerchief and wiped
the beer up. I would not for all this world have offered him
that cloth; I knew the tear-ducts were choked. Or something
like that. I just got up and went to the men's room, causing a
diversion, especially from a blonde in an orange dress who
came up and said, 'What a sweet little man! *What* do they call
you?' I went in and relieved myself. You wouldn't think a
small guy had a large bladder, but he has. It could be the

tears that get suppressed. And I waited there a while, among the stink of urine and carbolic, the running water and the decaying pipes with their white crust. From my pocket I took that old false moustache and my sun-glasses, put them on. Then I turned up the collar of my coat and stuck a cigarette in the corner of my mouth and lit it carefully so as not to set fire to the false whiskers. I checked my appearance in the mirror. Then I marched out, all of me, pretty tough and wishing I had a hat too. They all laughed and when Papa saw me so did he. I kept my disguise on and ordered two more beers. I was getting hungry and my scalp was beginning to itch.

Both of us had forgotten Lacland, snug back there in his crate, mumbling after nothing but bread and water, and thankful to have his boots off at last. Or so I thought. I was wrong. Papa had started drawing in the beer on the black wood of the table. First a square, then a great big square round it; then a man's shape in the small square, with long legs sticking out. 'That's *him*,' whispered Papa. 'I gave him a bucket tonight, just to see what he would use it for. After all, with that food—even such food as he takes, he'll need *something*.' I don't know what got into me just then, but I dipped my finger in my own beer and wrote a big cross cancelling the drawing. Papa narrowed his eyes. 'Draw it again!' When he spoke in that tone you did not argue. I drew the two squares again, with the man inside, on my part of the table. Papa wiped out his own with his sleeve. 'Yes, yours is better, isn't it? Like a man in a coffin. In peace, in safety. Like an animal in its hole. We must do something for him, and soon.' Wiping off my own drawing—which had almost dried into nothing—he took my arm and said it was time to move on.

Papa Nick

THAT MORNING it hurt to look at the sky. I mean that it jarred as if you had broken a fingernail and caught it against a silk scarf, magnetizing you with faint shock. To stare at that sky made your eyes water; it was an unkind silver, just the sort of sky you expect on days when things are destined to go wrong: anyway, when they do go wrong. It wasn't the sun burning at the cloud-cover as often happens in summer; rather, it was a dead light like magnesium, making the iris wince, so that the people you met looked spasmodic and garish in motion. Perhaps that is what they always look, but on this particular day they crossed the eye's view painfully, like visual discords. I think of sardines in a shallow can: they lie there, stiff-tailed and plump-bodied, at peace, lambent with oil; and then, suddenly, an electric current passes through them and they bristle upwards out of the can, awkward and contorted, the tails stiff and sensitive as springing wire and abdomens twitching for lack of a head. And because I can never see accurately when the light is harsh, I could almost persuade myself that the people I met that morning on the avenue were newly beheaded sardines, their pallid stumps looking crude. I stared and then my gaze rebounded, all obscuring tears and hurt retina. A bad-looking day, and what was to come bore that out.

I have this bad habit of living in the present and the past at the same time. I remember that morning: how I sat there looking at the bums as they lay around on the mattresses. Derelicts was the polite word, but they and I never bothered much about the superficial things because our relationship was

47

elementary. It would have been easy, after the first few years of looking after them, to work myself up in my own eyes into a pastor: my flock and staff, and all that. Instead I saw myself as something almost mechanical: enter a bum and I would feed him, bed him down for as long as he needed. But while developing this mechanical charity—which is not to disparage it, of course—I became even lonelier. There were limits to what you could talk about. It was one thing to read aloud— Rimbaud in English or the Bible; it was quite another to try and talk about these things. The same went for my favourite recordings when I brought them out of hiding and permitted Brahms to flood the room and assault the fragile, intimidated ears of the men on the mattresses. I could talk to Lazarus, the dwarf, and I suppose he is a credit to my informal system of education; but he can go only so far and then he becomes hysterical, like a man who has walked along too many tight-ropes. He listens, at any rate, and when he talks back he can be as original as I need him to be. Sometimes I feel like Frankenstein; perhaps I should have left Lazarus in his minor night and not filled his head with questions. But you can't go through life without imposing your talk on someone, and I think he's gained from it as much as he's lost. He tries; I just wish he didn't have that wild, unco-ordinated streak. His eyes enlarge, then bulge, and his eyebrows begin to signal violently up and down. It wouldn't be as bad if his eyebrows were the same colour as his hair; but his hair is silver, somewhat dyed, somewhat naturally so. This gives him an odd air of distinction even in the wrestling ring; he looks much older than he is, and tempts you to think his few feet of body might be frail. Oh no, though, he bounces and cavorts like a chimpanzee; except that, as I say, he is an emotional chimpanzee.

I sat there on that morning in the approximate silence of deep-embedded coughs and the throat-clearing. A few bums were still sleeping and a few were conversing (if that is the correct word) very quietly. A scene of almost monastic peace; a flop-house idyll. I watched and yet I saw other things more immediately. Back in the villa, or rather on the balcony in the evening with a long undiluted Scotch on the high circular table beside me, a pack of Gauloises and the mosquito-bomb: I was slumped low in my deckchair, vaguely overcome with food—too much spaghetti that night, and somewhat lonely. Out over the Mediterranean the moon lolled evocatively, illuminating just a narrow strip of the still sea as far as the horizon. Somewhere a baby wailed. Voices floated across from the bar opposite: French voices in systematic debate, but muffled and distorted because the body of the villa was between me and them. I sat there and floated. Now and then I squirted the bomb into the night air as the needle-whine of the mosquitoes came near. Moths flopped unsteadily at the lighted windows of the living-room. The lizard was looking out from his commanding position at the top of the window; if I made a sudden move he would vanish into the roof. No telephone and no company. It was a disturbing kind of peace such as you can stand only when you've had a surfeit of relationships. There was no wind, no murmur of sea; only the lingering, humid heat of the late evening and the usual thick-wrapped darkness. It was enough to make anyone sentimental —in the best sense of the word; even a young man looking back on Princeton, Oxford, and a few months spent in a canning factory where you sorted frozen pineapple until you didn't know whether your fingers were pineapple or not. I had worked in that factory to try to 'make contact'; because if you have money you make only a different kind of contact, and that is no contact at all. Lucky in one sense to have money, to go there, to write and read and even to try to compose music, I felt as if I were sitting on God's eyelid, looking downwards at the world. Then I discovered that you make contact not by slumming, nor by cutting yourself off, but by discovering in people something you respect; and something which you can also see in yourself.

These things always come back. It is many years since I was there and I shall not go back. There are the bums; there will always be the bums; and here am I at the most disreputable station on my journey. Yet it is a scruffy heaven of sorts in which an unpretentious peace wanders in and out of the days, creeping up on us and then fading away only to reappear as if by accident. Some days there is Lazarus when he has expelled himself from his lodgings and his landlady; some days there is Rachel, the over-wrought Jewish girl who was in Buchenwald and is supposed to be crazy; other days there is

Doc Rumboldt, always in a hurry, just calling in to check on the most infirm of the bums; and then there are the days on which I go across town to visit Venetia, still an actress, and very much so when she sweeps into this place on a wave of mink and Chanel, electrifying the bums and dispensing alms: cigarettes, candies, gum, tobacco, papers, brown bread she has made herself and liver pâté. I have always refused to let her give the men transistor radios (this was her latest idea). I think they would stop thinking altogether then; not that they would disturb one another—they would use the earphones of course, but they would soon be living in another dimension. That bad habit I reserve for myself.

I recall once how some of the men got high; I think it was the day I presented the 'community' here with an electric razor. I happened to go out to the store, and when I came back they had most of them shaved. They were dancing, or something like that. Here was Rachel, with an intensely con-centrating face, in the throes of a gentle, strict dance which took her from foot to foot, metronome-like, and made her hair swing. On either side of her, much more rapidly, to the sound of a simple jazz rhythm from the radio by the window, the derelicts were celebrating. One, with a shawl round his head, kept jacknifing at the knees. He was moaning slightly. An-other, with a dumb-bell above his head, was (it seemed) parodying the routine of the weight-lifter. Yet another was wobbling his belly and tossing his head back. They were all out of step, out of tune. There was no co-ordination, no balance; they wobbled, heaved, tapped and swayed, all with very little noise and painfully intent on their performance. The belly-dancer took a few little steps across the room, tapped his toe on the knee of one of the less energetic bums, and then scurried back to the others. A stray laugh or two stirred from the depths of a throat. I stood there with the tall brownpaper bag, just watching. Soon they elaborated the routine into a formal bow and pirouette in front of the Jewish girl, taking turns. Then she began to spin and at about the fifth spin began to squeal, 'Going to the garden in the morn-ing' closely followed by one of the bums who half echoed, in a baritone, 'Goin' fishin', too!' This held for about five minutes, a grotesque private rite which celebrated and made a protest too. I wondered how long they could go on extemporizing like that; they were tiring, I could see, and when someone emerged from the bathroom with a sheet tied bridal fashion around his head, they all ran to pick up the sheet trailing behind him and followed him to the other side of the room. It was a small, temporary and very dignified procession. Then, just as quickly, they all sat down, the sheet was rolled or folded up, and everything was calm. They expected a rebuke, I think, but I just reported the fact of the food in the bag I was still holding and went out into the kitchen. I would not call it fear; but there was something in the energies on view there—a small whirlpool which opened up and closed over again—that perturbed. You expect it now and then. The Jewish girl left soon after, her thin face bright with semi-hysteria. I was glad in a way that Lazarus had not been there. Set him bouncing and he cannot stop; he means no harm but he has no limits, no speedometer after fifteen miles an hour. He mutters to himself a great deal and whips his head around constantly, as if he is being trailed. It is his smallness that does it, I suppose: he is on the defensive most of the time, a stern custodian of himself. You have only to watch him train at the gymnasium: he punishes the punch-ball, he thwacks the mats, he thumps the horse, he percusses at everything. But there is no one gentler with a hurt bird or even a house-fly. He will always open the window to send the fly on its way. He once kept a bird in his lodgings for a month and cured it; at least it was well enough to fly away.

Thinking of such matters, I recur to Lacland as we called him. It isn't every day that you find an inarticulate, helpless bum at the top of the subway. If you did, places like this would be crowded. But this man had obviously been jailed or imprisoned somewhere; you might even say bottled up. Lazarus and I did our best. Then it occurred to me that he couldn't stand light or noise, so he really needed and merited his crate in the cellar. It took me longer to realize that Lazarus terrified him; I cannot be sure why; nor can I be sure why I eventually decided to give him absolute privacy and peace. The cellar has a false wall; it is what used to be beneath a stairway, now covered over. So, hoping I was doing right, I moved Lacland from his crate, put the mattress in the small space under the stairs and covered in the entrance with fibre-ply board. I worked on the board at night, cutting a small space for a door and fixing hinges with screws. This had the appearance of a cupboard-door and, left open at night with the cellar-door locked, it gave him enough air. In the daytime I kept the cupboard locked except when, to keep things private, I went next door and down through their basement into my own. Then, again behind locked doors, I opened Lacland's little door, fed him brown bread and skim milk, and emptied his bucket. You may think I was too secretive and possessive in this; it may be so. But as I saw it, the man was not ready for community and I had a duty of care which consisted in sheltering him while he was helpless and, perhaps, although this is less certain, of helping him to emerge one day into society. He emerged all right, but only after a long regimen of brown bread, milk, emptied buckets and locked doors. I would feel easier in my own mind if he had gradually developed to the level of the bums above; but, after some tedious months of my nurturing him—all of this in secret or at night —he began to show an interest in speaking to me. I cannot say that I made an absolute secret of his presence; but everyone regarded my slips or hints as a small local myth concocted and sustained by an ailing old man. Equally, I never advertised him. Only Lazarus seemed to have any suspicion and he never asked exactly what had happened to Lacland. When I think back now, I see myself as over-zealous, playing the omnipotent a little and yet, for all that, justified, managing a careful passage from darkness to light, from animal to human. I will not deny that, about once a day, a thrill would suddenly course through my arms as I handed in the thick slices of brown bread, the feeding-bottle and reached in for the bucket which, eventually, he learned to hand out to me as soon as I arrived. An odd mixture, you might think, of nurse and demiurge, of the apocalyptic and the satanic. It was moving and rewarding to see this creature, like the first amphibian, get his bearings, graduate to meat and potatoes (which of course is when the bucket became more repugnant), ask for more and more light, occasionally laugh with a goat-like noise and finally begin to speak. He learned his words as if he had known them before; he forgot nothing and we very

rapidly progressed from my naming the plate by torchlight—
'PLATE! PLATE! PLATE! BREAD! BREAD! BREAD! MILK! MILK!' and
so on, to simple sentences: 'BREAD AGAIN?' as I motioned at
the slice and pointed to his mouth, or 'CAN YOU SEE?' as I
indicated my eyes and the flashlight I always carried. He was
emerging, coming out of the night of his ancestors; like some
dark fish soaring up from the coarse river-bed to butt his head
against the surface of the water and into the magical region
of air. No discoverer, standing on his peak or untrodden sands,
has known a thrill as acute as this. One man, one near-man,
soon to stand erect, was quietly taking suck in a clean cellar in
the most plangent, most unreal of cities. I think of this as a
rebellion against the concrete, the steel and the gasolene
fumes. I was making the organic fit to withstand the in-
organic; the sturdy buzz-fly able to fly confidently against the
glass of any window, to rehearse and rehearse until one day
the glass would be lowered and out he would sail into the
corrupt ether. The creative will understand; it was like
watching the granite take shape under your hands or the
paint develop lucid configurations on the canvas. Here I was,
like the man tending his farm in wartime, arguing no allegiance
for cabbages, no policy for turnips, no pacts for livestock, no
amnesty for the regular tide of manure. Call it fidelity to the
God-given; I am reluctant to dignify too much what I did,
right or wrong, in all this. When the outcome is unpredictable,
but when you hope and trust what it will be, you take the
risks, assuming they are yours alone. In this I was mistaken.
I never thought of myself as jailer, though it was true that
Lacland could not get out. Slothful, seemingly at peace, he
lay there, occasionally stretching and yawning and laughing
deep in his chest. I would have said, had I discussed him at all,
that he was coming to life in every sense.

This far he had expressed no feeling about dirt. I would take
him a wet face-cloth and a towel, but most of the time I had
to clean him up myself; and of course he never shaved. His
beard was vivid, a reddish brown with wild streaks of what
looked like silver. One night, as I went downstairs, I thought
I heard a strange noise; not a growl or a moan, but in between.
I unlocked the cellar door and went in. There was no light.
By this time—he must have been down there for three months

—I knew my way in the dark and so hadn't bothered to switch on my flashlight. I was carrying the plate with my thumb clamped over the bread, and I had some Gruyère cheeses wrapped in silver foil in my pocket. I walked up to the cupboard door—to where I knew it would be, and reached out for the lock. I found air. Then I moved my hand sideways, thinking I had made a mistake, and scraped it against an enormous tuft of wiry hair; then a sharp pain struck my finger and, as I switched on the flashlight in panic, I saw Lacland, his face swollen and his eyes rolling, biting on my hand. When I snatched the hand away, he roared with primitive glee; the small door swung uselessly on its hinges, the lock suspended by a single screw. I think I shouted at him to get back and raised the flashlight as if to strike him (a move of which I now feel ashamed, but it was instinctive). He thrust his head even further out of the small hole that was no larger than fifteen inches square. He was like a stertorous horse glaring out from his box. I was not ready for what came next: his massive, filthy hand reached out and snatched the bread, squeezed it, crumpled it and then flung it in my face. More wild guffaws. I flinched back and stared at him as he half crouched to push out his head and his hand, with saliva dribbling from his wide mouth and his free hand against the fibre-ply partition. He wasn't trying to get out, but he was angry. I could find no words for some time. Then I pointed the flashlight at the ceiling, and his eyes followed the beam.

'I've come to feed you,' I said as calmly as I could.

He stared, grinned and shook his head.

'Aren't you hungry?' I looked at the empty plate, still in my hand, and his eyes came to rest on it. His jaws were working violently by this time, beneath his whiskers, as if some animal were shuffling in the brush. Then he made a long, spittle-thick sound like 'Ah-h-h.' This was nothing new. What he did next was.

'You bastard,' he grunted. 'You bastard!'

I looked and looked. Either things were coming back with a rush into his stirring brain or someone had been with him. He repeated the words.

'Who did that?' I asked, pointing at the door, the small one.

'Bastard did that. That bastard.'

'It was you, was it?'

He laughed crazily. 'Yes, bastard; bas-tard; you did that. You did that.'

'Lacland,' I said, my voice higher in pitch with excitement, 'who smashed down that door?'

It was obvious that he had thought the answer out, 'You smashed, you bastard!' Then came his most ambitious statement ever: 'You think I can't talk. I *can* talk and I *can* think and I *can* smash a door and I *can* bastard you and I *can* bastard that Lazarus and I *can* get out when I want——'

'Stop it!' I shouted, although I cannot say why. He had never spoken connectedly before. But he stopped. I told him it was never part of my intention to imprison him; he nodded at that, and I felt easier. Then he shook his head and said, almost modestly, 'I kill.' I don't know why, but suddenly I knew that Lazarus had been down there, had spoken to him God knew how many times and had taught him I hesitated to guess what. 'Look!' he shouted. With his left hand he reached down, inside the wall, and came up with a sheet of paper which shone in the light. It was a pin-up, gaudy in pink bikini and rippling with fat. He patted the sheet gently (I noticed how long and discoloured his nails were). He told me that this was his woman, that I could not have her and that she had been there all the time.

'Lazarus bring me this woman,' he shouted with unnecessary and almost peremptory force. 'Not his; this *my* woman! What do you do with a woman? What do you do with this woman?' He began to shake the wooden partition and beat his bearded chin on the lower rim of the gap. I told him to calm down, to put the pin-up away, to eat his bread—although that was in remnants on the floor—and to take his milk. Surprisingly he took the milk: in one gulp. Then he told me to watch, and he bent down. His face did not reappear but, out over the edge of the hole, like fragments coming back to earth after an explosion had flung them upwards, there came hurtling a large bone, a knife—a carving-knife—several newspapers and periodicals, some of them torn and stained with what looked like excrement, a piece of chain, a hammer, a small coping-saw, a pencil, a ball-point pen, a whole roll of toilet paper and an empty bottle of Johnnie Walker. His head came up again, smiling devilishly; then his left hand, with a flashlight in it, which he switched on and turned into my face. His right hand held something small, in leather; I could hardly make out what it was, but suddenly I knew for I heard a click and the cellar was filled with Dixieland music—a throbbing beat to which he paid no attention. He was looking for my response to his revelations.

'Well,' he shouted, 'how you like that? Lazarus, he told me about the bums up there. Hey! you think I'm a bum? I'm no bum, you'll see. No bum at all.' I told him to switch off the light and the radio, but he took no notice.

At that moment I felt sick: sick of the cellar, of Lacland, of the human flotsam upstairs, of Lazarus the twisted retainer, of all I had ever been. There he was, his chin shoved hard into his chest so that his eyes seemed deeper in his head than ever, with both hands raised half threateningly, half imploring. Poor bare animal; sample of the underprivileged. And I felt impotent. Here in his cell (yes, I now saw it as that) he had learned up on the twentieth century from which I had thought so charitably to extricate him. He already had the apparatus of fun and indulgence and here I was bringing him milk and bread, Gruyère cheese and a bucket. Some of our hopeful kindnesses are more bestial than we ever believe; I knew this, but I also knew I should not release him to run amok with a hammer and a knife and a raw shin-bone and a taste for Scotch. Why, he could speak and read; he had outwitted me with little effort, hadn't he? And the thought ran through my mind that this lamb could be a dragon. Whereas I had previously sheltered, or thought to shelter, I had now to protect him from himself: which was possibly a new twist in hypocrisy but one I had to live with. Then I thought of Lazarus, who must have sneaked down behind me or got in some other way. Lazarus had meant well, I thought; but he had overstepped. I went up in a vortex in which I lived to believe, believed to live, lived to love, loved to live, believed to love, loved to believe—my head spun. Though we walk through the valley of the shadow, I murmured to myself, we fear—what do we fear? We fear the lie that isn't always evil, the good that is not always wise. We fear possibility. We tie down, strap up, we fasten. We are afraid of running loose; so we incarcerate. We make incarceration our principle. Oh, the way we live; the way we pretend to live when we are afraid to live. We do more damage with our pity and our good motives than a sabre-toothed tiger would in the nursery. Here was Lacland in his nursery, which was new-grown into bear-garden. Here was I, custodian become jailer, man of light become oppressor.

I automatically fumbled about on the floor to pick up the bread, and I realized how cold it was down there and wondered if I had associated cold with virtue, chill with discipline. With my head down, I felt hang-dog; and, when I looked up, there he was, his face bulging and working at the aperture, mocking and nodding. Outside and above us, the decent night must have settled by now; there would be the calm scrutiny by the stars, the bland moon, the homeward drunks and the cops patrolling. Quiet men and women with buckets and mops would be swilling down hallways and marble corridors. Once again, I wanted to escape to the island paradise which of course was no paradise but only a certain kind of luxury misleadingly associated with certain colours, sounds and names. I asked him for the bucket; he handed it out, twirling it between strong finger and thumb, and the handle squeaked against the enamel. The stench was sharp, and I turned to carry the bucket back upstairs.

'What about my things?' I almost dropped the bucket as he shouted. 'Gimme back. Come on! Gimme!' I put the bucket down and looked around. Carefully I handed back the news-papers and the periodicals, the toilet paper which flapped loose as I passed it across, and the pencil and pen. The bone, chain, hammer, saw and empty bottle I dropped in the bucket with a series of splashes. He still had his flashlight and radio safely inside somewhere. He did not protest at being deprived; I imagine he thought he could get Lazarus to replace what he had lost—with God knew what. I thought of razors, revolvers and acid. Lazarus, in one sense, approximated to low (which was all right) but also crooked life, and there was no telling what experiment in psychology he might dream up: such as getting his own back on the master-race of the average-sized. With Lazarus you usually knew; but not always. He had, as I have said, that unsteady, fervent streak such as would unhinge a less cynical spirit and perhaps transform into intermittent saint a person of more positive morals.

And then, at once, I was out of it; back among the bums with their loitering eyes, unco-ordinated limbs, phlegm-thick monologues, whisky-veined eyes, badly cut hair, foul breath and careless self-indulgence. I had emptied the bucket and I walked back into that upstairs room like Adam reparadised. I obviously looked worried, though, for one of them—it was Edgar the Time (so-called because he always wanted to know the exact hour)—came swaying up to me and said, 'Papa, you wear the worry on your face.' They all talked some kind of stunted idiom learned in the shadows and perfected during tipsy monologues to themselves. Yes, I was worried, I said. I told him I was worried about a friend of mine who had fallen into bad habits—liquor, women, knives and so on, and how was I to get him clear. Find him a new bad habit, he said. Find him some person with an outlandish and shocking twist: then he would either reform or destroy himself the sooner. I could see the sense in this; I wondered what Edgar would say if he knew what I had in the cellar and if he knew that, until very recently, I myself had not known. I asked him if he had seen Lazarus that evening but he hadn't; Lazarus was, he thought, wrestling either tonight or tomorrow.

'We should do sumpn for you,' suggested Edgar. 'Like buyin' you a new watch; for the time—for the time being— just for being, if you follow me. Buy you sumpn.' I heard this routine daily; nothing ever came of it. 'Say,' he called down the room, through the cumulus of tobacco smoke and the slots between his remaining teeth, 'we should buy Papa some present!' A straggling chorus of assent stirred up and down from the mattresses where most of the men were half sleeping. 'We'll see tomorrow,' someone called out; and while they were settling down again, with assorted grunts and releasing of wind, there came like the sudden outpouring of a cement-mixer on to a metal platform—but with pebbles crashing in the cement—a long, incensed roar from way down in the foundations. Somewhat muted, it could not have been said to be a human noise; I knew what it was, but Edgar, the only alert bum at that time, cursed about the subway and the lousy buildings and (of all things) the high rents. The roar must have lasted twenty seconds. Probably Lacland wanted whisky or meat, a woman or whatever you can guess. This might have been how Lazarus discovered him; and whether or not he frightened Lazarus or Lazarus took pity on him, the unkempt unredeemed in his minor cave, I knew not. I decided not to go down and, half expecting Lacland to come bounding up the stairs, I walked out after telling Edgar what the time was and that I would be back soon. It was ten exactly. It was a matter now of finding and questioning Lazarus; easier said than done.

He had wrestled and was relaxing in the changing rooms at the Gardens. The effort had made him almost voiceless; his cheeks twitched, quivered, and streamed with sweat. He nodded a greeting, buried his face in the towel, looked around him at the other dwarf wrestlers who were giggling at me, and announced that he had lost—or rather that he and his partner had lost the bout. 'No use tonight, Papa; they rowed the boat on us and my groin-muscles are ruined. I should give this up.' I glared at him. 'Have you been visiting in my cellar?' He studied the nail on his big toe and then insolently and innocently said, 'Visiting who?'

'Lacland!' I burst out with it; 'Lacland! Who else?'

'I don't recall him. He must be new. I never could keep track of all the new ones——'

'You know very well who I mean. The man in the crate.'

'Oh yeah, but he went.'

'He did not went—he did not go. He stayed.'

'Upstairs, was it?'

'In the cellar. Down there.'

'I saw no one'; he had said it before he realized.

'So you *did*! You went down there, you sneaked down and pushed your nose into something that concerns you not at all. Do you realize what you've done?'

'My partner and I,' he said, smirking, 'have just lost a wrestling bout. That is what I have done.' All three and a bit feet of him.

So I gave up direct questioning and just told him that Lacland was wild and excited, that I had seen his trophies and that I had a problem on hand. And Lazarus, with hardly so much as a blink, changed position at once:

'I thought he needed something to—well, play with; have fun with. Meant no harm.' I don't think he did. It was no use expostulating about the possible harm to come from a knife in the hands of a savage inspired with Scotch; but I did want to know something.

'The bone,' I said, 'what about the bone?'

Lazarus scratched his head, the hair lying sleek with sweat. 'T-bone roast from Mrs. Pomeroy,' he said lazily.

'That was no T-bone roast. What was it?'

'Well, some roast, you know. Just a roast, part eaten.'

'He didn't leave a scrap of meat on it.'

'So he was hungry, then. Give him more.'

And that was how the 'interrogation' went: Lazarus, fractionally contrite but really baffled because he thought I was exaggerating. I slapped him on his well-covered ribs. 'Get dressed. I want you to see him. And hear him. Who taught him to speak? The radio? You?'

He can't talk at all. Not as far as I know.'

'I tell you he talked.' I spoke with angry vehemence. Was Lazarus being honest or just joking?

'Then, if he talked, he learned from the radio. Sure, I gave him that. What did you expect him to do all day? He ain't got the materials to *think* with.'

'Hasn't he? You come with me. You'll hear some talk, and stuff he couldn't have picked up from the radio.'

Lazarus shrugged. Then he flipped the towel at my face and stumped across the room. 'I need another shower now. You got me all excited again. Why you bother me right after the bout?'

I decided to wait. From behind the partition he shouted, 'You talked a speech yourself the other night!'

I could not understand this. 'Talked? When?' I asked.

'In that bar, after the movie; the war movie.'

I told him that was three months ago.

'Yeah. Like I said; the other night!' and I could hear him laughing as he soaped himself and stamped around under the water. Before you lose your sanity, you have to meet a few of the sane to compare yourself with; before you know you've lost it, that is. Bums all the time, shuffling and expectorating and whining and holding out the eternal hand of mock-need. I lit a cigarette and walked out into the corridor where two dwarfs eyed me with disdain and distrust. They were just leaving, each carrying a gaudy bouquet. Then they burst past me, sniggering: 'We got these from admirers. From admirers. From admirers. Fans!' They disappeared into the exit at the end of the tunnel. How strangely metallic and fey they were, all of them, always compensating and usually doing so by inventing little jokes and plots they thought no one else could reach. I waited a while, then went in and called Lazarus. He had vanished. I called again and he emerged from behind a cupboard. He was transformed: a cream tuxedo with a large carnation in the lapel; his hair waved up high and slicked with grease; a speckled white shirt with silk embroidery catching the light and a narrow pink necktie clipped to his shirt with a glittering metal hand as big as a half-dollar. On his feet he had lemon-coloured suède shoes; the trousers looked black. As he came into view he was sliding a large ornamental ring on to his finger. 'Phi Beta Kappa?' I said. 'What else? How'd you know? How'd you know?' he said in his high-pitched giggle. 'I'm the most educated small guy in the whole city.' Well, if he stayed with me long enough he would learn something. And soon. Then he posed for me in the centre of the room, waiting to be admired. With a small white comb he corrected the slope of his hair—did this by feel. I told him he looked beautiful. He continued to stand there, leaning against my impatience, and suddenly he looked the most derelict, hopelessly veneered wastrel of them all, tiny and erect on the water-splashed board floor and yet king of the sweat-aromatic room where I was a patent misfit. 'O.K.,' I said quietly, 'shall we go?' 'I'm waiting,' he said, and we left.

Out into the night we strolled, with all the other strollers nudging one another as we went by. But we were accustomed to that and within fifteen minutes were back at the brownstone. I paused at the pillars and asked him, 'How did you get in?' He shrugged and said he couldn't remember. He was tired, he said, and wouldn't be in bed before midnight at this rate. So we walked in and down. I unlocked the door of the basement-cellar and switched on the main light: it was the first time I had done that since I first installed Lacland where he was. There was no face at the opening in the board. I called through it but Lacland failed to answer or appear. I called again. God, what if he had collapsed from over-stimulation? Duded Lazarus was hovering uneasily at the door; then he came in and said we shouldn't wake Lacland. I was watching his face, his pale, ferretish face as he said this; when he changed expression and stared, I knew Lacland had appeared. And he had: but peculiarly altered, like Bottom transformed, because he had somehow tried to cut off his beard. The result was hideous, as if wild birds' nests had sprung out from the texture of his face; it was a kind of straw acne. 'You like the looks of me?' cooed Lacland, enunciating very clearly. 'You'd be so nice to come home to! It takes the pain out of shaving!' His eyes were wild and blue; his lips were moving constantly and his teeth showed not yellow, as we might have expected, but shining white. Lazarus gaped and then whistled a long self-conscious, nervous whistle. 'He talks!'

Lacland leered. 'Talk! You two haven't lived. I got things coming back to me that civilization itself can't understand!' I suddenly felt afraid: my insides fluttered. But Lacland was talking, fast and clear: ' "Always, my dear man, when you take a bath, your shirt with yellow oxters swells in the morning breezes above the mud-messed forget-me-nots! Love gets through your customs only lilacs"—oh what crap! "And the wild violets, the sugary sweet spittle of the dark nymphs!" ' All I could say was: 'Where did you get that?' At once he showed me: he held up a book—*Poems of Arthur Rimbaud*. Then a bottle; Scotch again. 'Listen to this!' he cried, 'just listen to this! "The ancient beasts bred even on the run, their glans encrusted with blood and shit. Our ancestors displayed their members proudly by the fold of the sheath and the grain of their scrotum! I used to observe the shape and performance of our arse——' " He stopped because Lazarus was howling with laughter, laughing so hard that his head wobbled and his neat quiff of hair fell forward: 'Of—all—the—bums!' gibbered Lazarus. 'Just get him, pretending he can read from that book!' I told him that it sounded as if it did come from the book, from Rimbaud indeed, but most remarkably of all from Lacland. And then, very gradually a shocking polyphony began to build up as Lacland snatched at phrases and the dwarf jeered and shrieked abuse and I tried to quieten them.

'Roll up, roll up,' shouted Lazarus, 'ladies and what you have along with you! Meet the *Reader's Digest* man and Phi Beta Kappa! Phi Beta Crap!'

'You calm down,' I said, 'you just give——'

' "Dark and wrinkled like a purple pink, it breathes," ' declaimed Lacland, ' "nestling humbly——" '

'Nestling humbly!' echoed Lazarus, 'of all the bums you meet! Roll up, ladies and funtlemen; an offer never to be repeated!' And on they went with Rimbaud's conneries mixed in with Lazarus's gibes—little wand of ivory, roll up folks, down into the basket goes the head, all fall down, all stand up and howl, all shriek, all declaim, the scarlet skullcap in which ancient noses lie a-drying, of all the bums, of all the ancient drying bums in all the flophouses in the world, or roll up and see the newest wonder of the world! It was bedlam, made by two: the weird, hirsute ranter from the dark hole in the plywood and the stunted miniature man dancing up and down, half mad with glee and half crazed with envy and malice. Lacland ranted on and the dwarf began making sallies across the room like some small terrier dog, snapping and sizzling his spittle. Lacland roared as the dwarf approached, then hyenaed as he leapt back. It had to stop, so I put out the light. But there was Lacland, wild with inspiration now, holding his book to a flashlight and suddenly pronouncing with impeccable authority, ' "It is raining softly on the town." ' Lazarus stopped in mid-charge; stilled, abased. There was a moment of immaculate peace. Lazarus said it again: 'It is raining softly on the town. On this town. Papa, it is raining softly on the town.' I told him that could be true; but that was the wrong thing for me to say. He wheeled round on me in the faint light: 'How do you know? You don't know. You got the book? No, you ain't! You couldn't tell if it's raining or not. You're the Gestapo!' Lacland took up the cry, and they both chanted away for some time.

Then, without warning, Lacland bent down, reappeared with his whisky and a burning magazine. He threw the paper on to the stone floor and splashed the whisky into the fire; there was a violent flash and Lazarus ran screaming up the stairs. Then it was dark again and Lacland called out that he wanted to sleep. It had been an exciting evening, he said, and thank you for calling on him. He would like some meat for breakfast; and good night. He would be there whenever we cared to call and would we please bring our own drink. And some more for him. Bring down the boys, he said; he'd like some company, preferably some he could read to and who would keep quiet. And then, like the Ancient of Days, he rose slowly up with the flashlight held at his ear, anathematizing me in the foulest, most inventive filth I have ever heard. 'Don't you offend me,' he said; he had powers and would soon set all of us to rights. And now good night, followed almost at once by snores. Then a grunt, a commotion behind the wood and an empty bottle hurtled out and hit me on the head. It clinked and rolled against the wall. I turned and walked out, taking care to lock the door behind me, and walked up the steps with a dominant image in my mind of the vastness of Lacland's horny, clawing hands and his terrible, working face pitted with whisker and polished with sweat.

I stood for a while, looking up and down the street, taking deep breaths to quiet my racing heart. There was no sign of Lazarus; he would be safe by now in Mrs. Pomeroy's dignified, precise establishment—all crisp white cloths and shining silver, stuffed foxes and parchment-shaded lamps. I envied him while I listened, only half attending, to the city. Dull, brutish hooting from the river; the swish of cars on the avenue at the end of our street; the harsh, jangling laughter of teenagers out on the spree; the petulant crying of tomcats; the gentle hiss of wind in the wires; the churn above the buildings of a non-jet aircraft; the rustle of wrappers along the gutter. There was no rest in this city; no cease. And buried beneath it was a—a phenomenon which two someones had created somewhere, and then launched on to the stream of flotsam. Had I let him go his way, what then? No one could know; I had kept him, tried to do something vague but well-enough meaning, and he had begun to loom like a prodigy. I wiped the summer sweat from my face and looked up at the big fat eiderdown of the sky: violet and mauve, punctured here and there with reflected light and the aerobatics of pigeons or angels. It looked reassuring; enough to sleep comfortably in for the rest of my days. So I turned round, walked in (I never locked that door) and walked upstairs to my camp bed and the worst of my sleepless nights. My insomnia is to sleep what the lack of decent conversation is to my day. I sometimes accuse myself of masochism, although of the sumptuous kind;

I do not have to live anywhere in particular, but I have continued on here, a talisman to riff-raff and a warning to all do-gooders. I stretched out on the camp-bed not bothering to rearrange the blankets; and in consequence part of my shin and shoulder remained uncovered. I knew someone had been in this small shelter of a room because as I had entered I fell over a book just inside the door. I picked it up and put it on the bed, in case I needed something to read.

It was time to review the situation (how pontifical and military that sounded, coming from me, the most disorganized and least epauletted of pseudo-leaders). First, Lacland was here and was remaining in the cellar only voluntarily. I wondered why. Perhaps he felt safer there, like a gestating child with several months to go. Whatever he had been, whatever had been done to him, he was developing with the speed of panic; no longer a vegetable slug, he was attuning himself and diffusing vibrations of menace. Yet who could honestly say that Lacland was someone, something, to be afraid of? I would do better to be afraid of my own meddling; what failure in me, what deficiency, had led me to harbour this man—not against his will, but against sane judgment? I had wanted to protect and I had done so. But I had also been catalytic, just as Lazarus had been: I had, for some dark reason, kept Lacland down; oppressed him even. Lazarus had given him too much too quickly; and now, what with my own austerity and regimen and Lazarus's plenty, we had a problem (another dull, depersonalizing word, like *situation*). Somehow Lacland had to be put on some rails, either back to the aboriginal dark —which was apparently impossible—or onwards to a code by which he could manage himself. The wild thought occurred of abdicating; making Lacland king of the bums! Train him for office, put him right about banking and provisions, introduce him to the regulars and warn him about the irregulars, and then I could make a final exit and go to join Venetia in her pent-house. Lacland could even have an unofficial salary— but I shuddered at the thought of Lacland in charge, however feckless I myself might be. No, I reached out for the next downward stair of thought and stumbled: I was downstairs again, and the jolt was sufficient to return me to my inquiry into myself. Why did I do it? How extricate both Lacland and myself without causing a public scandal or a local nuisance? Or even worse. It was a decision calling for more than nice judgment. I realized I was sweating, and that was because I had already decided somewhere in the recesses of my mind that I was going to make one of those approximately tidy decisions: to keep Lacland to myself—to ourselves, and yet not to suppress rumours. I had no idea what Lazarus had told already or what he might go on to tell. There was no point in asking his silence; he could not appreciate such a request. He composed his life from day to day, like a child playing with building bricks; and upon a whim he would topple the lot or perversely decide to plan ahead. You never knew.

I reached out and pulled on the string tied to the light switch (one of my little efforts at luxury: I could switch on or off without leaving the bed). The walls were distempered pale green, as bilious a colour as chemical art and natural accident could produce. I picked up the book which was lying on the edge of the bed; it would have fallen off when I turned over. It was the small collected Shakespeare, dusty and scarred, with a postcard marking a page: 'Temple of the Sun. Carlsbad Caverns National Park, New Mexico. One of the more spec-tacular formations in the Big Room, this pair of columns does form a natural shrine.' (Implying, I supposed, that some pairs didn't.) 'A delicate peach, its colour is much like that of a dawn sky.' That was a small inspiration to arrive in the small hours; a ticket to somewhere, where dawns were peach and columns paired off into shrines. I badly needed Venetia now, for advice and consolation, for the sluicing cool of her mind, for the calm diapason of her shoulders when she decided to play on the piano (or to iron my shirt then and there and no objections stood for!). I began to review again. Lacland was now as unknown to me as the abominable snowman; an un-known quality rather than unknown quantity. I must try to anticipate him—not so much head him off as beguile him through indirection. Lazarus had to be made to feel con-spiratorial in a plot that transformed him into a hulking pro-tagonist before whose expert machination the forces and agents of darkness itself would quail. Grey, bulging birds re-turning with no evident pleasure, but holding their formation all the same. Such thoughts, these, migrating always to the easier regions. Venetia had to be told and brought in; so too, I fear, had Doc Rumboldt in case of emergencies; but not Officer Rooney—not yet, if at all. Then I thought of the bums and their unwitting, rumpled faces with skin like paper that has been screwed into a ball, then retrieved and smoothed roughly out. Creased faces, punctured faces, wandering minds and unco-ordinated bodies loomed out of the corner of the room : there, on the other side of the thin wall, they all slept (I had surveyed them often) in diffident surrender, coarsely mattressed on trust and shabbily covered by a counterpane of communal non-aspiration. Some came never to go; some of them had even died there, although the majority for some reason disciplined themselves into dying in public view—in the subway, on the corner, or during a rare visit to the barber. Others kept regular terms, like lawyers, while others arrived, spent a few days refuelling and vanished into the traffic again. A roll-call was as futile and as brutal as counting pores in your skin. Lacland belonged to none of these: I could not see *him* stumbling back, out of breath and blinking savagely with conjunctivitis, but also bearing on high a bunch of violets with which to dignify our private limbo, or stealing picture-post-cards to pin on the wall like surreptitious windows into Samarkand. No, he was a burgeoning intelligence; malign, perhaps, and powerful. A faint shiver ran through my shoulders and neck. It was all very well feeling apprehensive; but what to do? I felt that we should all be doing something positive. Lacland should be out at a riding-school somewhere, rolling along with a crisp ease over the mossy turf; or negli-gently flicking the wheel of a muted, giant automobile, all gleaming pink and chromium while the crowds fell around him like confetti. Lazarus should be spearheading a vast posse of gabbling dwarfs who would overpower Lacland's horse or car and drag him down to devour. Doc Rumboldt, wetly chewing on his spatted cigar and bouncing with gregarious-ness, should be calming Lacland with a deft syringe. Mrs. Pomeroy, with Lazarus out of the house, should be preparing an enervating cocoon for Lacland, her new lodger, of ermine sheets, cream cakes and gently tended coal fires. And the fire's own purring sibilance would make him drowsy, gradually drowning him until all he wanted was to succumb utterly and loll back, at which point we would all help the cause by severing the head cleanly from above with the portable guillotine. Small hope. We would wall him in with Edgar the Time as company and then flood the chamber after having told Edgar what the hour was, and thus return to diluvian the antediluvian. It was a bizarre kind of natural history but justified by the unnatural history of the foundling this far. And all I could think of in addition to these vengeful fantasies was the First Symphony of Brahms and the turmoil of its opening in which the contending forces of the first creation rant and boil outwards as if to the rim of a crater and then subside briefly in froth, only to surge and quarrel upwards again because the demiurge is determined to conquer. I suddenly terminated these reveries by beginning to perform the one decisive act I could think of: filing my nails so hard that a faint, putrid smell of heated bone wafted up. I was transmuting the frail shell that guarded the finger-end; imagine, then, how we must reek if we file at our ankle-bones or jaws. Ah, *ongles délectables*! All the lovely uncles filing at their elbows like demented cellists. The main thing was to bury the parings and filings; for, according to custom, if your enemy gained possession of them he could necromance you to death. And I did not wish Lacland to have more power to his name than he had already.

My course of action was clear; exactly when it had clarified itself to me, I cannot say. I suspect I had assumed it from the start; otherwise these reflections would have had more of the pertinence of urgency. Lacland had to be humoured; and civilized too. It would be like taking over again after the barbarians had departed, exhuming the *corpus juris* from the *corpus delicti*, and setting all to rights before the world came to its next end. But in order to humour, I required allies. Now, Lazarus, both craven and meddlesome, both erratic and a creature of habit, had won the man's confidence: or, at least, had so far evaded his mistrust. I could call on him for footnotes to the enterprise. Rumboldt: he was too jolly for anything and he would want the man to become a Rotarian and be bland. No; when you have a cuckoo in the nest—a wrong bird in hand, keep your eggs away. But enlist him later on, if only to make him feel important. The one person to count on for agile advice was Venetia: she knew enough about acting to know what kind of front to present to Lacland (especially if, as I thought unlikely, he was himself putting on an act). She would toss her tapering face backwards, as if someone had suddenly peeled an almond and tilted it, and opine while her eyes accelerated into a green morse of implication. It was easy to forget that she was about fifty, had two girls intermittently away at well-bred colleges with regularly mown lawns and had acquired those green thumbs from oil-paints, not from lawns or green-rooms. The only trouble was that she relished her own wittiness too much, and made the most of opportunities for it; so much so that a worthwhile idea would suddenly disappear beneath a coruscating display of verbal ingenuity and you would come to the end of a long conversation feeling rewarded and gratified but vaguely out of touch with the world. It was like going into a dime store for a minor but essential item—a key-ring, say—and emerging with a Tiffany bracelet on to which your keys just would not fit. All the same, the glitter beguiled you into condoning the absence of practical purpose. Her intelligence operated smoothly; it would glide on satin runners; and it was up to you, the auditor, to extract the germs of sense before (or while) she raced ahead into ingenious baroque. Yes, I could depend on her for advice; I could also count on her for a means of escape: we would seem to be concentrating on the matter in hand but all the time be shying finely away from it. In other words, earnest debate with her would be both a stimulus and an anodyne.

I have often wondered at my continued presence in the straw-pile that this place is and, in my most bizarre moments, have thought of myself as a turkeycock sublime, stumping and rooting around merely to fool the opposition (always the nice-minded; the bourgeoisie, if you like) and encourage the others. I thought how my despotic tutelage over Lacland had already given my personality a new twist; in fact had twisted it just enough to enable me to retain control. This was just as well: had I not thought that, what could I have done? Have the creature-man shanghaied, deported, done away with? Installed in some credulous museum-curator's collection or in some unscrupulous circus-master's retinue? It did not bear thinking about; not at this hour of the morning anyway. I was tempted to creep downstairs again just to check on Lacland.

But then I thought: if he has gone, I can without too much burden on the conscience forget him; if he chooses to remain —because obviously he can escape whenever he wishes—then I have nothing to worry about. I will not pretend, however, that the thought did not occur of his ascending the stairs in search of his tormentor, unspecified weapon in hand, lusting to make an eggshell mess of my skull. I dismissed the thought, and thus reassured myself that I retained a measure of self-control and therefore of control over him too. About then, sleep came, even while the light shone, and dispersed only at dawn, which meant I had slept approximately four hours.

The dawn was fickle pink, degenerating into nacre smothered by brown salmon. By nine, as I was fumbling at the coffee and the bums were making their first snorts, there was thunder and the sky became bruised purple. The coffee hurried cheerfully to boiling and I pulled the thin curtain across the kitchen window: perhaps out of nothing more than distaste, but more probably out of bone-deep superstition. I did not wish to see the lightning. The air was lank and putrid; my sinuses throbbed, and for once I took my spoonful of cider vinegar in water to ease the aching. After a carelessly fried and therefore burned egg, I made way for Edgar the Time, always prompt in the kitchen with his can of sardines which he then fried, causing the abomination of abominable smells. I shuffled in what I used as slippers (an old disintegrating pair of suèdes now shiny with grease) to the main room where an extraordinary sight stopped me just within the door: to a man, they were huddled under their bedclothes while, at the large window facing south, lightning blanched and thunder complained. They huddled, like animals in undergrowth, coughing with being awake, but determined not to see; it might have been pentecostal fire warning them of its inde-fatigable rent-collector's interest; or an augury of hell, which some of them no doubt deserved (but only as much as we all merit the dentist's drill). I stared down the room at the huddlers (perhaps a dozen that particular morning) and mused on man's turpitude and the cold feet of his meta-physical self. As long as we have a blanket to curl under, the next world and the inexplicable in this are easier for us; de-prive us of our blanket, that hair-shirt of voluntary blindness, and more of us would go mad than the remaining sane could count. Please God, I thought, that they should soon rise; that I might open a window on this sty. The room was its usual foetid self, heavy with stale breath, tobacco smoke and another odour I could never define: which, when I was being melodramatic, I called the foretaste of cerement—part the out-breathing of flowers, part armpit reek and part the smell I always remember of a fertilizer, a powder called Sangral, made from blood. Holy Grail indeed! it stank more like rotten black pudding. I looked down the room: frail cargo, this, as if on deck during the cataclysm, praying to the neighbourhood gods for surcease and free haircuts, for unlimited supplies of liquor and none of those alimony letters. Foundering, they rose with grey faces to meet the day: to them each day was a cheque drawn against an uncalculated account. Each day was a bounce or a careful endorsement of destiny. I can only stand so much of the precarious, or of thunder; then I have to move about with all the agitation of a panicked rabbit or just retreat into a book. I was in no mood for reading, so I went around awakening the men (or at least that was how I pretended). I poked at them, shoulder-shook them, harangued them, pestered and pleaded until they crept out. Not a one without a bottle under the covers and one had a hole burning still, with red rim, in his shirt from the cigarette he was fondling under his blanket. And this time, at about ten, it did rain gently on the town, on this unreal city of carefully aligned concrete and ascending fumes. The rain wreathed and veiled the town (well, the *city* if we must) until windows became mere mirrors and to look outwards was simply to meet an unexpected and not entirely cheering view of oneself. It was a lonely world in that room, a gentle indolence of functioning cadavers where the sight of a geranium provoked boys' tears and the recollection of some lost woman haunted and haunted until the walls themselves became planes of rebuke and the mattresses barren nests.

If I seem to be exaggerating, I am. You have to know at first-hand the accumulated pressure on the breathed air of men already tending themselves as their own memorials: some gibbering with hate, others frowning into the heart of yesterday as if into the crystal of a clairvoyant who has got things all wrong; and others, the most pathetic, who smile in such a way as to tell you they have surrendered—are members of the legion and go quiet-footed, mild-hearted and gentle-mannered towards the assembly-point for the next world. That is why I was where I was; not out of morbid interest but perhaps out of some feeling of affinity and even more of envy. Myself, still having the cash means of extricating myself, I envied their abjectness; they could afford to give up. I, on the other hand, still insured against my past miscalculations, felt obliged to project plans and deeds. It is quite pointless to hope to savour the beauty of failure if you are still obliged to the world of the efficient, meaning the world of money, thanks to my dear mother and what came to me annually in consequence of her foresight. But, vicariously, I belonged to them in much the same way as a clown belongs to the other participants in a circus: just another man in the act but, on-stage, an eccentric and amateurish bungler. I could impose upon them because I could feed them. But they were graduates; and I was a sophomore of uncertain promise. They never wanted to go out, except to the movies once a week, whereas I in comparison had all the spunky initiative of youth: longing for Venetia and yet unable to achieve what she insisted on as a condition, the break from all this. You can belong to a community, however stale and disreputable, more than you can belong to an individual, however intimate your affinity may be. Most people die without knowing this; it is not, in fact, a matter of much importance because you serve the community instinctively, without knowing, whereas you serve the individual rigorously and in almost complacent awareness of what you are doing. As it was, Venetia disapproved and was lonely because she disapproved; she must have loved me intensely to reserve judgment on me for so long. I felt grateful and had I been a butterfly or moth, rather than a Lacland-fosterer, would have skimmed in that second to tell her that all was for the good in the long run and that she too could glean something from my minor underworld. But, as she once said to me, all radium eventually turns into lead, love's light—unreflected—into a weight in the heart. Shall I say we disagreed about contexts, and leave it at that? I cannot because on that morning I was to have with her one of our most crucial exchanges, one of which

I am not proud but about which I endeavour to be honest.

Her penthouse overlooked the river and we spent many hypnotized hours following the progress of barges, small steamers and other craft, and speculating about their purposes. In her day Venetia had starred in about half a dozen films, when she was spectacularly black-haired and discontented-looking, tight-mouthed in the fashion of those times and magnetic. Yet, for some reasons she herself had never been able to define, she had never been quite right: it was her intelligence that troubled them and her penchant for knowing better than them all—the privilege of all reasonably educated women, of course, but singularly awkward in a high-pressure *kitsch* industry which punished heresy with exclusion. Well, she paid her price, and then married a sea-captain, saw the world with him (as they say), bore him two girls and had just settled down with him in Connecticut when he died of pneumonia one morning after the girls had just returned from school. Before long she had moved back into the city and taken up music and painting and dynamic conversation. Her sadness, if any survived, was always carefully tucked into the folds of some expensive silk or worked beneath the surface of an abstract painting. To the girls, she was a spirited and daunting mother: not so much the ciné-queen translated into humdrum devotedness as a much older sister slightly impatient because they couldn't grow fast enough to catch her up in age. As I say, she was a witty woman, and this scared them most of all, for she toppled their idols and creeds before they had had so much as a chance to make a mental genuflection.

I took out and put on a new drip-dry shirt with a faint blue check; it felt too respectable for me and the collar was stiff as cardboard. But it was a gesture to the occasion and I thought that a gesture was in order. Then I found my blue bow-tie with the white spots; splashed shaving lotion across my face and the bald zone of my skull, and descended the stairs. I always visited her by cab, with a cigarette lolling in the corner of my mouth and some small gift in my hand. On this occasion I stopped the cab long enough to purchase her a new cigarette-lighter, a neat one with purple glass embossed in the form of a queen's crown. Then we swept up to the mighty glass doors and I passed the uniformed doorman with what I hoped was a wave as debonair as usual. I rang, spoke with her through the tube and took the elevator right to the top. She was waiting with the door open, looking somewhat thin in a frilly dress of violet and black. She waved to me with her long billiard-cue of a cigarette-holder: '*Chéri!*' she exclaimed, and gave me a peck on the cheek. I caught a faint whiff of Scotch and perfume, in that order. It was eleven o'clock.

'Now,' she said, bustling and beaming, 'we have much to talk about, and it is *so* futile on the telephone. I haven't seen you for weeks!' She had not, but that was nothing unusual. I had to feel just right before visiting her: capable, that is, of emerging intact and keeping my hands off her until, and if, she gave some encouragement. She was a professional flincher; even her deliberate movements towards you suggested that she was flinching from something invisible. Negatives alone appeared to provoke her positives. I noticed that her dress had a fur, possibly mink, collar, very neat and young-making. I said so and she nodded amiably while pouring my Scotch and casting a quick eye at the thermostat embedded in the wall. The floor was all white pile, thick and soft as cotton wool and the walls were hidden with canvases, some vilely gaudy and others almost empty save for a line or a circle. I always felt puzzled in this room and I always, eventually, walked into one of the long low tables she kept scattered about. (She painted in the next room, from which you could watch the river.)

Conversation was now about to begin. I gave her the gift and she cooed at it, held it to her as if to suckle it, and then leaned sideways to kiss my brow. This was very gratifying. I felt like an old, battered truck, waiting on the lines for the shunting-engine to catapult me into the depths of the truck-pool. It was like being left in a quiet, newly painted country station while the rest of the train phutted off into the land-scape. Birdsong and champagne elation held me tight, and through the gloom (it was still thundering outside) I saw her hands begin to gyrate and signal to me. 'The one thing,' she said in preliminary to her skeltering patter, 'the one thing I cannot stand is having to search for matches, having to use them, having to suffer the feeling of hell being so close while the phosphorus burns. The smell pollutes any cigarette. Don't you agree? And then the bother of where to put the matches when you simply are not the kind of person who remembers or the kind who places little ornamental boxes of them on the arms of the chairs lest the guests be inconvenienced! See, it works beautifully!' She flicked and flicked the lighter; it lit seven or eight times and then failed to. 'My God!' she screamed, 'what can be wrong? Did you have it checked before you left the store?' I said I had had it filled but had forgotten to bring the butane cylinder with me; it was still in the store, I supposed. Then, we must telephone at once, she said, and was half-way across the carpet before she had another idea which brought her back. 'Flint!' she hissed; 'that's it. I do believe I saw it jump out—or what was left of it.' I took the lighter from her, flicked it and it lit perfectly. She smiled. 'Well, then, there's nothing for you to get bothered about, is there?' as if I had been a small, ordure-encrusted infant running amok with a meat-axe.

'No.' I reached inside my nostril, took hold of a long hair, closed my eyes and with enormous force tugged. The whisker came away and I flipped it behind the chesterfield. I knew she was staring and I let her continue. 'What were you saying,' I asked, 'before all this?' For answer, she went to ensure that the door was locked. Then she began some involved tale about the stock market; she had bought at the wrong time; now it was down and it would fall further, and she had lost money and she couldn't sell. I told her to try horses next time. My tactic was to let her expend her gathered-up energy because, as I knew from many wasted expositions in the past, to try to reach your own muttons while she was in spate was hopeless. *Yes, I see*, she would say as she gaily slammed your offering back towards you. So on she went, plumping up the cushions as she prattled, smoothing the back of her hair (French roll today and most appealing), reaching forward to press my hand like some excessively animated official with a seal. In the grate the small coal fire cast lazy shadows on the white tiles, sputtered, and gave me something to look at when I looked away from her. She liked, she said, to look right into a person's eyes when she talked. I supposed she could see her sentences going in like darts. And then it was over; Salome had discarded her first verbal veil; and she shifted her position, sat close and asked how I had been. 'Not your health, but the way your thoughts have been.' I relaxed a little: this would be a good way of getting at my point. 'I feel,' I said, half-formally, 'a tender regard, as well as a hell of a lot of irritation.'

'Because I talk?'

'Partly; partly because I need to talk more than you do. And something has to be *done*.'

She stared at my face, itemizing it, travelling round it clock-wise. Her beautiful small tapered hands gleamed in the blurred light: they were never dry, and the nails shone like exquisite china—pink china.

'If you have something important to tell me,' she began in those crisp, good-broadcasting tones of hers, 'then risk it. Tell me. Or is it ask?'

'As a matter of fact, it's both.'

'Very well, then, tire me out with it. Talk it out; you look worried—not your usual frown but something a bit sharper. On edge.'

'Well,' I began unsteadily, 'the derelicts, you know; they mean *something* to me—something which makes me do things now and then which——'

'Have they gone? Have they mutinied?' She was off again briefly, sliding along the skids of her own quip.

'No one has. One of them, the worst, his name is Lacland——'

'You were never one for names. Strange to hear you being so specific!'

'We found him on the sidewalk and took him back with us. Lazarus and I—the dwarf.' She nodded cynically.

'Now,' I said, with an increasing sense of my own idiocy, '*he* was rather a special case. Inarticulate, lame, a vegetable. I finally put him in a crate in the basement.' I could tell from her face that she thought Lacland had died. 'He lives down there,' I resumed, 'and I have been feeding him just what he likes: bread and water; some milk.' She was studying the carpet in some bewilderment. 'All right so far,' I said. 'But the other day I found that Lazarus had been feeding him meat, giving him things—a radio, magazines, whisky and so on. Also a saw and hammer.'

'What's wrong with that? Poor devil. But why a crate?'

'He needed to be enclosed; he couldn't stand the light or the noise. In fact I boarded him up and dealt with him through a small door I kept locked.' She looked angry and suddenly bored.

'You've been there too long. Too long. It's going to your brain,' she murmured. I told her it always was in my brain. 'I was just trying to give him the greatest sense of peace and safety. And now I find he can speak; he reads and recites Rimbaud; he is wild and fierce and possibly dangerous—and he is as articulate as you and I.'

She tightened her mouth; back to her movie-days. 'Is this a joke? Are you trying to entertain me?'

'The thing is, what to do? He's still there but he's broken the door down; God knows what that dwarf will do next. In fact, the man—not the dwarf—is imperfectly civilized even if he can speak and read. It's as if he's suddenly remembered all he'd forgotten. There was a letter in his pocket saying he wanted to join the cavalry. What can anyone do? I could be charged with kidnapping or attempted murder through attrition. Anything. And if I let him out—or rather, if he comes upstairs, what then?'

'Tell the police. Do they know?'

'Well, I said Lacland had gone away.'

'And all the time you had him in a crate in the cellar?'

'Yes.'

'You fool. I sometimes wonder . . . Can I see him? Would it be safe?'

'I couldn't guarantee. He has a pin-up there, and that arouses him quite oddly.'

There was a long silence during which she crossed and uncrossed her legs, exposing slight veins like commas or parentheses on her calves. Then she seized the poker and ruptured the main mass of coal in the fire. A new flame burst out and made cavorting shadows which reminded me of the mattress-room and childhood animals made by combining hands into shapes.

'Is he really dangerous?' She seemed to have made up her mind about something. 'Would he attack?'

'He bit my hand the other night. I don't think there is any way of treating him gently. I went down there this morning

before I left, but he was asleep. At least, he didn't answer me
and I heard snuffling.'

She took my hand and sandwiched it between hers. Then,
as if in some kind of pedagogical trance, she made her points
by pressing each of my fingers in turn. (The bird, I recalled
from a film of Cocteau's, speaks with its fingers.) 'You did
wrongly to put him down there at all. You did worse to board
him up and tell lies about him. You have probably been taken
in by a practical joker. You trust that dwarf too much—he's at
the back of it, of course. You should send the man packing at
once. And you should give up the whole squalid business. I
mean the whole notion of a flophouse for bums like something
between a cathedral and a circus with yourself as ringmaster-
cum-priest.' She was nodding to herself now; the narrow veins
at the side of her temples appeared to be wriggling; but that
was just the fire-shadow.

'I don't want a lecture,' I said roughly; 'I just wondered
what you thought I should do for the best.'

'Well, now you know. I can hardly believe it. You, an
educated man with means. If you *had* to take him in, was that
the best you could have done for him?'

'It seemed the most suitable thing at the time,' I muttered
lamely. I knew how feeble and erratic it all sounded. It was
hard to credit. 'Be tender,' I said. 'Be reassuring. I know how
idiotic it sounds. I just want to know what comes next.'

Almost as I spoke she eased my head against her shoulder
(the bone felt thin and stubborn) and stroked my forehead
with her rings going over it coolly like the runners on a sled.
A slightly desiccated pair we made, with our taut limbs and
tightening skins. She pulled at my bow-tie, murmuring '*Nice*,'
and it fell apart, like a spotted wish-bone dangling from the
spoon-hollow at the base of my adam's-apple. Then she
twisted the top button from its hole and the pinging noise
went from my ears. 'Cuddle,' she whispered, but the sound
was that of a wave breaking in my ear, and I could feel myself
sinking deep into a periwinkle sea, arms useless as a dead
seal's flippers, all resolve and dignity annihilated into the
schmalz of dotage. I yawned and she said how tired I looked.
More at peace, we kissed each other's fingers and I felt the
skin between my eyes unwrinkle and the pocket of air that

never seemed to leave my lungs made its way up and out, in pure relief, and her breath was peppermint from the lozenges she always kept beneath her tongue. Like the child who has invaded the candy-shop, I suddenly became heir and usurper in one: pink and white stripes, gay-flapping awnings in the wind, succulent jelly-candies and miles on miles of pallid gum. From far away, beginning with a faint vibration of half-lost memories (a child kicking at last night's fireworks after the rain has sodden them—yet still somewhat afraid of a belated explosion or spurt of fire) and continuing into a rhythm of a galloping horse, grassy-hooved, and breathing in shudders, there came something vestigial and reflexive. We lay close, unspeaking, each giving the other time to listen to his own self beating—beating about in the brush of desuetude in search of a silver coin, a trembling platinum thread long lost, or the horror of forgotten cats' faces like gargoyles who risk being ridiculous and pay the cosmos one of the last of their carnal tributes. I felt sopping, hot, thick silk stretched tight and, determined to lose, wrenched it away like the net that has suffocated us all down the ages. Pistil and mastodon, I agreed with myself that she would agree with me, and there in the ember-light we renewed with our fingers and teeth an old habit which hardly bothered to call on us any more. *You cannot*, she said. *You cannot stand* and I laboured across the pitching deck to catch the mast as it fell, and once again the rigging was the net around my head and shoulders and I flailed to be free; rent and tore, with the terrible weight straining my arms and the core of my being cracking. And then suddenly, stiffening, and being able to carry the over-balancing mast right along the deck, trailing the tangled rigging and the smashed tackle behind me before aiming and then shunting the whole lot overboard and following it myself with a swallow-dive clean into the foam, where I almost stunned my head on the floating mast which had not gone down.

It was a shock to wake face-down in the hot sand, gasping for air and blinking sweat away from my eyes. A new alloy of the spirit grew up from my ankles, through my rocking knees and into my groin, thence into the caverns of throbbing air in my chest. I kissed the tears from her eyes, masterful again, and madly scratching at the sweat in my moustache. There was a long violet silence then, during which I heard the fridge click on and off three times. We both slept, I believe, made newly free of the area in which parrying and thrusting is irrelevant and only the will, the surrendered will, counts. In these very human abdications we had to make the most of the time left to us before a peculiar mixture of pride and self-pity set us closing opened shutters, winding up the skeins of exposed personality, as well as reconcealing the dank strands of intimate hair. There was a headlong, headstrong rush back to the polite world where we persuaded each other that we had not been trespassers: old meat cutting loose; mutton shamming at lamb; insecure teeth clicking in skeletal punctuation; ill-wrapped bone crossing and tapping the current of the main supply.

Vous êtes fort, she said in her French persona. This reprieved her to the extent of ten years: just enough, making her feel just a little bit of a tartar (no tart, though) and making me smile at the untruth. Her Modigliani face was tilted back, all her face muscles relaxed, looking oddly vulnerable and childish. Whose nest had she fallen from? Grey, thick hair had fallen back from the conspicuous ears and the faint mask of rouge had slipped—had been redistributed, so that her face seemed to have no convexes at all. At peace, her peasant breasts (on so slender a body) reminded me of sitting white fowl, intent on the egg, and there was no sag. Beside us, on the expensive carpet, our discarded clothing reflected the fire and looked like a mountain range, like alps flown over. Dark villages of seam and button clung to the slopes; a giant might have swung his arms and broken the electrical wires, thus plunging the mountainside into darkness.

Over the white Alps alone, I murmured, and thought of John Donne in his cell. Then of Lacland and of how very little advance we had made in that affair, to which I had now to return, after a decent interval and a new peace made with Venetia.

'Your frown has come back,' she said playfully, although she had not been playful about it before. 'You owe something to yourself: to *us*. Sometimes I think we know each other intimately but not superficially; you have to have both.' I nodded, as I always do at the most serious forms of truth, and grunted myself erect in order to poke the fire. The calm, lapidary face on the chesterfield caught and held my gaze.

She was wondering. Here in our cocoon there was no reason to break the peace: no envy, no malice, no wrong noise. But out there in the pigeon-plastered city, where dinosauric buses belched and the people continually struck sparks off one another, obligation was raising his dirty head and asking, What now? Suddenly she got up, breasts bare, and raced into the bedroom. Within a minute she was back, radiant in a kimono and brandishing a pile of travel folders: maps, timetables, lists of restaurants, even a currency calculator. 'Let's go,' she burst out, 'let's go! Let's go where we can sit out the rest of our days in the sun; out of the soot and the fungus of it all.'

The same idea had crossed my mind too. I picked her up bodily and sat her on the piano-stool; she still held the leaflets. 'I'm going to do what I can,' I said thickly as she began to trace a dissimulating melody down the still, white keys. 'What I can.' I went into the bathroom and arranged my appearance; then I returned and slipped on my few clothes, noting how shabby the jacket was and how taut her face had become with her hand stationary on the piano. 'All I can. And more.'

She nodded and said with a strained brightness, 'Soon?'

Then I realized that she expected me to stay for lunch and took off my jacket as she began to mention my staying. While she busied herself in the kitchen I walked into the studio to look at the river, black as pitch today, and to think about Lacland.

I must have dozed off, my mind nervously bounding like a klipspringer over the undulating ground. What woke me was my name being called: over the address-system, my name in a muffled blurt. *Would I, please?* Would I what? The loudspeaker, wherever it was, crackled and seemed to include the marble waiting-hall in a dissatisfied and temporary silence. *Would I please?* Then with an abrupt click, the silence, the new silence, was cut off and the old murmur and dead reverberation of women's heels walking was resumed. Yes, I thought, these people should be ribboned, escorted, have trains of silk held behind them and be greeted by slaves bearing baskets of convolvulus. They walk whitely to weddings, jostling at the backs of those in front of them. They are eager to board their trains and I see them settled at home the day before the journey, confiding to the chintz and the rumpled beige antimacassars where last night the daughter-of-the-house's love wrestled with her visiting wooer's love (their daughter, this, on the threshold of life). I myself am catching no train; but train or no train, we are wafted into the void, with only our innocence and makeshift wisdom to cushion us and our timetables flung long ago into the bucking wind. We fling the millions of times of departures and the telephone pad and the reservations, all these transient records of ourselves, we fling them skywards. Conquerors on every superb Saturday we contrive to have ourselves hurled away from the metropolis and hope that Sunday will not bring thunder. And, one day, with some surprise, we discover tucked into a side-pocket the exceptional vestige in the form of a ticket torn but not this time thrown skeltering on to the suburban gusts. This time, having found it, with all the emotion rubbed off its face, we throw it into the fire.

I sit on the hub of the spinning wheel. The spokes are gun-barrels down which, at the word, all the unloved and the cherished, the diseased and the hearty, shall be puffed coast-wards like flies. *Would I please? Please would I?* altering for emphasis. *At Track Seven.* And then the same change of silence. If it were my train, I could sit here and they would not mind. But it is not my train; they have never called my train yet, although they keep on calling my name. And now I would never go to the barrier when it was called. All I have to do is sit here in immovable bulk for one unthinking second, and then even if I ran I would fail to catch it and the pattern of my life would remain. I am not culpable; there will always be others to use the trains.

The unspeaking face with two sterile fingers shows me Eastern Standard or Greenwich or Pacific Time: all of time. The people who watch the clock have no characteristic that is attachable to time. They wait. They wait while a glacier in the north assembles behind the suburban avenues. The old man on my left with the underslung wet mouth open like a football bladder exhales his air unsentimentally, clutching against his spittle-scarred and imprisoning blue suit his news-paper; he hugs the headlines. He is waiting for a train so that he can make the incontrovertible journey back and so have a fact to give his friends. Under the neon lights the murmuring

tide of travellers ebbs and surges; they travel through their
own minds, minds remote as the moon, about their own
business. A coloured woman is sleeping over there. Within her
arms her child stares with implacable black eyes: a cherub in
tar in the rumbling paunch of the busy world. And *he* has
arrived, just now, brown from his efficient tour, embracing the
children as they peck him with welcomes, and his wife, en-
circling them all on tiptoe. Talking crisply now from his view-
point of executive health; yet I saw him palm, briefly, fur-
tively, divinely, her buttock. The negro woman is coughing
but the child is unperturbed as the volcano of phlegm writhes
itself into gradual peace deeper, even deeper, in her throat.
She does not spit. And now she is standing in front of me, her
face strangely segmented as if in rose-petals; and I am returning her smile successfully. My version of the general situation
is coloured by what the columnists call a private grief. I could
well sit here in the company of this maltreated but unquench-
able woman and say: There is a debris standing to our credit.
Let us not overspend nor seek the credit of further debris. Just
then a crowd of boys in torn sweat-shirts came scattering
vociferously down the river-bank, vaulted the rails, exploded
across the field and dwindled into the distant end of the em-
bankment. For an instant the landscape reared in sterile
threatening—a storm-sea in paralysis, and then all was safe
again. I answered to my name, which she must have been
calling for several minutes, and went through, holding her
hand lightly, to scrambled egg, bacon and sardines on toast.

'You ask if it is Saturday,' she said over her shoulder as she
switched off the coffee. 'It is. You *are* getting vague! But it
doesn't really matter.'

We ate English style, using knife and fork at the same time;
then I scooped up with my fork, reserving my other hand for—
for nothing. There are times when the hallucinations mount
within me like water which cannot find an outlet; and I swim
or flounder, depending on whether I can relate what mounts
to what is outside me. I am aware of not always trying to relate
the one to the other, mostly because my hallucinations always
seem to evoke loss, absence, being bereft, being motiveless and
having no place. To tie all these in with my daily world would
be too painful. Take the loss of her conversation, which even

now was chiming and punctuating, and the allusive smiles that accompanied it. At bottom and buried deep, there was the resentment and the disappointment she feels that I am not different, that I have not behaved differently. I thought of her as she once was, sitting like black narcissus in her canvas-backed chair (her name in large lettering across the back) and growing increasingly impatient with interviewers and advisers; until, forgetting her own maxims about inflicting one's temperament on others, she hurtled away pouting and announced the next day that she had had enough. Of course, she resumed work a few days later, but with a blistering impatience enough to ensure that this was her last movie. And for some time she lived alone at the edge of a desert (a place called Rapallo Springs) with only a ginger cat and a Mexican maid for company. This I had pieced together over the years, from her talk, from her album of cuttings and from fragments of nightclub chatter. I had already begun to feel ancient before she married her captain—this being yet another form of oubliette down which she could dive. *Oubliette*: it wasn't, but it *sounded* like the companion to *alouette*: it was the forgetting bird, not the view-halloo bird or the bird that said, 'I can go anywhere with *you*.'

'You are very thoughtful today,' she was remarking—not for the first time, I suspect. She had finished eating and had poured the coffee. I told her I had a slight head, which was true in a punning sense, but I could not begin to tell her that the future kept eluding me: that as I neared it, it sank away, and I found myself chewing on dusty straw of platitudes, lavish vacuities such as people on beaches speak merely to defy the heat. I knew how it all should have been; I knew in appalling detail because I had spent the major portion of my days compensating with exotic idyll for the inwardly roasting sense of failure; of chances missed, obligations renegued on, admissions never made and inertia enthroned. She had once arrived, down in the Bahamas, exultant at my postcard of invitation (as if I had wanted the postcard-reading world to know), and I had gone out at dusk to meet the small boat. She had taken a boat for the last lap, simply (she said) to savour the prospect better while sailing up on it, but also (I was sure) not to seem over-eager. Such were our cautions in those days!

Somewhat shaggy with incipient middle age I had left a
simple meal of minestrone, fruit and wine which I had been
too excited to eat in the lonely, panelled dining-room, and had
driven down to the quay in my rope-soled shoes. 'Careful,'
she said, 'you'll spill your coffee.' I had spent the day in
scowling restlessness, mis-hitting every golf-ball, mis-reading
every sentence, and finally walking round and round the
house, pausing only to sit and smoke by the windows of the
cool rooms, gaping at the blue of the sky and sea and shuffling
the years like cards, tensely and aimlessly, and speaking her
name. There were few other guests in those days. I tested the
fresh paint of the landing-stage and found it still tacky. In
that heat, what else? The small boat grew towards me, and a
couple who had been embracing on the seat got up and
drifted towards the landing, like slow-motion ballet dancers.
With a lurch and a sudden back-churn, the boat made contact; the timbers groaned back into place and almost at once
a squad of mahogany children burst up the gangway and
scattered noisily, their parents in pursuit. Burdened adults
followed. There was little light, and the air was like velvet,
caressing the face and wrists.

'You looked thinner than ever, in those days,' I said to her,
sugaring my coffee.

'I've already sugared,' she reminded me. 'It would never do
to be *grasse*. Or so I used to think. When you're half peasant
anyway, you haven't much chance!' This was her way of
generalizing about the Irish blood she had. I remembered
looking at her slender body and noting the heaviness at the
bust and hips. As if some vast hand had squeezed her round
the middle, forcing the weight upwards and downwards. Nine
chimes rang from a small tower; you could almost see the
chimes ascending. And I remember how she had eaten the
warmed-up minestrone without a murmur of complaint and
had given Jack, who warmed it for us, her autograph with an
almost oxy-acetylene smile.

I lit her cigarette. Or rather she blew out the flame. So
much for new lighters. This time she inhaled instead of blowing, and the tobacco caught. Then I went back. Given an
ivory tusk to handle and linger over in a sunlit but cool room,
it would depend on the person as to what pleasure he got from

the handling or the lingering. To start with ten tips of the fingers ringing the thick base, and then to trail them slowly down, narrowing the ring until the fingers fell together as the tip gave out into nothingness, that would move different people differently. You could be disappointed when your fingers slid off. Or you could find the tusk-point a piquant and refined extreme off which to glide into bliss. The coma followed the too long delirium. But of course it was always different. Standing alone in the sun-flooded morning room I saw the tusk on the mantel as no more than an ornament. She made it seem mineral and dead. Outside, in order, the geraniums, the terrace, the shore, sea and sky lined up in strips. Down by the quay, a man was hammering at an empty boat. Then there came a brief chime, a jolly waterfall of chimes: it was Sunday. Be praised, she had not gone grey. I stood for a while, musing, balanced on the balls of my feet, curling my toes in the thin canvas shoes.

Later, with the saucer wobbling, I took her the coffee. Mellow and satiate, she had assumed a foetal position under the one sheet. She moved easily into the waking world; there was no transition. Dishes clattered from the other side of the kitchen and, like a zombie, I rose and began to dry. She stared at me, began as if to say *How silent you have become*, but then changed it and exclaimed, 'A labour shared!' She could have left the dishes for the maid, but she had always been a little fanatical about dirty dishes. So we worked at speed and then set the coffee percolating again.

To fish there was no need to transact for a boat. Fish abounded, gargantuan as in the old maps framed on the walls. As I looked at those old maps, I saw my own face: presumably what others saw too. Face like the true Druidic stone and the hair beginning to lose heart. In those days I still had the urge to write music and even an image of myself shambling around the festivals, attenuated and grizzled, with a rhapsodical white carnation in my jacket, shovelling tobacco from a battered tin into a foul pipe. *When he conducted (rare), he loomed over the orchestra like an overhanging cliff, getting his way not by inducing awe but by suffusing about him a heavy yearning, like the passion of a monolith and not to be denied.*

She, part-source of the yearning and the pretentiousness,

knew most of this. Once she, understanding the ruthlessnes,
needed (they say) in love and art, had snatched from me a
whole set of written sheets which I had decided to burn. To
her it had seemed fixed, settled. But I had blazed after her, up
the stairs, scoffing and reviling, saying she was trying to mis-
represent me. And it had soon become intolerable, for I
eventually became shy of putting anything on paper and
would walk round unspeaking, aching to dismiss the sound
from my head: just to be able to disentangle a solitary thing
that would stay. So she had gone. And she had not dared to
return. Finally, after many futile sorties in this field of stones
and flints, in which there was no music that would speak back
to me, I gave up and began to read books instead. I knew she
had travelled, trying to land and leave suddenly, with grief
raving behind on the shore like Dido. But grief, like some
hideously faithful wet-nosed collie dog, had always caught up
with her. And now, this time as we looked out at the swimmers
in the passive water and the orange blossom of the sand, we
had come to terms.

'Funny, the wind,' she said, feeling at the breeze with open
hand. We were near the middle of the bay, in the centre of
the burning-glass. I itched all over with sweat; I dug at the
roots of my hair and scraped viciously with both hands. The
glands were protesting against over-work. Then she burst out
laughing, the sound rising hysterically like a saw biting into
tougher and tougher wood, thus losing just a few revolutions
each second. The yelp of her laughter echoed across the water.
She allowed hysteria to possess her entirely; I shouted at her
to stop, something abusive, but she merely raised an arm and
pointed, waggling her forefinger up and down. I too could
have, should have, laughed at that moment; instead, I waited
and began to make fun of her, the movie tradition, the glamour
rat-race, the star-cult—almost everything. Once again, the
hysteria went echoing out. We ate in silence and a day later,
against all my pleas, she caught her plane. I drove her, certain
that the last overture would work. It didn't and I returned
to the house, checked that no one was standing outside and
threw the ivory tusk through the main window, cutting my
hand in the process. Thus the paralysis of shame and the
bullish panache of not really knowing how.

One of the main penalties of being human is that you never quite trust a truth. I have already alluded to Venetia's wittiness and her cool mind; but perhaps this was merely compensatory self-encouragement because she was, in fact, facetious, and bird-brained, both stalely amusing and erratically discerning. I wonder about this because I might well have distorted for myself all the facts about Lacland; and I exonerate myself (no slight process) by sticking to my belief that occasionally things happen to us which cry out for interpretation—which sometimes arrive with an interpretation ready-made. This, for better or worse, is the sort of person I am. Add to that a growing weakness for hallucination and you have all the makings of a madman's dream. I mean the kind of vision, ludicrous because undernourished and in competition with a hideous reality, which the millions of prisoners in all the jails of our century must have witnessed, with the water-soup served in garbage-pails, enlivened now and then by the up-floating of some unrecognizable head—cat or puppy, while the roaches and bugs collected in the hollow pipes supporting the canvas hammocks and the rat safari began regularly after curfew so that the diet could be augmented. Hang a hunger-banner behind the bars and they machine-gun you while you hold it. It is no wonder that our helpless, numbered political misfits have conjured up visions that exorcize terror itself and find meaning in futility. Yet, I, who had known what is sometimes called the good life, was metamorphosing daily; creating a fact and then twisting even that, and subsequently deforming still further what I had twisted. And Venetia: was she the strong reassuring arm of the ally who helps unbidden, who intuits before you have explained, who beguiles you with wit while she does her serious and useful thinking behind that façade? Or was she less than strong, less mature than I, and simply casting frantically around for a means of evading a new predicament? It was about this time that I really began not to be sure of my accuracy; if I closed my mind, there grew wild visions in imprisoned luxuriance; if I opened it the least bit, the world flooded in and I began to relate everything to everything else in a kind of paradisal synopsis. And the few things that I held to— the mattress-room, the congealed past, Venetia's penthouse,

Lazarus's desire to educate himself and Brahms's God stirring up creation with a Mixmaster—these were sliding into the quicksand where all the cranks had disappeared: all the messianic, unhinged purveyors of virgin births, immaculate self-worship, second comings, visions of Fatima, indivisible loaves, talking statues, virtuous lions and all the rest of that forlorn retinue.

I paused and took stock; took stock of my shop-worn stock. What I had done with Lacland had been a blunder; but it was irrevocable now. At least he had had time to collect himself, whatever and whoever he was. He was now more fitted, more properly equipped. And slowly there grew upon me the fantasy of expulsion: he was to reappear in the world, take his place, if on a low level only. If, of course, he wanted to emerge; and I could hardly see him not wanting to. Out from the egg, then, this belatedly precocious chicken, sponsored by those who abandoned him and those who mistakenly had held him back. I confess that I would in some ways have preferred him to remain as an embryo, at peace down there, performing his few elementary motions and knowing little of the other kinds of disillusion: other than what he had already known, if indeed he had been aware at all. As I pondered on the matter, comparing with my efforts to mould the young Venetia and my failure in that, I began to gain confidence. Two wrongs cannot make a right, but a wrong could be mitigated: I had merely miscalculated; had, on the basis of little clear evidence, misinterpreted. I had forced an incorrect timespan on him. I recalled how the human baby and the chimpanzee develop in parallel for their first two years; well, if you had never made the comparison before, you would not know that the human soon outstripped the chimpanzee. And I thought, what if God Himself still doesn't know? What if, each time one of us is born, He waits to see how we develop? What if what we call human has been a prolonged aberration: something not intended? The human baby takes so long to reach active maturity, and Lacland somehow parodied that slow progress. He was also, now, parodying the speed-up after puberty; he was the earthenware embryo who suddenly exploded into the retarded truant man of wit. I could make plans for him, guide him. And then I thought of the plans I had offered to Lazarus, their intermittent and overall failure.

Between the organic thing's own laws of growth and the nurture we invent, there is a vast wasteland of vainglorious prescription. It is as much an effrontery to nurture as it is a cowardice to leave all to nature. The Kikuyu woman despises her bare breasts and takes to *braziru*; she does not know yet that we can conceive of a thermonuclear way to freedom. We may get vertigo, but the growth goes on; so must the nurture. Even at this time I had little feeling of tampering: to leave well alone would have been to saddle Lacland with all my ignorance and none of what skill I had. I saw clearly that I was to lead him out now, doing my best to forestall the wrong kind of consequences. Thus, the vertigo of wisdom, the middle-aged boy who intones the rhyme about the moon: *I see the moon*, but forgetting the next line: *The moon sees me*.

By now Venetia, not surprisingly, was very quiet. I could see that she was fatigued and needed her afternoon rest. The thin black lines beneath her eyes kept tightening up, like thin springy wire, when she blinked. These sudden contractions were a danger-signal, a twin twitch that I had seen before. Paler than usual, she was staring hard at me and telling *me* to take a rest. I think she meant I should go away with her 'to the sun', as she always phrased it; and at the time it didn't seem a bad idea except that I had too many things to attend to. Over the years, her exhortations to pull up roots and go had become a stylistic exercise for her, and a burden to me. I wished I had gone years before, or used the time better when we were both in the sun to start with.

'How silent you have become,' she murmured, cupping her chin in the palms of her hands. 'There was a time when you talked everybody down. And now you keep going away. Is it nice in that private world of yours?'

I thought at first she meant my brooding but she really intended the mattress-room. I nodded, then shook my head. 'There are problems you never look for: not problems of managing, coping and such, but problems of being yourself.' It sounded lame, and lamer still when I qualified it with 'It depends on who you think you are to start with. I used to think of myself as some kind of missionary to those men; then I gave that up because it sounded pompous even to me. But until just lately I had always thought I was doing some good.

It seems now that I've been developing an inflated notion of
my own power—and a poorer notion of their rights.'

She said nothing in reply, but her look said that she
agreed. Indeed, she went further, tightening her mouth into
a papery-looking ellipse of disapproval: it was obvious that
she wished me to remember what she would not waste time in
repeating. I imagined how the words flickered among the
cells of that nervously alert brain: shiftless megalomaniac,
overdoing it, being cruel to be kind—in other words a waste
of time and also of her life. I squirmed a little on my chair, as
if a rebuked schoolboy. She had always had the knack of
making me feel hopelessly junior: a sudden hardness of
manner, shedding her gentle self, would take over, and she
appeared to become a species of calculating machine. She did
not need my presence at that moment, for she was sinking deep
into thoughts of her own in which my presence was marked by
a sign, some inanimate hieroglyph which said little about me
but neatly recalled for her my predicament, my assets and
drawbacks. And during the whole time I took to rise, kiss her
cheek (tasting powder), visit the john, kiss her cheek again,
take up my coat and walk to the door, she said nothing. 'Call
me. Glad you came.' She said that as I stood at the door; she
knew that I would have called a cab had I wanted one, so
she had no need to mention that.

I punched the buttons in the elevator, thinking how she
was reliving old disappointments; these come keener only
when you realize that nothing has taken their place. It was
misting along the river. The grimy world had resumed its
tainted aura and I felt desolate. I used to be able to persuade
myself that there was more self-solace in concentrating on the
immediate than in daydreaming an escape. First of all you
looked at the world's unredeemed items; then you scanned
even more closely, itemizing each component part until you
had gained all the knowledge the casual gazer (and the casual
grumbler) missed. It was a form of penetration leading to an
eventual mastery; and at one time I thought I had achieved
that mastery. But I realized as I walked along the river, taking
deep breaths of the water-laden air, that such relief comes
only because my kind of scrutiny had been a way of ignoring
significances. I could lose myself in the texture of a man's face,

or the topography of a wart, until I almost forgot what I was looking at. And now I was riding my own personal pendulum the other way, yearning to interpret and yet, having dared to interpret the once-inarticulate Lacland, had struck fairly deep into error. Yet, even to call it error was to pretend to know too much: I did not know everything, therefore I must cease punishing myself. I paused to light a cigarette, shielding the match inside my coat-collar. A posse of boys fled past me, hysterical with laughter, and some boat on the river made a bull-like noise from which they seemed to be fleeing. They outran it. I walked on, blowing smoke at the swirling grey of the fog, perhaps wishing that I could disappear with the same ease as the smoke and the boys. Before long my knee had begun to tighten up and ache, so I eventually stopped a cab and told him to return me to the brownstone. I had work to do.

I was still worrying about Venetia when I walked up the stairs past the room where those two boys shared their girl-friend. As I went by, walking slowly, I heard a song, or at least a percussive snatch of it:

'What I need is a brand-new man
To make a brand-new woman of me.
I feel like finding a new man:
I need a brand-new new man,
To make a woman of me.'

It could have been the girl, who was Amy or Aimée or something like that. It didn't sound like a radio. I wondered whether Venetia herself might not have backed that sentiment when she thought hard and honestly about her wealthy layabout with his three staid Christian names, still haunted by a dreamy lonely boyhood, a hoarder of broken typewriters and unlikely books. I wondered about my hands, neat in shape, but calloused and only rarely, as on that morning, manicured. Listening to Brahms with a sardine in my mouth; a bad shaver, so that tufts developed high on my cheekbones until I swept them off on a vigilant day; prey to demoniac, excessive outbursts of laughter; whipping out a nostril hair at any provocation; taking out my teeth for sheer ease and forgetting where I had put them. I was an odd consummation

for the ritual that began with cuffless trousers, stiff collars,
black ties, fresh attacks on the gym, red-dog and poker. Oh
Princeton of Cottage, Ivy, Cap and Gown, Quadrangle and
Cannon, with your perfected rites of horsing and your con-
fected emaciations of the soul! I was even odder to have
graduated from that aquarium set which ached to possess
pygmy elephants and Arabian saddle horses and howled
'Great!' in unison as some ingenious water-skier sailed by,
like a miracle, skimming the water with the soles of his feet.
Look, no skis at all! Isn't that something! And wasn't it something
relevant that a couple of hired and sentenced killers had
requested a last dinner as follows: shrimp salad with Luis
dressing; tomatoes; avocados; garlic bread; lobster thermidor;
top sirloin; fried oysters; frog legs; baked tomato with sour-
cream dressing; Mexican fried beans with cheese; as if squalor
could turn back on itself and wonderfully, finally, disdain
the gourmet pleasures of a whole class by commanding such
labour of preparation not long before the digesting body was
stopped by a surge of pure energy, thus aborting those other
juices, the digestive, and telling all of us what dream tantalized
these two men while they endured. I tossed the newspaper in
for the men to read, picture of the Cook County execution-
chamber and all, with the iron hood (slotted for the nose)
poised above the rodded chair and flanked by bare brick wall.
That would give them pause, and maybe I would have some
unusual, ironic requests for a new diet. 'T'ank you, boss!' One
of them, his face raw as canned tomatoes, took up the paper
and trudged across the room. There were about a dozen of
them lying around and smoking. The air stank of fish and whisky.
I walked in and looked at them, at the weird miscellaneous
anthology of freckled hands, punished noses, rheum-thick eyes,
lips drawn tight, hair left where it fell, teeth decaying like
cracked bathroom tiles, neckties somehow hauled on and
round, shoes unlaced and faces unshaven. One of them, lying
flat, resembled a pregnant woman, with a little melon-like
protuberance rising from his shirt and belt. Another was
scraping something from a plate; it could have been gravy
or soup. Some of them would freeze the soup and sit there
sucking at their popsicles, marvelling as the soup-flavour
warmed to life in contact with their scarred gums and cracked

lips. That day's collection looked poor; very poor indeed. Apart from Edgar the Time, Johnny Sligo (he walked bent double, having, it was said, been a coalman), and old Alan, over eighty and distinguished by a large bump, shaped like a poolball, on the top of his bald head, I knew none of them. A few raised their hands in frail, brittle greeting that was part sycophantic and part timid. I nodded, discovered that they were fed and comfortable and went into the bathroom in search of aspirin. My head was full of hammers, and now I had to go and interview Lacland. With this in mind I slipped a thin piece of steak into the pan and slid an egg after it. The frying noise cheered me somewhat and through the steamed-up window I could see quadrants of blue sky forming into a convoy in the afternoon haze. It had stopped raining. My legs felt hollow and my voice seemed hard to pull from the depths of my throat; when I don't talk, it sinks down there and I have to practise to summon it back to full power again.

I can't say why, but I expected Lacland to be wandering around, and not in his hovel. When I arrived, switched on the cellar light (I reckoned he could stand that now) and called him, he appeared from behind the plywood partition and grinned, looking very pale but cheerful.

'I thought you'd never come. You're late,' he said with no trace of annoyance. 'That smells good.'

'I didn't expect to find you in there,' I told him as, handed him the plate and cutlery. 'You wouldn't like to come out, would you? There's nothing to stop you, anyway.'

He chewed and violently swallowed. 'No. Safer in here, I guess. A nice, lazy life. But I guess I would have come for food if you hadn't come by five.'

'You have the time?'

He nodded. 'I'm thirsty too.' I handed him the Coke I had in my pocket and he stooped, disappeared, and then rose again, the bottle to his mouth. 'I can open these,' he said with some pique. 'And just as well that I can.'

It had taken him about three minutes to finish the egg and steak. I felt guilty, but perhaps he slept most of the time.

'You've got lipstick on your face,' he said suddenly. 'You been out?'

I wiped at my cheeks. 'No, your chin,' he said. I wiped again and he roared with laughter. 'You had no lipstick on you! You old goat, you ought to set a better standard of behaviour!' I flushed at that and told him to mind his own business. 'No,' he said, 'you made *me your* business, and now *you* are *mine.*'

I watched him leering and winking, then wheeling his shoulders forward like a fighter shadow-boxing. It was no illusion; he did look menacing. 'That dwarf,' he burst out, 'he's been here. He has duplicates of all the keys. And he brought me cheeses and beer.' He reached down and slapped his stomach: 'Now that's a good feeling; nothing like food for calming a man down!' Again the wild fireworks of his laughter. 'Tonight,' he announced with great gravity, 'I am being launched in society. We are all—Lazarus, myself and you— going to the wrestling. Lazarus has a bout.' I told him I thought this was Sunday, but in a flash he corrected me: 'You must be getting too old to tell the time; today is Saturday, and you are invited.' It was unnerving to hear all this from our late vegetable. He knew I would have to accompany them, out of obligation, curiosity and sheer anger. 'You know,' he said viciously, 'you don't even bring my food regularly and you don't know one day from the next. Why, I could starve to death down here before you got your calendar straight.'

I barked at him then: 'Well, you have only to walk up and ask!' It was the wrong thing to say; he scowled and said he did not intend to ask. I had brought him here, imposed these bizarre conditions on him and now I was his servant. All this sounded very much like words supplied by Lazarus. I didn't answer him but took the plate and the empty bottle. I then began to walk up the stairs.

'Hey,' he called. 'Hey, fruit! You going back to your boys? Don't you like my company? You scared of me? You know something? You don't like guys who can talk back to you. Or even just talk to you.'

I turned round and walked back. 'You don't have to stay if you don't like it. What you get here—ALL you get here, is free. If you don't like the service, find a different hotel.' He cackled and kicked away at the board: 'Now I love you,' he bellowed; 'you have a sense of humour, so now I can love you!' Abruptly he quietened: 'Now where did I come from? You found me up by the subway. Where did you say I come from?' I shook my head and told him the little that I knew.

'I don't believe all that,' he snarled. 'You're keeping something back. But I'll find out and then God help whoever it was got me into this. God help *him*! *Them!*'

I asked him if he was coming upstairs, just for the walk. It would be as well to do it while he was fairly quiet. With a tearing crash the plywood burst outwards and he was by me, motioning me to precede him. 'No, wait,' he said, and reached into the recess for his shoes; his sweat-shirt was ruddy with spilt gravy and egg yolk and his trousers looked mouldy. He contemplated the shoes a moment and then threw them back. 'I can manage without,' he said quietly, and we started up the stairs, continuing up the next flight, past the Amy ménage (for once the door was closed) and to the doorway of the mattress-room. I pushed him before me and pointed to the bathroom; he stank abominably, and again I felt guilt in my insides. 'Why don't you clean up first?' He paused, took a long look down the long room, pouted and slouched into the bathroom. I followed him to give assistance, but he slammed the door, shouting, 'I know, I know, I can manage!' And he did, eventually achieving a monstrous din by singing loudly, beating on the wall and suddenly opening the door, saying: 'Come here, saviour! Show you something!' I thought he was bent on something lewd; but no, as soon as I appeared he raised both legs high, like two hairy tapered tree trunks, and crashed them into the scummy water. Two columns of water shot up and I got some in the face. He shrieked with delight and began to beat time with his legs, plunging them down and jack-knifing them up again. I closed the door on him and I heard him continuing his sport. Once again, I wished and hoped and prayed that now he would leave us; go out into the world like a giant refreshed and quietly lapse back into being a salesman or whatever. And then I recalled his Rimbaud and went as quickly as I could down the stairs to see what he had in his cave.

I flicked on the cellar light with a negligent push of my arm and peered in, round the corner. At first I thought a vast white rat had leapt at my face, snarling and breathing harshly. But it was bigger than a rat and very solid; something struck the pit of my stomach and I almost vomited, but not before crying out, I remember, 'God!' I sank to my knees, gasping, my eyes pouring tears. I shook my head and shoulders and finally made out two thick columns of coarse cloth, swaying and buckling. I looked up and, level with my face, saw the twisted-up face of Lazarus, tongue out and eyes squinted up.

'We're the same height today, master,' he shrilled at me, 'just the same height. I was here all the time. I thought you'd come down here to spy on that poor guy. You might even steal his books or his transistor!'

I stood up slowly, wiping my eyes and trying to breathe deeply. Then, systematically, slowly, I abused Lazarus, ending up by calling him a little toad. He listened with exaggerated attention. 'You know,' he smiled, 'I don't care what in hell you say. I could pee on you; it's people like you who cause the trouble in this world, prying and snooping, locking guys up who did no harm, keeping their friends away from them, telling lies about the lies you've *already* told.' I told him to shift, but he turned his head slowly from side to side. 'I go when you go.' Behind him I could see a mound of objects, with some paperbacks obvious and what looked like a bottle in the corner. I took a step in and recoiled: there was a carpet, and a thick one at that. 'I got that from Mrs. Pomeroy,' he said. And I began then and there to wonder if he might not be right: perhaps I had been oppressive, mindless, cruel, thoughtless, domineering.

'Does he have all he needs?'

Lazarus nodded, and then I heard footsteps coming down the stairs. This would be Lacland. He had not been long.

When he appeared he was wearing one of my shirts and his own jeans; he was still barefoot and his toenails were sallow and long. He stood a moment, looking in, and then spoke: 'I saw your bums.'

'Some bums!' screeched Lazarus. 'Some bums, those! They're just dead men in living clothes!'

'Yes,' said Lacland, 'I guess we'll all have to do something about them, the living ones. I took your shirt; is that all right? Now, if you two will oblige, I would like to return to where I prefer to be. O.K.? I thank you, and I will be ready at seven if you will let me have some socks.'

With this said, he squeezed past me, shoved Lazarus away and told him to replace the plywood wall. I was amazed;

perhaps I had not been so wrong at all. And while I stood meditating on the event, he switched on his transistor radio and I hastened up the stairs before I heard any more of the song that blared out: 'I feel like a new man.' It was just a coincidence, of course, but a distasteful one. He shouted after me: 'A new man! A new, new man!' I heard Lazarus coming up the stairs behind me and waited at the top to intercept him and to put some questions.

I put questions to him and he evaded them all. Why, he wanted to know, did I ask questions when I had something to look forward to: my adopted man was coming out—and at a wrestling arena. I have always noticed that Lazarus responds to strain by becoming either over-animated and gay, or by getting morose and rude. In one sense, I thought, his mind was sometimes like the stores which keep their lights on all night. You walk by on your way out or homewards and half expect to see clerks and girls moving about with files and papers. But no, there is no one to benefit from the blaze of light; the desks are empty and the counters have no one behind them. His mind occasionally left its lights on when there was no one, no thing, there; he emptied his mind, or his mind emptied itself. So it was futile to question him or to try bullying answers from him. He left the building and I was just going to wash, in preparation for the evening's wrestling and whatever followed, when two thoughts came into mind: I realized that Lazarus was probably strung-up about his wrestling bout, although he usually took such things in his stride; the second thought was that the caretaker was ill or at least had not shown up (he had always refused to live on these premises), and therefore the downstairs furnace, not oil but coal, had to be stoked and tended. To ask one of the bums to do this was to ask to be frozen one night, because one of them *had* forgotten. So I went down, took the left-hand turn into the furnace-room instead of the right-hand turn to Lacland. The furnace itself was quiet: a faint hiss of pipes, a creak from the expanding or contracting old iron of the furnace-frame, and a scurry of some invisible animal or current of air. I took up the shovel and plunged it into the pile of coal—small coal, it was, such as they used to put into the stokeholds of destroyers. Six shovels was enough. I then realized I had forgotten to rake and poke the burning mass, and I should also have allowed the coal-gas to burn off. But I was out of practice and I just vaguely remembered to pull the chains which operated the draught so that the fire would rally again. It occurred to me to ask Lacland to undertake these chores, but he was dressing (as he said) and I didn't want to perplex him further at this time. I shelved the idea for future use: for a future attempt.

Lazarus would make his own way early to the arena. About an hour later I went downstairs and found Lacland reasonably immaculate—for him, in sports jacket, unpressed pants and my shirt. He had no tie, but that was beside the point. What he did need was a coat, and I told him so. With extraordinary meekness he agreed and followed me upstairs. A few minutes later we left the brownstone, took the subway and arrived at the stadium in good time. Lacland said nothing all the way, but drank in all he saw, especially the chic women in the subway car and the cops outside the stadium. He seemed to be humming to himself—not any tune I could recognize, but a kind of tonic sol-fa of his own. Nothing he did or did not do could surprise me; or so I reasoned with myself. Lazarus had given me tickets, so I presented these and we sat. Then we stood again to remove our coats after having greeted the seats with our buttocks.

It was well timed. The first bout began almost as soon as we resumed our seats in the smoke-full, thick-throated arena. A tall negro entered and loped towards the ring in a pink satin dressing-gown with EBONY boldly lettered on the back. Then came a short, obese-looking Oriental with long fingernails and a dressing-gown covered with yellow dragons on black. The lights dipped.

Lacland was concentrating hard and gripping the sides of his seat. The microphone was lowered for the dapper M.C. in his tuxedo, and he announced: 'Ebony Mountain from Ohio, at 260 pounds was taking on the Nagoshima Bomb of Japan, at 250 pounds. Twenty-minute bout: one fall.'

The two contestants met in centre ring: Ebony Mountain, very sporting, offered to shake hands but the Nagoshima Bomb spat at him and turned away in order to perform some elaborate ritual. He knelt, bowed, knelt and bowed again; then he stamped both legs hard on the ring floor. Before beginning he removed his robe, revealing salmon-pink tights at which the crowd hooted and jeered. He turned to face our way and shook his fists and bared his teeth. All this time Ebony Mountain stood amiably in his corner, gently marking time with his long black legs and making one wonder if his white tights were safe. Before long Ebony was bleeding from one eye, having begun well by a series of crotch-holds and slams. Whether or not he could see was beside the point; certainly the bout went as if, after some vicious-looking close battery, he could not see at all, and the Bomb soon applied his claw-hold, which consisted of a two-handed grip on the stomach muscles during which he appeared to be kneading bread. Ebony howled in agony and the three-count came; but the Bomb continued kneading until hauled away by the referee, a balloon of a man called Tiger Maloney. The Bomb, always suspected of illicit holds and dirty play in general, left the ring to boos and a few hysterical old women followed, expectorating towards him and cursing him. All this time Ebony Mountain writhed on the ring floor. He was eventually raised to his feet and led out after being helped through the ropes.

Lacland looked hard after him: something was puzzling him. 'That negro never gets to win,' he confided to me. 'He always loses and that's why his skin is black.' I did not follow this—if I heard it correctly—so I simply told him he was right and promised him, little that I knew, that the next bout would be better.

It was. Two three-hundred-pounders called Gene Sloan and Sugar Samson grappled and bellowed and sweated for the full half-hour. The previous bout had lasted only five minutes. There were wrist-locks, hammer-locks, full Nelsons, scissor-holds, step-over toe-holds and even one aeroplane (in which one man spins the other man and then swings him round by the feet). All this was accompanied by ritual shrugs and belligerent advances to the audience, which was now beginning to cat-call. The match ended with an Indian death-lock by Sugar Samson which appeared to cause genuine agony in Gene Sloan. The bell rang, Samson gave his bull-roar, flourished his biceps, smacked his chest and departed to boos. Sloan staggered to the corner, sat down, was helped up again, and finally was helped out of the arena, walking as if both legs were broken. After an interval, one more match and then we would see Pee Wee Lazarus, who *always* bounced up again.

I got Cokes from the aisle, and Lacland meditatively sucked on his straw. 'Does Lazarus tackle big fellers like these?' I told him of course not, and explained that Lazarus was one half of a dwarf pair which wrestled another dwarf pair. 'Then why don't the big guys wrestle in pairs?' I told him that they sometimes did. But not tonight. The air was pale blue with smoke, and the smell of beer wafted across the buzzing arena. Over on the far side the television commentator was talking fifteen to the dozen although there was no action at that moment. It was some ring-gossip, I supposed. To our left, in fact next to Lacland, I noticed an attractive blonde who made a great show while the lights were up of crossing and uncrossing her well-hosed legs; Lacland was watching like a pupil with a metronome. She smiled at him and he first of all looked at me; I turned away quickly. Then Lacland slid his hand beneath her coat and I looked away again. I decided to buy more Cokes, but just as I reached the aisle the warning bell went and I had to return. As I came past, the girl simpered at me, and Lacland, his hand and arm deep under her coat, began to withdraw his arm but then thought better of it. I bundled past and sat down.

The man next to me whispered, 'That's him; he was on the TV in the interval,' and I looked towards the long approach: I could just make out a youngish figure with a broken, very Roman nose striding diffidently towards the ring while small boys screamed acclamation and adults cheered. This was Jack the Ribber, a clean fighter, and a major worker for crippled children. He vaulted high over the ring ropes and bowed to all corners of the house. There followed a heavier, shorter man with white hair (it was dyed), who approached the ring with a wild heaving motion as if at any moment he might run amok into the crowd and eat several of them. As he walked, he kept flexing the muscles under his jaw and tossing his head sideways as if in slight epilepsy. He received boos all the way. This looked like an ugly wrestler, in both senses; and he was. He reached the ringside and suddenly pretended to assault a jeering fan who promptly left his seat.

The chalk-faced announcer rang his silver tongue round the

usual formula, all the vowels vibrating in his nose: 'This bout-ah, most falls to curfew-ah; thirty-minute time-limit-ah. In the red cornah, Jack the—Ribbah,' from somewhere in New York State (but the young man was obviously of Italian stock and had many Italian fans there that night), 'weighing 235 pounds. In the white corner, from Pennsylvania, Avalanche, weighing 250 pounds. Your referee, Sam Wiesner,' at which Sam Wiesner clambered into the ring and towered over both wrestlers. He lifted their robes in an oddly sexual, titillatory way, and then inspected their boots. At this point, Avalanche punched the other wrestler viciously in the kidney, but Jack the Ribber merely laughed, did a backwards somersault and began to limber up by hauling at the corner ropes. There was a pandemonium of cheering at this display of competent contempt.

'Good old Jake!' shrilled a small, high voice; it was the blonde next to Lacland. She was waving her arm at the ring but Lacland still had his arm deep in her coat and would not let go. She turned to him as the lights dimmed, and he did something, I know not what, to make her wince and then sigh. I looked at the wrestlers again. Jack the Ribber was the epitome of correctness and poise; as well as being a polymath he was a syncretist of religions and a boon to charities. The blonde must have been thinking of a similar-looking wrestler who had also appeared here. The Ribber was still doing gymnastics in his corner while Avalanche was circling like some hound-dog, actually salivating (I could see the wet rolling down his jaw) and uttering animal sounds. The bell rang and at once Avalanche charged, roaring, and flailing his powerful short arms. The Ribber merely twisted, caught Avalanche by the arm, reversed the hold and began to twist. Avalanche snuffled and roared. The hold went on for a minute or two until Avalanche burst free by pulling at the Ribber's shorts on the referee's blind side. Then, hog-like in charge, he took the Ribber by the eyelashes (it seemed) and began to twist his ears. Lacland and the girl were in a throbbing huddle by now, neither distinguishable from the other. No one noticed. The Ribber was on his back, subject to a punishing hold whose force he expressed by thumping his one free hand against the ring floor. Avalanche shoved and roared, shoved and roared.

It looked almost over until the Ribber, with a callisthenic triumph of a somersault, pitched Avalanche high into the air and caught him on the fall with a back-breaking hold which easily went to One, Two, Three, as all the small boys in the world seemed to cheer and the women in the arena shrilled moistly from their very loins. Jake had won again, screamed the blonde. Well, it was Jack the Ribber, but who cared? Avalanche, too obviously cast as the ogre, had met the valiant knight and had been worsted. Jack the Ribber turned to leave the ring and received an Avalanche charge, fist and teeth, in the back. The bout, despite the bell's renewed insistences, began again. But not for long: with a glorious, non-samaritan heave, the Ribber pitched Avalanche towards the TV commentator's position, where the ogre hit the cement floor and then ran wild among the spectators. Guards appeared; Jack left; Avalanche climbed into the ring again, shouting and raving, and was finally persuaded to leave so that the midgets could begin. He left, bucking his head, shadow-boxing all the way, waving and roaring to the accompaniment of tired boos and a few bottles badly aimed but falling near his feet. Lacland was deep, by now, in his new-found girl-friend's confidence, and I began to feel like the mother who for the first time finds a strange, new female smell on her boy's collar. I meditated on this for a short while only because, almost as soon as Avalanche had gone, the biggest roar of the evening announced the arrival of the dwarfs, pattering quickly up the ramp like ancient gnomes.

First came a small, stern-faced dwarf in Indian headdress; this was Talking Tomahawk, closely followed by his ally for tonight, Colossus O'Keefe, a wild, bouncy, tiny man with wobbling eyes. Then, to equal cheers, came Pee Wee, in a yellow robe down to his soles, followed by a relative unknown called Gulliver, who wore a tin helmet from some war, presumably as a metaphor of his precarious condition and emblazoned with the motto: 'Tiny Giant'. His robe was black, and he minced his way forward, like a reluctant debutante. There were the customary cheers, boos, murmurs of indifference. Lacland was attending hard now, and the girl, shocked at the sudden withdrawal of his attention and of his arm, looked piqued. She was nudging him in the ribs. Then she

floated a hand towards his groin, but he kept his eyes on the
ring, conceding his arm only as a somnambulist might, in the
slowest of slow motions. The bout began, with Pee Wee
Lazarus and Colossus O'Keefe; the other two, by the so-
called rules, had to wait outside the ring until a touch-off (of
hands) could be managed. The bout began with a great
amount of gratuitous acrobatics, Lazarus vaulting on his
opponent's back and then somersaulting off to confront him
when the bewilderment had worn off. The crowd responded
gaily, half-pitying and then only a fraction pitying: they saw
a devil-dance, I think, performed by minor Rumpelstiltskins
in the clear light of the arena. The sawn-off bodies with the
powerful legs and shoulders bounced and percussed across the
ring, over the ropes, under the ropes until finally, as he
tired of this preliminary display, Colossus O'Keefe touched
off Talking Tomahawk who, with his Apache hair-ridge,
whooped into the ring bearing a non-talking axe. The referee,
a vast man called Funk, impounded the weapon while its
namesake did a petty war-dance before him, soliciting the
crowd's sympathy. But the crowd, even yet swayed by some
racial memory, supported him little, and he then walked
across to where the hard-pressed Lazarus was trying to release himself from a toe-twist applied by Colossus O'Keefe,
whose hair was now a mass of greasy coils, surely obscuring
his vision as he levered away at Lazarus's leg. Lazarus was
howling, and Lacland was emitting bestial noises which suggested he might race up at any moment and intervene. But,
perhaps because of the blonde, he stayed where he was.
Colossus O'Keefe and Talking Tomahawk now arranged
Lazarus between them as a human ram, and charged across
the ring, launching him like a dart into the turn-buckles.
Lazarus collapsed in the corner, but at once they picked him
up and hauled him back in order to repeat the process. His
nose was bleeding. Gulliver, unnoticed, had crept round
behind them; he slipped under the ropes and, as they gained
speed, tripped them with his leg. Again Lazarus went headfirst, but this time less painfully. Lacland was on his feet, the
blonde urging him to sit down, but he was bellowing un-
couthly. The referee ordered Gulliver from the ring, waving
a hortatory finger. Combat then resumed, and Lazarus,

outnumbered, received some face-mauling and a good deal of discreet thumping. Gulliver prowled the edge of the ring like a lynx. Eventually Lazarus escaped, tapped Gulliver on the hand and retired to catch his breath and wipe his nose. Gulliver fared worse: he was shot across the ring; they rowed the boat on him—stretching his legs and arms ruthlessly, and they even did a double toe-hold by which his legs were twisted simultaneously in different directions. After a few minutes of this, Lazarus burst illegally into the ring and assaulted Talking Tomahawk with a small stool. The resulting mêlée proved hard to stop, and before long all four were scattered over the person of the referee who, like a Goliath, snatched at the flies and roared injunctions. The crowd stood and roared its delight. Lacland was on his feet again, hooting and waving at someone—presumably the referee. The blonde clutched at him, as if she were having a fit, or pecking at him with a bird-beaked hand. (For no good reason, I remembered a horror-movie from my youth: *The Cat and the Canary*.) Then they all five fell apart, brushing their eyes and foreheads. The referee, Mr. Funk, admonished them all in turn; but the crowd was happy, having seen this Michelin man crawled over by the puny.

Orderly combat began again, with Gulliver opposing Talking Tomahawk. By a swift manœuvre, Gulliver touched the hand of Lazarus, who bounded *over* the ropes and immediately organized a stretching followed by a sling-shot; Talking Tomahawk's shaven head hit the corner-buckles with an impressive thud, and he collapsed. They dragged him to centre ring and sat on him, waiting for the count to begin. But, again illegally, in came Colossus O'Keefe, wobbling with self-conscious malevolence, and vicious in attack from behind. He took Lazarus by the hair while Lazarus was thumping Talking Tomahawk in the stomach, and hurled him against the ropes, picked him up on the rebound and hurled him again. Lazarus sank into the ropes and flopped back, held up only by the impetus from the ropes. Then he collapsed, more dazed than hurt. He sat staring at the crowd.

The other three began, not to fight or to wrestle, but to perform one of the rituals: they each began to race across the ring, gaining speed and momentum with each impact against

the ropes, until all three and then Lazarus, who did not wish
to be left out, were criss-crossing crazily, missing one another
by miracles. Suddenly they all collided, and Lazarus failed to
rise. The other side, spotting their opportunity, at once felled
Gulliver with a series of timely blows to the throat and kidney,
and then arranged him against the ropes: indeed, tied him
up in twisted ropes so that he was held there, a helpless target.
They then picked up Lazarus and charged across the ring
with him, ramming his head into Gulliver's belly. The shock
released the ropes; Lazarus catapulted into mid-ring, where
they leapt upon him, put him on his back, and waited for the
bell. But, for some reason, Gulliver revived at once and upset
the manœuvre with a charge of his own, upending Talking
Tomahawk into the corner and finally chasing him down to
the cement floor. Then the bell rang. Lazarus was still in
mid-ring, dazed and furious; Talking Tomahawk was wandering wobble-legged among the audience and the remaining
two were trying to find each other. The massive referee announced a draw, and Lacland at once burst from his seat and
climbed into the ring, punching him viciously in the face. The
crowd cheered, and the blonde screamed, half excited and
half terrified. I decided to stay where I was. By this time the
referee, well schooled in such eventualities, had shoved
Lacland out of the way and was busy throwing dwarfs off his
person. They all rebounded and butted him again until he
fell, hopelessly trammelled, and then they took Lacland and
slung him off the ring to the floor below, where he landed,
unhurt, and climbed back. Lazarus helped him. Then began
the brief final skirmish: Lacland, Lazarus and Gulliver
tangled with the referee, Talking Tomahawk and Colossus
O'Keefe. The bell rang and rang, and finally the ring personnel
climbed in, stripped them all apart and ushered them out.

Something touched my hand: it was the blonde, saying, 'He
did right, didn't he?' I told her that I thought he had done
something foolish in the extreme, and the last I saw of him
was his back, disappearing between Lazarus and Gulliver into
the changing-rooms, followed by the other pair and the irate
referee. I decided to find Lacland and left my seat, only to
notice the blonde, with her child's face and electric-blue coat
tagging on behind. 'Gee, I hope he isn't hurt,' she whined as I

hurried along. The evening's wrestling was over. It often ended like this, in uproar, when there were dwarfs; but it was rare to have a full-grown intervention other than the referee's. We hurried down the aisle and into the dressing-room corridors.

The blonde and I, she breathing heavily and sweating at the tip of her nose, arrived at the entrance to the dressing-rooms. We could get no further as the entrance was jammed with reporters waving their cards and badges and scratch-pads. Some large-shouldered man was trying to keep them at bay, but after a few minutes the crowd shoved him aside and poured into the interior corridor; the blonde and I followed, she holding to my elbow. In the crush someone's cigarette caught the side of my face and, involuntarily, I wheeled side-ways, went off balance and tripped over someone's foot. The blonde swayed with me, but we could not fall as there were so many people. Or bodies, at any rate.

The first person I saw was Lacland, flushed and dishevelled, speaking excitedly to some of the Press. Lazarus was perched on a high stool, swinging his brief legs and appearing to await his turn to speak. The noise was stultifying. The blonde raced out to Lacland, who turned, caught her in his arms and embraced her violently. Cameras flashed and the indis-criminate hubbub gave way to spasmodic cheers. Lazarus stared, seeming offended by this display of perfidy; but then he recovered his grinning composure.

'No,' Lacland was bellowing, 'that was no draw! I could give you a thousand reasons! No draw, no sir!'

'What's your girl's name?' someone called out. He asked her.

'Mimi. Now isn't that a nice kind of name?'

'M-I-M-I?'

She nodded and asked, 'Did you all take my picture?'

'You'll be in the papers tomorrow, honey. You just see.'

Lacland was now speaking again, with exuberant gestures of his arms. 'No, Pee Wee is my friend and I just cannot bear to see any friend of mine get such a raw deal as he and that other little guy received out there tonight. If a man can't stand by his friend, especially a *little* friend, what kind of world have we got?'

This provoked a roar of delight. Everyone wrote speedily.

'It is a matter of ethics; would any of *you* stand by and see unfair play?'

A thin, worried-looking reporter spoke up: 'I would like to ask one question. Did it occur to you that you interrupted a bout in which you had no scheduled part?' He pronounced it 'skedooled'.

'I'm glad you asked that question,' said Lacland, fondling the girl's upper arm, 'because I have the answer; and that is: yes, it did. But I just could not stand by and see this small guy humiliated.' How formal and prim he sounded.

'Hell, it was just a wrestling match; it happens all the time,' said the worried-looking reporter. 'You never seen a bout before this? With midgets?'

'No, I have not,' said Lacland. 'And I don't care if I never see another.'

'Say, what's your name?' asked one aggressive-looking man in a white raincoat.

Lacland suddenly caught sight of me. I made no sign. Let him answer and explain; this was none of my doing.

'Lacland, John Lacland,' he said. 'Without the K.'

'Where from?'

'I've been away, and I've only just come back.'

'You live in town?'

'Sure, I live in town; that's where I see my friends.'

'You a college boy? You speak well. You're not a wrestler.'

'Of course I speak well; I read all the time. My friend here,' and he motioned to Lazarus who appeared to have calmed down, 'buys the books for me, and we study together in the basement.'

'Study in the basement? Where?'

It was obvious he didn't know.

'Mainly the poets,' he said, 'the French poets. Rimbaud and some others.'

'You and him?'

'Not that I like to talk about this—it's private, and I have my rights.'

The blonde's eyes were glazed with admiration.

'You from out of state?' asked the worried-looking reporter.

Once again he ignored the question. 'Can't a man do good,' he shouted, 'without being pestered? Can't he help a friend without writing his biography in public?'

'Don't you worry, bud,' said one man, 'you're among friends. We just like a story. Will you and the little guy pose for a few more pictures?'

They posed, and Lazarus assumed his most serious air. Lacland looked smug. Then someone called out, 'What do you do for a living?'

'I save little guys who might save me,' he answered with sanctimonious earnestness. Heads nodded approvingly; other heads shook with silent laughter.

Before long, someone had asked him and Lazarus to appear on a TV magazine programme; they accepted and were given written instructions on how to reach the studio. I winced at what might follow from that.

When, eventually, we all struggled out into the rain, the reporters, the blonde, Lacland and Lazarus, we presented an odd body: Lazarus was leading (people gave way before him as if he were a goblin from hell), with the girl cemented to Lacland's side. I followed, saying nothing, and wondering how the bums would respond to the news. Here, out in the open, was an alliance to test credulity. Whatever Lazarus had done in the basement, it had worked a potent charm. Lacland was now, even in his own eyes, a saviour, and I was the mere keeper. An argument began about where to go: the girl wanted to dance with Lacland; Lazarus wanted to eat and drink, but not to dance. She suggested the Bird Cage, and Lazarus, happier in the lowlier dives, mentioned the Tijuana, where he often went. Could they dance there? Yes, they could, said Lazarus. No one asked me, and I didn't care anyway. So to the Tijuana we went. And we went there under an umbrella which Lazarus produced from nowhere; I think he picked it up in the entrance as we went out. It was a woman's umbrella, pretty and light green with scarlet markings. So, clustered together, and getting different parts of us wet at different times, we reached the club, negotiated the steps and reached the fug of the interior—dim lights and the sound of 'Sweet Georgia Brown' played inaccurately and percussively by a negro trio. A slatternly Puerto Rican girl with rosetted breasts and a towel knotted at her groin was trying to sing. Our table, after some involved banter between Lazarus and the proprietor, turned out to be about one foot from her, just below the height of her navel in which there was a black and white dice, the six outwards.

A waiter with noxious breath leaned over us and inquired. Lacland said, 'Whisky,' in a loud voice, Lazarus adding, 'Scotch.' The girl had a rum and coke. When I looked up again, everything was orange—as if there had been an explosion too loud to be heard. I rubbed my eyes; but they had just altered the lights, and we were catching the spot-beam trained on the girl. She ululated and undulated, crackily mouthing the words against the twanging of the trio. We would all soon be too deaf to care and too blinded to object. The trio bumped on, the crowd talked against the singer and the drinks arrived in grimy glasses.

Lazarus asked for the bottle, inspected it, smelled it, and then tossed it, open, back to the waiter, who caught it without spilling much: 'Take out the tea!' said Lazarus, 'and take these back too.' The waiter poised himself a moment, between refusing and hitting; then he caught the manager's eye and took it all back. After a few minutes he returned with clean glasses and an unopened, sealed bottle of Scotch. Lazarus nodded like a general receiving fresh supplies. The girl had already drunk her rum; she asked for and was granted another. The crooner wobbled her backside at our faces; the younger members of the crowd whooped, and she finished. The trio calmed down and we looked at one another.

'Now *we* dance,' said the blonde brightly, and she hauled at Lacland's arm. I watched with a grin. He stood and preceded her to the floor. Then, with a few other couples, they bumped and stumbled for a few minutes before having words. When she brought him back to the table, she was saying, 'And you never told me you didn't know how,' and 'I could have shown you in just a few more minutes. Let's go back and try.' But Lacland sat down firmly and sulkily; his eyes were bloodshot and his cheeks vermilion. The crooner reappeared, this time wearing soiled arm-length silk gloves and some exotic flower in the top of her towel. I drank my Scotch straight down and poured another. The music sounded as if some drunk were leaning on his car-horn; I could detect no pause or break in the sound. There was a slight pulse—a badly kept rhythm—to which I tried to attend. Then Lazarus and the blonde were on the floor to the amusement of the patrons and the discomfiture of the girl singer. She awkwardly bowed, swept her hand towards them and they held the floor for five minutes, Lazarus stumping about two feet in front of the girl—largely because she moved away whenever he came near her, dancing to herself as if she were under scrutiny from a harsh observer miles away. It looked like the Twist, but it was really Beauty and the Beast. Lacland watched morosely, twitching his right cheek and eye. He leaned across to me and whispered something I could not hear. So he shouted, 'Maybe I should fetch her——'

I stretched my arm across the table to restrain him. 'No, you stay here; she's all right and you'll offend Lazarus.'

He nodded at once and took another drink. His breath was sawdusty and rancid. He looked around, and then loudly said, 'Oh, the way people live!' That was all, so I nodded, echoing whatever he meant.

It was then, I suppose, that I began to get drunk. Lazarus and the girl came and went; then Lacland went with them, and they all danced together. Another bottle appeared on the table and I poured from it automatically. Two female crooners appeared as if glued together and stood behind the microphone, thus appearing to be one grossly wide woman bisected by the steel tube. A negro spiritual began, but all out of key. Someone emerged and began to juggle a plate on a stick, and then another and another until the whole stage was a galaxy of wobbling and spinning plates while he bustled them on and caught them always just in time. I may be wrong, but a man in a bearskin appeared and was tamed by the girl in the groin-towel. A tumult began in which heads—tight curly negro and wavy greased Latin—soared and fell before me like pool balls on a bumpy table, and a tap-dancer like an endless automatic pistol fluttered into and out of view, his arms waving like snakes and his head flopping as if from a broken neck. Next thing I knew I was on a cold road in the early morning, helping to pack a severed underarm artery by the light of a flashlamp while a crescendo of crooners got in the way of the light and kept nudging my arm. The armpit bled and bled while I tried to make the bleeding bear lie still. Venetia appeared with a cigarette-lighter and her underclothes in her hand; hurry up, she told me, the police will be here soon and we can be away into the sun before anyone knows who did it. I asked about her daughters but she said they were married now and we need not worry. The whisky spilled and caught fire and Lazarus was doing backward somersaults on the small stage, with the others standing by to catch him if he fell. But he never fell, never once interrupted his helix of motion; and then I was wrapped in the sodden bearskin, lying on my back, and I asked furiously about the bear. They said he was home by now, it being his early night. Now Lazarus began to snake along the wall, writhing and mouthing while everyone screamed and tried to escape. Back and forwards he went, howling 'Na-a-a' in a high-pitched voice which made the top of my head lift. I was trapped in a sewer, suspended high in a well above the black, invisible, rat-infested water, and hanging from one finger which protruded just an inch above the manhole cover. I waggled the finger to attract attention, but no one saw it, and suddenly someone walked on it, crushing it, and I fell into foul-smelling water, down and down, into mud and ordure, swooning and stifling. A rat faced me, his mouth like a purse, opening and shutting at once as if he had it on a drawstring. I began to speak but when my mouth opened the rat leapt in and we fell struggling to the bottom below the bottom, into the oldest ordure of all where we would always remain, safe so long as my teeth were firmly clamped round the rat's abdomen, giving the rat my breath to breathe with and the rat giving it back to me. Deep under the slime we waited and held tight, a pocket of life and breath, waiting for the miracle.

I woke to find a Gauguin woman in a purple dress handing me a melon—a slice of melon held in such a way that it looked like a whole one. She smiled and said I should eat now. I said my thanks but poured out my questions from, it seemed to me, a thoroughly lucid head. It was Venetia, she said; but it did not look remotely like her. Yes, she said, she had had her hair tinted: from grey to auburn; and it looked ghastly. What about the furnace in the brownstone? What furnace? The coal-furnace. Then what about Lacland and the plywood partition? Had he gone back? She didn't know. And Lacland and Lazarus? Oh, Lacland was that man, was he? Well, about him she wasn't sure, but she had seen Lazarus on TV with a handsome youngish man when they talked about brotherliness and wrestling, and the young man offered to start a fund for retired midget wrestlers. Apparently the money had been pouring into the TV station all week—cheques and bills and even quarters in envelopes from children. The wrestling, she said, had a following she had never realized and she could never understand why I had never gone to watch Lazarus while he was in the ring. After the show she herself had sent in twenty dollars—just as a gesture, you know, and Lazarus had called her to say thank you, and they all wondered why you yourself had not made some offer. But they hadn't seen you for some time, not since the wrestling bout the other night when you said you couldn't go and watch because you had to see me. That was nice, but surely we could both have gone. And a pretty little girl, about twelve years old, appeared at the door and said she had brought flowers for you, and she too hoped you would attend the next wrestling bout when your head was better. Twelve years old, I asked; not a blonde girl as tall as you. No, only quite small—in fact undersized for her years (she told me her age). She is one of the children who have adopted the midgets on the TV programme, and who interview donors. They may look helpless, but on the TV they have more aplomb and words than you would think: so direct, you know, and unhypocritical. I have tickets; we can attend the show some night.

'Have I been delirious?' I asked. 'No, quiet as a lamb, for a change.' I felt at my moustache; it was neat and crisp. She had trimmed it for me, she said; otherwise I would be quite unpresentable to visitors. I didn't want visitors, I said; I was still ill. No, not ill, but tired; but that's all over now and she had bought the tickets. Wrestling tickets? Or TV? No, the plane tickets, silly, for the honeymoon. Oh, I said, had I agreed or proposed? No, I had not, but she took it for granted that after all this time I had made a sufficient gesture in coming round to her at that hour with an armful of roses and that lovely mink coat and that green, red-embroidered umbrella. To sweeten, keep warm and keep dry our late middle ages. 'Gravel Gertie', indeed! She still had most of her teeth. And as for me, well, I was just one of those lucky people who do not have cavities. I took out my upper plate in front of her just to make sure; it came out shining and moist as if it had been washed. It smelled sweet too. I had a strange, pleasant taste in my mouth too: yes, she had popped a mint or two in while I was sleeping. I saw the pilot and co-pilot walking down the aisle of the plane: 'Oh no, don't worry, we always leave the ship at this point; just a few urgent messages to send. If you get bored, just use the rear door. See you at the terminal.' They went out.

That was it; I was over Long Island in my sailplane, wafted and floating over the neat houses and the green squares of the suburb where fumbling children negotiated their first kite and skilled adults fumbled into the first motor accident. I caught the thermal, rode it and sailed out over the sea where the water shifted from green to dark blue and where, thousands of feet below, the green and white liner from Italy aimed gently in at harbour and where, very small and abandoned, I saw a raft with someone signalling. As my sailplane sank, bubbling quietly, I shook someone's hand and asked how he had been. 'Well, I'm more concerned myself,' he said, 'about that protégé of yours, vaulting down time and through the antennae, into the crowds in his expensive coat, and through them into those expensive receptions where he makes speeches and always ends with a quote from that French poet. I think he is just a bit mad, like all philanthropists. It's O.K. having simple tastes so long as you aren't a simple person'; and then that foolish, gutty laugh which had echoed in a thousand consulting rooms from Cleveland to Rome, confronting incurable cancer and coryza and boils and dermatitis and sheer, doddering age. 'Mad, but damned nice to the community! Strange no one ever thought of it before, a nice gesture like that—especially with the midgets so close, in one way, to the kids. In size, you know; ha-ha!' The laugh again. 'Nice guy; all credit to you for giving him the right ideas. A good neighbour to us all, even those he doesn't know!

'Anyway, before I go, here's the usual handout—don't lose it or you'll miss the next show.' He handed me a ticket and negotiated his raft towards the pink-looking sands. (I wish I had not lost that sailplane; how does he think I am going to get back?) Crawling on the bottom, I bumped my nose on two

vast spherical boulders which yet yielded as I pushed. I
pushed again and something wet hit my face, and a voice
echoed through the water, 'You dirty old creep, keep your
head out of my ——!' I won't say the word. I recoiled, apolo-
gizing. You find the oddest things. 'It's the last time *you*'ll
touch anyone,' the voice said; 'I'll report you.' So I took the
can-opener and began to bore it into my head; my, the bone
was hard—good guard for what brain there is, I suppose; and
I spent hours at this until I could pull at the cork by squatting,
there among the plaice and the sea-urchins, to pull with both
arms until, pop, out it came and I floated upwards into the
thinner, more goldfishy light where the keels of passing vessels
went by like turtles. I got a lift.

'No,' said the Captain, 'don't panic; the answer is on your
back. I can just make it out—the water has blurred it, you
see. Just a minute, I'll show you.' He turned me round to
the long military mirror set in the wall. 'When I have reason
to complain about my officers,' he said, 'I call them in and
stand them there, right in front of it. Then I say, "Take a
good look at yourself, and tell me what you see" ' I laughed;
they always expect you to laugh. So I did. Turning, I saw
my scored back, with the words, 'Tuesday, eight-thirty,
studio Five,' written in purple. 'That's octopus ink,' he said;
'talk about luck. You're lucky to be here.' I told him I always
felt I was lucky to be wherever I was, and he laughed again.
I laughed too. They like you to laugh. But if you seem to be
laughing at their own laugh, then they don't laugh very
long; they smile at you and try to think of another joke fast.
He rang a bell.

In marched two officers, their hats covered in scrambled
egg. I was to be clad, fed, equipped, lent a movie-camera
and today's paper ('But, sir, we have been at sea'—'Have it
flown in at once, and no nonsense, understand?' 'Yessir')
and sent ashore to a new car. I said thank you, but the two
officers, obviously well trained, swung their swords: up before
their noses, then down to the right, in a steel salute. I bowed.
They saluted again. I bowed again. They saluted again and,
not quite out of earshot, I heard a several-gun salute. I
bowed, they saluted and went. I told the Captain his officers
were most courteous; they had to be, he said. I saw and

laughed. He also saw, having himself made the point, and laughed so hard that he burped. 'My dear sir,' he began, but I knew now what to say, 'No excuses; pardon me, sir, but we never know when the enemy is *not* at hand!' He exploded with mirth. 'My,' he said, 'I could have used a fellow like you on those long convoys to Murmansk. Up there the ice is like icing.' He roared; and then he said a bit of cheer cheered up the loneliest vigil. 'At the top,' he said, 'it is always loneliest; the loneliness of command and all that.' I was not certain what to do now, so I clicked my heels and reached for a glass. There was a glass, with a toothbrush sticking out of it. At once he too clicked heels and reached for the ink. 'To the loneliness of command.'

'To the loneliness of command.'

We drank; I air, he ink. He could tell, he said, I had been well trained in my time—No, he did not want to know where; but it showed; every inch an officer—initiative, drive, P.A.O.M. (Personal Ascendancy Over Men) and P.A.O.S. (Personal Ascendancy Over Self). Those two, he said, won wars. Suddenly he frowned: of course it *was* me, it *was* I, who was swimming the Atlantic; I wasn't someone even higher—a chairborne admiral? in which case he should at once have had me piped and wined and two men hanged at the yardarm just to show good faith.

'We apply the law here,' he said, 'not justice.'

The air I had drunk went to my head: 'Hang them,' I said; 'I *am* an admiral.'

They entered, clicked, drew swords, saluted just once, thanked me for my sense of care of duty, said goodbye to the Captain, saluted him and me, then laid their swords on the table and waited. I decided to wait a little longer. Two ratings entered, cut-throat razors in their hands and black dots of ash, say half an inch in diameter, on their foreheads. Cut, came the order. They took their time, being careful not to damage what fell away and simply had to fall away because there was no longer any military support for it. Collar, tie (black), upper part of tunic and of undershirt, all came away. No nicks at all. It was tipworthy service. One rating's knuckle brushed the moustache of the shorter of the two officers.

'Sorry, sir,' he said.

'Carry on, rating,' came the loyal answer.

The rating stood back, clicked heels and saluted.

'Carry on,' said the Captain.

I too said 'Carry on,' with good grace and no malice.

The two officers were now bolt upright at attention. 'Splendid!' said the Captain; 'I would have liked such men with me on those long convoys to Murmansk. Up there the ice is like—Come!' He bellowed as the tap came on the door. Two more ratings entered, this time with nooses. They stood silently behind the officers and the other two ratings.

The Captain said, 'All is attached?' It was. Sir.

'Loop,' came the order. The nooses were slipped over the heads of the two officers. Neither flinched. I saw that the nooses led to long ropes which passed through the second rating's hands and out of the door. The nooses looked like dried, brown jugulars that had slipped from within the neck-skin. But they were quite loose; no blood was spilling, for this was a military occasion. I noticed that the Captain's cabin was neat and scrubbed; dotingly immaculate. 'Come,' he said, 'we will take some air.' I followed and was walking past the door when he stopped me with elaborate courtesy and apologized for the brusqueness of his act. We were to stand just outside the door, at attention, but only for a few minutes. He told me that once, at a party, he had heard of the discipline of the Turkish army; but his own men too, when spurred on by the national anthem or some patriotic song, could split a dried Liverwurst. 'Now watch,' he said. I looked to where the ropes terminated; I gasped and apologized. I thought, I said, the display had been magnificent and could Gilbert and Sullivan now be released and we would all have a farewell drink. He paused. Then he laughed; what a jolly good idea; I must have had some discipline in my day, he said, and he laughed loudly. He vanished. I heard clinks and swilling noises. He emerged from the cabin with two full glasses of Scotch. At least it looked like Scotch, or tea. *They* could not come out, he said, but *they* had glasses too. I had to excuse him for a moment. He darted across the deck, taking care to have his back to me at no point of his progress, and picked up the wall-telephone. A moment later he was back, and I was relieved. The ropes were attached, about fifty yards away, to the launching mechanisms of the flight deck; it was a carrier, as I had not realized previously. I was grateful the display had not gone further; there might have been an accident.

Guns sounded. I dropped my glass. He smilingly picked it up and attributed the accident to the vibration. I drank and, like the Captain, slung my glass into the sea—a good hard throw but I made it. In fact I bounced my glass off the rail, quite by accident; and the Captain laughed, whispering something about my being quite a ballistics expert. I agreed. As I stood there smiling at the joke, I saw the two officers coming gently into view, walking backwards as the ropes pulled against their Adam's-apples. I could see all of their necks, and they walked slowly backwards as if at a military funeral. The Captain said, as they went past us, both of them in exact parallel, 'Good luck, chaps.'

In strong voices they replied, 'Good luck to you, sir, and God Bless!'

He nodded and said they were good chaps. I nodded too; they *were* good fellows. (I hoped he didn't mind my switch in terms; but he liked, he said, *fellow* just as much as *chap*.) Drums began, and the two officers were now, still walking backwards, about thirty yards away, walking slowly to the flight deck. I thought we should end the ceremony and make ready for my departure.

Then I saw the officers ease themselves down, backwards, into some kind of slot. Again the guns fired and it looked as if it was all over. But no, there was another manoeuvre. The ropes were hitched to some mechanism and I heard the Captain's football voice echoing down to the flight deck, wishing the chaps good luck—and, to please me, good luck to the fellows as well. Then, in dead silence, a whirr and a surge of heavy engines. I saw two shapes catapult forward at colossal speed, going up at about seventy degrees, in strict parallel, until at about two hundred feet, like rockets, they both separated into two, the fuel-pack falling as it were, and the head of the missile going on in an eleborate trajectory far out into the sky and the sea. The men all cheered. The Captain apologized and explained that it was as good as they could do at short notice. Practice, he laughed, made

perfect. But I told him I had not meant—— 'NO, no, no in-
convenience at all,' he assured me, laughing. If his ship
could not oblige a visitor, it was not a disciplined ship. And,
he slyly and embarrassedly remarked, there would be no
need now to fill in all those blasted forms.

The helicopter churned above me and I climbed in, my
eyelashes blown to blazes with the wind. We were soon over
Long Island and I was let down, welcomed by a posse of
clowns, all in uniform with long-gloved wives, awarded the
transoceanic natatory cup and stood while the bands played
the National Anthem. Then I caught the local train, full of
champagne, and got back to the city too late to hand my
favourite shoes (these thoughtfully wrapped in a parcel by
one of the ratings) to the boot-repairer, for stretching and
seasoning. I remember wishing my mother had seen the
carrier with its lovely complement of sea-going jacks. Out
there, where the winds threw high and made long waves in
the air, she could have promoted all her maids for perfect,
immaculate drying of the washing. No smut for miles, and
everywhere across the waves the fragrance of frying bacon
and the pulpiness of ideally scrambled eggs. It was raining
when I reached the brownstone and as I walked up the steps
I paused, worrying about the furnace, looking at the silver
TV screens in all those uncurtained living rooms. Across my
sky no silver fish swam with such elegance as those two well-
disciplined servants of the Oldest Arm had shown as they
negotiated the alien sky, at such short notice and at such an
angle, their trunks getting so sluggishly into the air and their
heads bombarding the strolling fish only a few hundred yards
away. Such was life: big moments never announced themselves, did they, and minor moments always came heralded
in silly timetables and sillier bills of account.

I told Venetia and she agreed, handing me my milk and
vitamins. She had iron and yeast pills too. A thoughtful
woman, with I suppose, on occasion, rather more speech than
thought. I could hear drums, even now, as if they were beyond the partition wall; but she heard no drums, not now,
she said, although she knew there had been drums for me.
I told her I would like to speak to that Captain again; but
he was away visiting, she said, and would not be back for

a month of Sundays. I protested, and told her of the ratings
and the two orbited officers. She had not read about them
all, *yet*, but she did not look forward to that and therefore
would probably skip the news item when it arrived.

You know how it is, when you are deep in lotus jungle and
they all say you are in the parlour; or when you feel as if
you have been sucked into the vacuum cleaner and they
insist on addressing you as if you *are* holding a drink in your
hand. I might have been Napoleon, but she would have
addressed me as Caesar; I might have had leprosy but she
would have rubbed suntan oil into my skin. So I told her I
would like to see the TV please, because after all I had had
something to do with Lacland and Lazarus and their project
(their professed project because I trembled to wonder what
the real project would turn out to be). 'Those bums,' she
told me, 'are safe and dry, which is more than any of them
deserve to be. You have worried yourself into a coma over
those good-for-nothings you have gathered up; if you must
know, they are still where they were—none of them having
the initiative to shift, anyway—and Mr. Lacland, your
protégé, has returned and is looking after their basic needs.'
I told her I had not asked about the bums, although I was
glad to know; what I wanted to know was what happened
on the TV. She told me that I had been asleep again while
the show was on. Well, if I insisted, she would give me the
outline. 'That quaint little Lazarus, Pee Wee they called
him, was there in a very high chair, you know how small he
is, and Mr. Lacland was by his side. First the band played a
rather sickly tune and some famous comedian with a long
nose—not Bob Hope, but someone like that—came on and
wisecracked about being a sawn-off shorty with ear-plugs for
legs.' Tasteless it had seemed to her. Then things picked up
because a small boy, shepherded by Lacland (who wore a
tuxedo and a shiny bow tie), asked questions about wrestling:
Was it a clean sport? Was it a fake? Did it hurt? Did you
make much money at it? Was there much fan-mail? And
Lazarus, she said, answered with big smiles and every answer
was calculatedly nice. The children were charmed; and then,
as the gong went, the three latest contributors to the worn-
out wrestlers' fund (not confined to midgets) appeared on

the screen. One was a Bronx business man who donated a cheque; one was a small boy who brought a popsicle, which Lazarus licked and ate right on the programme; and last there was an old lady who said she never missed a bout (except when arthritis intervened). The amounts were not revealed, but the TV station had announced the legal arrangements for a fund with Lacland as treasurer; it so far totalled about twenty-five thousand dollars, which was not bad for two weeks.

So it was two weeks. Had I interrupted her during something important? 'Just sleep,' she said; it sounded like an imperative to me but it was only an answer to my question. I loved her, I believed, as much as ever. 'Yes,' she said, 'he made one funny remark—Mr. Lacland—he said they all had to play *chacun à son goût* but he pronounced it as *"Gaw-ut!"* ' I grinned. She said it was good to see me smile; it had been a long time. I winced. Her next sentences merged into an eiderdown of soothing platitudes, loosely evoked mutual memories, ancient rebukes renewed, current endearments replaced in the past, sly quips made solemn, witticisms made dull, trite comments metamorphosed into prodigious revelations. I was slipping away again. If I had listened to what mother said, I'd have been at home today.

'Too,' she said, 'there was so much liquor at your house in that upstairs room which has become a notorious flophouse.' It was a bottle-harbour, she seemed to be saying, in which hulks of men foundered among glass and stinking alcohol. Men rose only to imbibe; they lay down only to sleep it off. There were toe-nail clippings on the floor; the toilet was full of sputum; toilet rolls were strewn all over the floor; the smell was bestial and the noises were worse. Some of them had even taken to tampering with one another in the darkness. It would soon be—perhaps was already—a police matter. And my Mr. Lacland had promised to do something about it. If he did, they would all go; and that would be the end of them. It would indeed. Instead of a nasty sty of a home they would have a nice human tray which was not home; and they would soon be in the streets again, knifing and getting knifed. 'No,' I tried to say, waving an arm, 'leave them be.' But she was not listening and I was like a man at the telephone who finds himself slipping into the receiver: first it enters your head through the ear and then it sucks you up from inside, so that all you say goes echoing across very high vacant lots where only the pigeons have ears and only the steeple-jacks have any idea of proportion.

But it soon ended because, as I fell, Lacland and Lazarus in their Cadillac passed beneath, catching me neatly in the profound upholstery. I bounced once, and Lazarus slipped a cushion under my head, and we drove on to a vast building of steel and glass. This was Charity Enterprises, Inc., backed by station WTSR and the show called *Meet the Mat Men*. Deep carpet, busty secretaries in starched blouses scuttling with files, mahogany desks in offices full of cheques and lawyer's leather chairs. It was like a circus, especially because midgets were working the elevators and polishing the corridor floors. Other ex-wrestlers of much greater physical bulk were lounging in a room full of cigarette smoke and framed photographs. Then, at the bell, we all lay down and tried to touch our heads to feet, our feet to heads. It was Mr. Solly White, the backer, who had come to inspect the premises, twit the girls and explain his latest publicity stunt to Lacland who, neat in a black suit and silver tie, flashed his cigarette case and flourished bulging files. It was the hair-cream advertising this week, after the lawn-mowers last week. Hundreds of lacquered, inane heads in photographs were flashed across the desk-top.

'Yaas, yaas,' puffed Mr. White, 'yaas, yaas.'

'Not bad,' said Lacland.

'Not at all bad,' said Lazarus.

A high-pitched voice repeated all phrases, and it was the little blonde in a mink-collared suit and pearls. I had to run to the elevator to vomit, but the car was not there and as I leaned over I heard voices rising: 'I am Bulldog, don't forget me'; 'I am Jake Trask, you remember me?'

'Is,' I shouted into the echoing well, 'Edgar the Time there?' No answer; not even an echo. Then, from above, on a silver cable, there arrived not the elevator but four shoes, above which stood the two headless officers, floating in slow motion, attached to nothing, on their way down the shaft. As they went by I saluted and their chests turned left in response, then turned smartly back as they sank down. Fearsome cries followed, then silence.

It was lavish, I suppose, to be moved from the city to a small town upstate, with Venetia all in furs and jewels, plus a nurse of easily fifty years, all in another Cadillac with a uniformed chauffeur. I was being re-educated in my old style. The idea was to have me convalesce, away from the hubbub of the city, the presence of Lacland and the others, and the reproof of every brownstone building I saw from the window. Nobody knows you when you're down and out.

It was a white stucco house with green shutters, a double set of front steps and a porch on the side. There was a TV antenna on top but, I found, no set inside; that would come, Venetia said. It looked a lived-in house and it belonged to Venetia, who would visit me. There were books on the tables and of course on the shelves. There was a large, cinema-organ-like record-machine with a sizable stack of Brahms (glad), orchestral Beethoven (for during breakfast and dusting), Beethoven piano music (firelight) and much Mozart and Handel. When we entered the house it smelled like a deserted greenhouse, but it was warm and there were gay curtains at the windows. The chauffeur brought in my bags, a crate of canned supplies and the flowers which Venetia deftly arranged in various pots and vases. Things soon smelled sweeter. The phone worked. The toilets flushed. There was water. There was electricity. There was me. And there was also (at first) the visiting nurse, Mrs. Devine, a woman from maritime Canada with a vast laugh and an incomprehensible accent which, she said, was Bonavista Bay, Newfoundland. I took her word for that. She left me soon after ten p.m.; which meant I could sit up in the parlour and have a quiet drink and a read.

I always wished I could believe in the advertisers' truth. Facing the bottle of golden miracles with the red and gilt labels, I would always want to forget what the doctors said about this liquid's impact on the liver. *My* liver would be different. And on the bottle the gay-faced, slightly secretive man in the golden top-hat, red tail-coat and white tight trousers strode off home with his umbrella and quizzing-glass. Odd, though, that he himself had no bottle; I suppose he was hurrying home to his crate. Work out the world or wash it away. The sun should be golden, floating gently up across a turquoise sky. There should be well-drilled starlings doing precise orisons and immaculate wheels. There should be light, indifferent cobwebs resigning themselves to suicide and therefore wearing their best pearls in the starling-light. There should be porphyry and windows: windows misty to look through as delicate slices of cucumber or fat-transparent newspaper. I felt the ache of talking to myself between five and seven while the day like many other days ascended into harsh light. Slowly the objects of the dooryard returned and the night's erratic anaesthesia wore off. Survey the room, then. You never went to bed. In the grate the unlit fire: sticks diagonal, the old wrappers—from a carton of Lucky Strikes, last week's pink sales-announcements and some empty books of matches—and strips of cardboard, all drying and curling like Joans of Arc, despairing of the pyre. Yesterday's dust always looks grimmer and thicker and less likely to be removed. It gathers wood-ash and indiscriminate dirt, as if waiting for some footprint. The brown carpet has two scars where red-hot scraps of wood alighted. Beneath the carpet the felt has ruffled and here and there, by the window and the circular table with the false drawers, it bulges. Where the felt ends, about two inches from the carpet's edge, there is a line of wear and grease: feet have ironed down the pile, that vague and soft zone of foot-comfort, into a bare area of no fuss. Here the fabric fades, begins to expose its ribs, and the line crosses all, shadowed on either side. The brass fire-irons, clumsily stacked together against the matching stand, are like furred tongues stuck defensively at the sun. The white-painted bricks of the fireplace are dingy; there are soot stains and the impact-marks of thrown cigarette-ends. The stack of logs sits patiently, certain of prowess. The spiders I have let accumulate in the corners of the room and the angles of the furniture are still: they no longer panic as I approach. No flies feed them in this gauze-sealed house; but they live on, no doubt sucking the fabrics. Down below this room, the coal-furnace, where I shovel when I remember, must have begun to idle: the room is cold and not, as last night, tropical. Showers of birds are parading along the well-developed branches of the trees; milk has arrived and is patient for my disposal; the

street-washing machine has been by, drenching the gutters. Last
night's glass is rough and sticky with drying whisky; the ash-
trays are my evidences of having walked about; all are full,
like tiny extinct volcanoes dotted round with white butts and
the occasional boulder of a cigar blackened with uncontrolled
saliva. I put on a light but as quickly put it out: it looks
humiliated by the magnesium burst of daylight. I see my
weight remembered in the cushions; they have not yet
reasserted themselves to their original plump. I see little other
evidence of my having not slept. Had I sprawled on the
carpet, there would be no sign, or had I sat on the stove and
cooled my backside on the enamel, or had I hung all night
upside down from the mantel where the books are, or crawled
into the speaker to add my noises to the better devised ones of
Beethoven and Brahms. I know this room. When I lift the firescreen, be careful not to pierce my hand with that sharp
protruding wire. Always slam the side french window, because
the catch is feeble. In the drawer of this table there are four-
cent stamps and the cheque book. All over the cream-painted
room there is a film of coal-dust which filters up from the
basement when I shovel. I go down, put on the old pair of
gloves, open the furnace room, check the pressure and the
temperature, jerk the tubular handle, open the upper door and
stab at the coke with a long iron bar, then shovel in a dozen
shovelfuls of coal from the stack round the corner of the wall
(and above which I can see the daylight tampering with the
garage doors), then rake out the ashes from the small slit
below the ember level, and finally shovel out the chlorine-vile
ashes, marvellously livened with red coals, into zinc bins
which I leave out every Friday for the garbage men. This fills
in the time and means I won't have to listen to all the movements of whatever symphony I am using to terrify the
ghosts of the house's unending silence. And one day, from over
the hill, past the elegant stone-faced residences, they will come,
hundreds of men bearing coffins on their shoulders, grunting
with effort, just to enter by the garage door and tip the
contents into the furnace, while I shall rake and rake and jerk
the tubular handle owing to the supply and the length of the
tinder. I go to the phone which never rings: lift the receiver—
it purrs to me. Good, I am still in touch. I fear that one day,

when I lift the receiver, it will ask me what I want. And I shall say: an answer, which I have just got, so thank you, good morning.

Outside are the two greatest challenges: mail-box and milk-bin. I take the last first, unlocking the door and swinging the screen-door outwards, I flick open the zinc bin and pull in towards me the two brown bottles which preserve the vitamins, then flick back the lid. Mail will come later and, to be sure what I have, I have to grope down into the shallow metal box, down towards the spiders nesting in the dry bottom, so that my fingers catch on the open slot half way down. That will be later. First I have to learn to dominate the room again which has witnessed another night's loneliness and the whole orchestration of devices which goes with that. Violent speeches addressed to the corner lamp. Foul words into the fire. Off-the-cuff tributes addressed back to Beethoven and Brahms against the tide of their tumult. Small, lilac-feeling prayers whispered half-incredulously during a piece of Bach on a quiet organ. Minute-long attempts to be telepathic and disturb the world by sheer concentration and tight nerves. But they don't ring, they don't come driving in through the front doors in their cars. No, I would have to walk a gorgon or a unicorn down the avenue before they would look. But on that day when they come hoisting their coffins, because mine is the only house where you can burn anybody, then I shall charge avoirdupois for the stress on the wooden stairs down to the basement. And round the furnace I shall, at my own expense, install heavy silver-embroidered curtains of elaborate catafalque style. There will be spittoons for the weak-stomached, clean hand-cloths for the fastidious, smelling-salts for the agnostics, whisky warmed by the furnace for the morning-chilled and chocolate blancmanges for the hungry who have been carrying coffins all night across the state. All anthems shall be sung here to Sousa; all psalms shall be syncopated according to the bird of the moment because you can hear them so plainly in the basement (like standing in a vast dark shell with the sea of the birds' noises wobbling above you and likely to flood any moment). There will be seaweed, imported, for stopping the blaze from mounting too high, so that all the last reverential gestures shall not be hurried on account of the fire's voracity. This is why I stay up all night, keeping the furnace going, tending and raking and replenishing and shovelling ashes. I await that procession and I must have flame in readiness even though the dawns succeed one another like dreams, even though the white hip-bones of the weak lie around me and the empty eye-sockets of the long-skeletoned tell me to get breakfast. Down there, in the quiet, whispering furnace-room, where I catch the rats peeping at me and chop off their heads with one swing of the shovel, then toss them high against the white-hot ribs of the furnace mouth, I devote myself to the keeping warm of the house and to preparation against the dead. When the corpses come thrusting in from the neighbour graveyards, because of the overcrowding, I shall install my turnstile: this way to the fire; get your tickets on the right and at the word toss in as high and far as you can. And whatever you do, do not spill anything on the lip of the furnace: that is, no protruding permitted. Put in your leg, miss; too late to waggle it now. Pull his pipe from his mouth; he won't need it. Remove that walking-stick; he is horizontal now, the easiest position for all of us. Nor will such wood contribute materially to the blaze. Thank you. We have our troubles in these places. Move along, please, and those of you not busy, please try to shove back into the earth wall those human bones which keep arriving, through local pressure, from all the neighbouring graveyards: it is like living in a box of matches, with someone always trying to add an extra match. The pressure will crunch us all, and I do not wish to be buried among chop-sticks of withered human gristle. I wish only to be of service, stoking the last furnace so as to keep the earth clean. There are too many of us already slotted into the earth's surface, at the same depth, in the same condition, for ultimately the same reason, and we need peace in which to rest our bones. Failing peace, chaos. Failing space, ash. Failing ash, I ring God's number, which by then He will surely have vouchsafed to someone.

'Is it really you?'

'Who the heaven do you *think* I am?'

'Well, it's so early in the world to get a call——'

'Let me be the judge of that.'

'Well, you *are* supposed to be the judge of everything, so why the mock——'

'Were you interrupting me? I never could see why I take the trouble to——'

'No, I wasn't, but I've half a mind to!'

I dash downstairs to fuel the furnace; it is getting low and black, and I have to pump the handle madly for five minutes and then throw in wood to restore the blaze. There are no respites: the fire must be kept up.

Suddenly—if there *are* any actual degrees of occurrence—I recall where I am, that I am wishing Lacland were here to stoke, or that Lazarus the wrestling has-been would help me more. But why should he? He doesn't live here, or Lacland. I wipe my face with my handkerchief.

I know now, at least in my moments of repose, that the secret of life is to learn to exclude. To achieve fulness we must achieve a shut-out: these careers, that career; another woman, or women in general; that other God, or those gods. I am criminally slow to learn, but I have learned—since Lacland went and my folly became a byword—I have gathered all I can concerning the life which is minus what we wish we had. Soon, or late, you have to shut a final door on enticing avenues. If you do not, you will end up with—not necessarily nothing— but without the something you now cherish. Lacland has taken my pound of flesh; or rather his: we are one flesh in this. I look each day and he is not there: what spider-thick hell has received him now, or what paradise, I know not. I am, as some old sermon-writer used to say, in strange-wise repentant: life is a risk of this kind and the risker does not always lose out. Sometimes, I know, the bright silver shine of the slug's trail over a flat stone loses its lustre during the smoking of a cigarette. Sometimes, I have been told, it holds the sunshine and seems to crystallize the carefulness of God with things fleeting. On the one hand, the evaporation and oxidizing of fresh water; on the other, the arrested shine of a belated angel's passage. How I drool: but if I cannot colour what I know—elaborate all I believe in—I have no safety in this interim. And I am no self-sacrificer, I think.

This would go on for hours, in pain and tedium. My main dream was that I turned up on God's doorstep one morning and was taken in with no more fuss than if I had been the milk. 'You were lost,' He said, and I nodded. 'Well,' He said,

'you need not come in yet; where you need to go now is'—
and there followed the directions. When I look back—it all
fades quickly—I see an ex-sophisticate, rich youth, the con-
noisseur of islands and silky-holed women, smooth-bottomed
lagoons and well-chosen libraries, caught up into the street-
sweeping process with all the snorts of acid water and the
early-morning spittle of the street-cleaners. Phlegm on my
trouser-leg. Spilled scum on my fender. A rude endorsement
on my work-permit. When I was a student I would return,
very near dawn, to the residence and find the anonymous,
muscled cleaners hammering at the marble floor of the lobby.
The white spume increased, the mops whirled, the brushes
punched, and each man seemed to immerse himself into the
light tide of the day's foam: the pools of new water swilled
abandonedly outwards, the mops followed, and tough,
mahogany arms leaned and leaned as if to expunge the
merest bubble. Motion filled the hall as they stood, thick-
legged and blank-faced, getting that marble neat and spruce
for the day's thousands of walkers. And as I took the elevator
with a man in a numbered hat, I wondered about the necessary and soon lost the thought in an overdue sleep from which
no one waked me to cleanse me. When you walked across that
floor you were staining the bright patent of heaven, new-made
by private men in the salmon dawn with only a shack or
roach-thick apartment to return to.

I was free of thought when at last I lay down on the living-
room divan, having first disarranged my sickbed and thrown
a few clothes around the room. Dawn was ready to spill across
the window, so I drew the dark green curtain and then, before
sprawling out, massaged the back of my neck where the
muscles tend to congeal and even, it feels, calcify. They made
a sharp crack as I shifted them about; and then I settled,
hoping I was north-south rather than east-west. I was. So I
prepared to doze, but missing badly the hawks and spits from
the bums, and the creaks of the other house.

We were walking on the golf-course where not a person was
playing although there were snatches of sunshine and only the
lightest wind. It being somewhat chilly, we maintained a
crepuscular trot: partly because we were not seen, partly
because we were oddly released from living, being not young

but still capable of a friskiness of the mind. I noticed how we preferred the smooth mounds of the greens to the coarse green of the fairways. We spoke disjointedly and awkwardly for all our feeling of liberation. Ageing people do not flirt on a golf-course in early winter; they feel more unnatural than in the city for the city too is decrepit. I swung a slight stick as I walked, and she swung a looped red scarf.

'You are much better. Your face is less grey.'

'That is the cold air. When we go in, I shall fade again, like an old painting. I am too old for compliments.'

'There has been some trouble. Lacland has made the trouble; he has got that blonde girl into it.'

'No wonder,' I said. 'He would have impregnated her at the wrestling if she would have let him.'

'So you *were* there! Well. You don't have to be so crude.'

I looked sideways at her. 'What would *you* say?'

'Got with child! If you want me to be truly absurd, my truly absurd self.'

'Yes. Your true self. He should marry her. I can do nothing. You saw to that.' I looked at her hard.

She stopped, and as she stabbed her brown expensive shoe-toe at the perfect surface of the grass, she said quietly: 'Yes, I saw to that. I saw, too, to your being still alive.'

'I know,' I said, feeling ashamed, 'there have been doctors, nurses, flowers, books, long phone calls at my convenience, and all that. I am healthy, perhaps, but I have a fluttering heart. I am alive, but I have no function.'

'There is me; there has been me for a long time.'

'You are not a function. I mean something useful where I am not asked.'

'Thank you so much,' she snapped, 'I am not asking. I am hardly asking anything. What would I ask?'

'Oh—the time. The time of our lives. Joke.'

'Very flat, then. Try harder.'

We walked towards the deserted rain-pavilion and I was overcome with a memory of apple-trees in blossom where the children swung and the birds rioted. She was telling me one of her contorted parables.

'When Crispi died, in that frightful hospital from which no one had either the sense or the will-power to remove him, something became very plain to me. He had been living like an animal—to finish a score or something. He was once a gifted man with a brilliant future. He fell apart because he failed to take care of himself.'

'Why should I always have to speak the truth for you? He ate his heart out for you while you were busy with your children. Because you had little time for him spiritually, he could find no pocket-room for your money. It's as simple as that.'

She tossed her head as if threatening the wind. 'So. Isn't a mother to do her best?'

'Yes. All round. Not just as mother; as person. If you hadn't been interested in him as him, you should never have shown any interest. You must tell all people the same truth—if you *know* the truth.'

'Well, what am I to do about Lacland?'

'You? Nothing. Leave well alone. Let Lacland work it out for himself or, as is more likely, let the girl work it out for him.' It was a long time since I had sounded so robustly rude.

'Somebody must do something. Don't you care that he has got this girl into trouble?'

'No. I always, in my recent past, concerned myself with the sterile. You can always tell an old man but you can't tell him much.'

'Or an old fool either.'

I nodded. 'It fits.' She would have to do something and it was bound to be wrong. I was weary of that quietly quiet house and of the blank routine of being shelved. I was coming down the mountain again, and I was going to move back in. Lacland had removed to a smart, expensive hotel, but I suspected his new racket was by now not so new or anywhere near as profitable. The gimmick had worn off. The unreal city has to pursue a new, realer-seeming reality each week. Lazarus was safe in his lodgings: malevolent and feckless as he was, he still had to be regarded as not wholly responsible for his actions. Lacland had caught him up, outstripped him and was meeting him on the way back. It would be good in life if we could telescope what has to happen instead of waiting around for weeks and months while it grinds and skids and labours towards us. I saw Lazarus still wrestling, still suffering

mimed indignities, for his bread. I saw Lacland on skis, coming
rapidly downhill and therefore becoming desperate. I saw
Venetia, trying to help him, becoming involved in a snarling
farce which might end messily. I did not see Lacland with a
blonde, convex wife in tow. And I thought of disappearing
bums, or a declining population in the brownstone. Also,
there were rumours of the district's being replanned, and of
the brownstones' being demolished. If there is a time for sitting
still, there is one for revolt. I felt this was one for revolt. From
what I heard Lacland had already prepared for his descent
to the lower floor: my bums had gone, mostly, saving those
too decrepit or lazy to budge, and his own kind—much
flashier and less helpless—had moved in, with Lazarus as
their pet cockerel or ram or mascot or whatever. It had
become not quite a brothel or a brawl-room, but the clientele
had changed; surely I must try to restore it before the police
referred the whole thing back over my previous years. The
new rot must not corrode backwards too.

'You have already thought this out,' she said.

I nodded. I would have to go back, avoid exertion and take
my pills when directed. But I would have to go back even if
it meant extra ministrations from Venetia (whose heart was
gold surely) and a showdown with Lacland: my protégé, as
they called him. I would protect him no longer; or so I
thought. But then I began those old wonderings: if I had
brought him up better; if I had not enclosed him; if I, not
Lazarus, had given him the tools of life and the means of some
kind of self-destruction. Too late for all that, but not too late
for rearrangements. Violent or gentle. Quickened with the
idea, I began walking Venetia back, and when we reached
the house she began packing my things without so much as a
question.

Upstate or not, I was looking down on to a green, torn sea
which a shallow brown boat, now swamped into being invisible now tossed high on a pyramid of water, was crossing
by going crab-wise. Clouds like peelings from the surface of
an old painting, or pieces of burned paper, blew about wildly
and the horizon seemed to sway. Close by, erect and muscular
with a sinewy hollow to his back, stood a tall man with what
looked like a sack wrapped round his legs and a green, sodden

tunic round his upper part. Holding the sacking with his left hand, he was pointing at the boat with his right hand and seemed to be willing it forwards. In the boat two men were hanging out, trailing their hands in the water like children; perhaps they were paddling or bailing. Whatever they were doing was affecting the boat's course little, for the wind held it and drove it towards the trees and low bushes on the beach —a strangely green beach with a peculiar calm which the sea always turned away from and which stayed merely damp. The boat suddenly scraped in, and the shivering sopping men clambered out, hauled it safely up to the trees and spoke to the man. They all shook hands; I saw money refused; he gave them newspapers, from somewhere I could not see, and then walked swiftly away with a zestful motion, as if he had some cherished appointment for which he was already late. I was crushing a green grape in my hand.

Venetia drove the car herself; she drove with much display of cornering and speeding. She was angry, but that was no reason to kill us both on the highway; and I said so. She did slow down, but the tension of sitting with her during her pique was intolerable. And I had to spend the night at her place, I supposed, as I did not propose disturbing the men in the dead of night.

Later that night, in seclusion, I inspected my face: moustache looking brisker than usual, more bristle to it; my face was thinner, no doubt of that; my chin was more pointed and my eyes were paler and somehow more bulging. I reminded myself of some bedraggled bird pulled from the hay or some hay hauled off a bird. It was not a dissipated face, still less that of an ascetic. Rather, it was much used; all the weather and the gazes on it had striated it; but I know you can't striate hay or a bird, so it was a scratchy, itched-at sort of face which you would only remember for its having none of the usual compensations of a face. The nostril bristles had a wart-hog look to them and for the first time I noticed white bristles growing from the tops of my ears. Kind enough when I smiled at me; but when I smiled, *if* I smiled, at others? Who could tell? I had never achieved that greenish-smooth complexion of many North American men, with the facial upholstery riding easily on castors of fat. Nor had I managed that

aquiline look of some Italian peasants whose faces are all
impacted angles and tufts of hair. It was an in-between sort
of face, leathery and yet wispy, taut and yet with what looked
like air between skin and bone. A lifetime's moles pitted it and
made it look like the hands of some very old men who seem
to have spattered themselves with matt, brown paint. The
eyebrows had never tufted, either upwards or forwards, and
the mouth had never lost that old slightly disdainful twist,
although of course the lips had thinned and tightened. But I
had not yet sucked them in with worry or apprehension. I had
the feeling that if I were to apply boot polish this face would
give a scintillation or a glow; and if I covered the lower half
it would look more military; if I covered the upper, I looked
more capricious. Anyhow, I washed all of it and thus made it
look bleached and plastery. When you have had a plaster over
a cut for some time, the temporarily hidden skin looks just as
my face did on that inspection. To cheer me up, I splashed
shaving lotion against the skin and winced at the result. What
came next was sleep, but only after I had checked to see that
Venetia was asleep. She was. I tiptoed away, for all the world
like a father of something just a few years old, and tried to
sleep in the narrow cot in the spare room. Narrow cot, my
body lies in starch-sheet cramp and will remain with belly to
the sky until God reopens His inattentive eye. I have called
in my sheep, chased in my ancient chickens; there is no more
labour for this Hercules, and were there to be some tomorrow
he would not be Hercules. Good night, Venetia, lost in dreaming anger and swooning hopes. We keep on dying while we
sleep; the cells multiply and die as we snore. Sleep re-inserts
our finger in the dyke against a drowning tomorrow. Or a
baptism. Why does the heart speed up at night?

    I have not missed a dawn in years. This one came up with
a sickening patina; a blood-flecked green in which there
were delicate, consumptive fishes swimming and sharp
brambles interfering with the even rise. I blew smoke at the
window, estimating a clear four hours' sleep, counting the
creaks in the apartment, trying to decipher the sounds,
relate all the clocks to one another and determining not to
read. If you read you are cheating at insomnia. Oh God, in
not granting sleep you do by us as misers do by beggars,

for in sleep the roundness of ourselves as children comes alive again, and there are resting muscles where the day's tugging will insist. It is sleep on its many levels which tidies up the heart and heartens the fat in our hands. Climb gently down and kneel on this black velvet; shuffle forwards until it lures you down, and then fling it off tomorrow as a giant bridegroom might. I, instead, shell sleep like peas, squeezing its pod until it bursts and I can count out the dank, smooth seeds. I sow them nowhere, but I keep squeezing the pod and a myriad of schoolboys explodes behind my pillow. I am much taken with crypts and cellars, and I shall have cool plantain bending over as if to console even though there are loose heads lost at sea.

Venetia's alarm rattled on its metal plate. I listened, but she did not stir, although she must have been awake. When I heard her moving I would purify the house and greet the day with coffee beans, fresh-ground. And with waiting for signs and sounds, but getting none, I fell off in defiance of the gathering light and the first murmur of the tin parade on the street below. I dreamed again; in fact I dream so much that I can no longer divide my waking from my sleeping dreams. Lacland drove his car wildly through my first dream, and crushed Lazarus against a lamp-post. My second dream was of wholesome lightning over the sea, as if a distant wish has been granted and a child's eye has opened for the first time on the pageantry of a complete summer. All I know of miracles is this: when I cook and have to prepare bread crumbs, I take the bread and roll it between my hands, watching the crumbs fall into the saucer below. Then, when there seems no more to come, I open my hands and packed between some fingers and extending into the palm there are callouses of bread, smooth-faced and tenacious. But when I wrinkle my hands, these disintegrate into the finest crumbs of all, as at a commandment. My foot eventually found a way through the sheet and ended up against the wall, where, for the first time in my life, I woke to find it numb—not with cold, but from cramp.

After a quick breakfast I hurried round to the brownstone and took the stairs as fast as I could. The door of the mattress-room was open and I stood, looking in. There was no one visible; at the far end a bundle of clothes appeared to conceal a form, but there were no sounds. The blind fluttered and rattled against the open window; that was all. A party had obviously been given; the carpet was strewn with chicken-bones and bottles, cigarette-butts and wrapping paper. I went in and smelled the rank air. It was like going out in some suburb to mail a letter after dark: there are no children in the street but their toys still litter the sidewalks and you fall over handlebars and pistols as you stride importantly to the letter-box. I kicked at the chicken-bone and it skidded against the wall. The bottles were empty, all save one which was gently spilling into the carpet from some accidental angle that had kept it spilling, a drop a second, for several hours. No! impossible! I righted the bottle and stood it against the door. A snore scratched the silence and the bundle of clothes stirred. A face, an awful bleached-beetroot face, emerged from beneath the top blanket: it was Edgar the Time, struggling to open his eyes just like a wet bird struggling to raise its wings. Finally he cleared his throat and addressed me, still with his eyes rheumed shut, 'Hi, Papa; you've come back.'

I walked to the window and looked out. Drab nothing soared up from a maze of streets and anonymous automobiles wheezing gas. A bus belched by, squealed to a halt and then hissed its doors. No one descended; no one got on. It looked like the perfectly automated society. For one brief spell I could see no one at all, but suddenly a posse of girls broke into view, trying to beat the light and the bus, and succeeded. It was a grey, torn-looking morning, apt for some discreet funeral while the gutters were still wet and empty. Then I looked back into the room. Edgar the Time had gone back to sleep, and other sounds came filtering into the room. The men had found an old accordion and were having a senti-mental and malorganized quiet sing. A man was posted at each window, outlooking on to the corn and the wood that hid the road and the rest of the warm, moulded landscape. And then, just as I was listening to the sentimental thin sounds of the music and thinking of a sad tune, a cabaret thing which exacted tears and diffused pointlessness, there came in some man whose name I could not remember, and quite out of breath.

'I looked round the back first,' he said eventually, with his lungs still labouring. 'Convoy just passed . . . troops in trucks . . . some armoured cars.' He was breathing hard. 'How many?' He said about twenty vehicles. They were going north. It was beginning again. No sooner had I patted myself on the back for having survived this one, than something else arrived: petrol on the petals of rest while I sat pondering, and fingering my face, moving from the stubbled jaw to the strange unstubbled patch around the ear, that patch so smooth to the hand. Once again my postcard scene had come alive, like one of those old dioramas.

I watched this man struggling to collect his breath.

My fingers manipulated the skin as a barber would.

Another man's hand had a broken nail, ripped deep into the cuticle.

Another man seemed asleep, his pipe lolling empty in his down-sloping mouth; soon the pipe would fall to the board floor.

The world revolved; birdsong trickled into the mill. There was an occasional gust of wind like a large person running past; as if he wore a clerical cloak, making the broad wind priests make when they are hastening.

From another corner of the room came a tuneless and dis-embodied whistle; the sun had shifted round now and struck at a different angle on the wall. I fumbled out a biscuit. You should eat something, I said to someone. Edgar the Time groaned and turned away from the light. I had to walk away to the slit in the wall lest I thrash his vegetable head against the half-fungoid wall. I fingered my cheek again, knowing how tired and distracted I was by the cross-pull and under-tow and involution of events and the spaces between events. Then I heard voices, thin and querulous, coming from the stairs.

'He won't come back.'

Then, more throaty altogether. 'He will. He's a regular; a real regular; you can always count on them. He'll be back.'

'He'll swear we gave him nothing.'

'He sure will swear; he sure will.'

'So, then, what happened?'

'Well, it went like this. They tried the wine and seemed

better for it, you know. We had some sandwiches and then sent out for the chicken. Then we drank some more and they all began to talk; some began to fight, and Lacland got high: so high he had to go out for a while. But he soon came back and began to give the boys a sermon, which they didn't care for at that time, and they called him down.'

The voices faded into a mumble, still on the stairs. There was a strong smell of garlic, then of candle-wax and camphor. My forehead felt dry and tight and I couldn't sweat there; the rest of my body was sweating profusely. The skin on my forehead felt rough as sand. Then someone, lower down than the voices, began laughing—perhaps that thin unsmiling woman who called in for scraps to give her cat, although more probably to eat herself. I think what I liked best was the smell of cigar smoke which came wafting up the morning stairs, and I thought, although I knew I was wrong, that I heard cypresses clashing in the evening breeze.

Then we were climbing uphill. At one place the bank jutted out and a bird went calmly planing a long way below us, like an arrow crossing a map. It gave a delicious feeling of being severed from everything. We met no one else until we saw the slanted small vineyards and the women carrying baskets on their shoulders. The pastures were small. Higher up the road the cobbles ended and it was white dust in which only saints should leave their footprints. There were two donkey-carts ahead of us, loaded with baskets. One of the carters was singing gutturally but he stopped when he saw us in our uniforms. The sun was cruelly hot. I tied my handkerchief round my neck to stop the burning on the back of my neck. Then we met a donkey returning on its own and carrying two little boys in two of its empty baskets. The boys were very brown and kept shouting and slapping the donkey's rump, but the donkey did not change speed or gait and it was coming down about half as fast as we were going up. It was lathered in sweat and carried above it a cloud of small flies.

Someone got to his feet, blood welling from a cut on his lip. 'It is a misunderstanding,' I said, not quite realizing what had happened. 'Where is that louse of a Lacland?' he said, standing unsteadily by the window; 'I shall murder him.' It was Mazzini, the old, bald man who each day gathered up the trash, thrust it into a basket, using his feet and his leather-gloved hands. This was the unappointed man who kept the sidewalk and the street clean. With quick, loose-limbed movements he would pile the litter into wire rubbish-baskets which were fastened to the lamp-posts. Some days he carried a broom. He must have been sixty but was nimble as an ape. A stranger would stare at him, but he worked with a monotonous frenzy, mad with a passion for order. Emerging at seven-thirty each morning, he scoured the district in a grey sweater until dusk. He smelled of peeled oranges, and he was still bleeding and muttering. Lacland must have hit him, though I could not see why. I was only just waking up and beginning to see what I had been looking at. I had to take what I could see and build on it fast, and even if it fell down I had to be glad about that too.

Before long I realized that the bums were coming back, and that several were standing in front of me; and one of them had been in some kind of fight. They would tell me no more. No, they had not been here last night, and knew nothing about the bottles. Edgar the Time was too drunk to remember and too vague when he was sober: he would say that some men, and perhaps women, came in and drank while making a great noise. Then he would report that he had passed out. Obviously Lacland and Lazarus had thrown something in the room, probably with a full complement of their new-rich friends. No one had seen Rachel the Jewish girl for days; their last sight of her had been during the previous week when she had walked in, deposited violets on one of the beds, uttered a series of incomprehensible words and then departed. No one among these men knew where anyone lived, and they were accustomed to not seeing her for weeks on end. At one time she said, in a lucid interval, that she had been taking courses—by which I think she meant something not academic but therapeutic.

I then remembered to look downstairs, in Lacland's former cubby-hole. It was empty, as I expected, and all his belongings had gone. The plywood partition had vanished. Even the crate had disappeared. There was not a sign of all that had gone on down there. I felt at the walls; I fingered the light-switch, and even looked for stains on the floor. Nothing. It was bewildering, but perhaps only to one such as myself who

had tried too hard to see something worth seeing. It was a
chapter concluded, part fantasy, part wish-fulfilment. I spent
the remainder of that day helping the bums to tidy up the
place so that they could then disarrange it to their own taste
all over again. It was the natural thing to do. I called Venetia,
who was angry at the time I was spending away from her.
Then I went out and bought cheeses, soups and bread, plus
some sardines for myself and a carton of cigarettes. Neither
Lacland nor Lazarus came near, but I expected to hear of them
soon enough, through the wrestling fraternity or the TV. I
wondered what Lacland had done about his blonde girl-friend.

Several days went by. I called Venetia regularly but could
not appease her. As far as she was concerned, I had reverted
to disgusting type; and what I camouflaged as charity she
denounced as sloth, a craving for mud and a general lack of
taste. She was probably right. As the days went by I noticed
how short my breath was becoming; there were fewer hallucinations, but I found I could exert myself hardly at all. So
I just didn't exert myself: a wise therapy, surely. He who
sleeps on the floor need not fear falling out of bed. Gradually
the nondescript, easy routine came back to the place; there
were no intruders, no cops and not even Venetia arriving in
a mink-wrapped rage. We sat and smoked and boiled the soup
and read the newspaper in pieces. There were some shaves
and a few alcoholic long conversations of no great logic.
Winter was tightening up and the bells were beginning to
sound on the radio. At this time I preferred to avoid stores and
to turn off the radio. But the bums liked the Christmas rig-
marole and I let them have their way: bells, carols, and all—
well before the season had really begun.

What happened next has to be told carefully, and in the
right order. Otherwise it may not seem as odd as it did to me
at the time. Doc Rumboldt phoned me one evening in a
hoarse, troubled voice. Would I come round to his surgery.
Apparently Lacland had reeled in, bleeding from the head
and quite dazed. He could not explain to Rumboldt what had
happened. He had, in fact, as I discovered later, been missing
for days, whereas Lazarus, whom I had telephoned briefly, had
said nothing of this. Lazarus at Mrs. Pomeroy's, safe again
among the old parchment and the ancient paintings and the

bleared chintz, was a ludicrous enough conception after all that he and Lacland had achieved together. They had quarrelled, however, about something Lazarus would not mention.

As I walked round the two blocks to Doc's, I tried to clarify the record. Their TV show had ended, the charity company had melted as quickly as it formed; Lazarus was still in training, so to speak, and could still be seen performing at the stadium. But I had no wish to see Lazarus, performing or not. When Lazarus saw the truth, his eyes bent. So I was left with Lacland, now on the loose again, and the unresolved question of his expectant girl-friend. Venetia's source of information was an anonymous phone-call (probably from Lazarus), which she had later checked with Rumboldt who had seen the girl and refused her pills. Where the girl was she would have to find out.

Rumboldt looked pale when I arrived and removed my snow-caked rubbers. 'He's in there. Had some kind of a fall, but he's conscious now. Coming round slowly. Take it easy with him, won't you.' I asked Rumboldt what he thought I was going to do: harangue the man? After all, what had he done worse than I had done to him? I went into the side room and saw Lacland, full-length in underclothes, and looking remarkably hairy. His eyes picked me up the instant I went in. He made no sign of recognition.

'Well,' I said, slipping off my heavy coat. 'What have you been doing all this time?' As far as I knew, he still had his apartment downtown. He stared at me as if it were I who was full-length on the couch; and then, slowly, his voice gaining in strength he made what must have been a difficult speech.

'I let you down. I let you all down. Thought I could do something useful, like you. Just let you down. Made all that money, and spent it. I'm sorry.'

'Fine,' I said. 'I suppose you want to come back.' He shook his head. 'I don't qualify,' he muttered, turning his head away.

'No one ever qualifies in there. They just happen along.' I thought that sounded right, but I must confess I was troubled at the prospect of his returning.

There was a silence, during which Rumboldt came in and gazed at both of us. He told me to sit down.

'He's had a fall, not a very big one, but enough to give him that.' He indicated the four-inch plaster on Lacland's fore-head. 'Where did you get it, boy? In traffic? Did you walk into something? Nobody hit you, did they?' Lacland stared upwards. 'He won't answer. I don't think he knows.'

'Lacland,' I said, in my quietest voice as if to suggest it was himself speaking to himself, 'what happened?' He shook his head slightly. Rumboldt was drawing something on a pad and making calculations; he saw me staring and grinned, like a schoolboy: 'Just applying some of my old police experience!'

I tried Lacland again, but he refused to speak. 'Look,' I said, already beginning to tire of this one-way song, 'is there *anything* I can do? How is that little blonde I saw you with?'

The transformation was shocking. His face filled with purple, his legs began to quiver and his voice burst out like a radio turned on from silence to maximum volume. Tears ran from his eyes and his mouth began to dribble.

'Judy,' he said, lingering on the vowels. So might a fallen bird twitch in the gutter. I was sorry to find him in such a condition, but I could see no remedy until we had some kind of information to go on. So I asked him what about Judy; I had known her as 'Mimi', but presumed this was she.

'Do you know where she is? Is she all right?' I realized I should not have asked two questions. He shivered and shook his head. That answered nothing, really. Rumboldt had stopped his scribbling and was listening hard, nodding at me to go on. I paused, and then tried again.

'Do you know where she is?' I give what followed as clearly as I remember; it did not come to us clearly at all.

'Do you remember——'

'There was a bridge . . . a new bridge, with . . . foghorns. We had been quarrelling and she had rushed out of the apart-ment . . .'

Rumboldt propped his head up and gave him a glass of water.

'Was that bridge near here?' Rumboldt was officious now.

Lacland nodded. 'She said she was going to jump into the water . . . and I didn't believe her. I didn't believe her! Can you blame me for not believing her? We argued again. It was all about what happened after that night . . . at that club.'

Mercy, I thought, I have been away longer than I thought.

Surely, then, the girl cannot be far advanced in pregnancy; it all seemed slightly overdone. After all, without being too cynical, and despite what Rumboldt had refused her . . . I abandoned the thought for he had begun to speak again.

'Lazarus. You know what he did? Do you know? Do *you* know? I know. He took advantage of her while she was drunk at some other place, some party we went to afterwards. I was there, and she made fun of me because I was too drunk to speak. Then Lazarus, and he was drunk, I guess, went off with her into some room in this guy's apartment.'

Rumboldt looked sick. 'So you quarrelled. When? At that orgy you had?'

Lacland groped in his mind. 'That was a sort of quarrel; she didn't stay long enough with me to make a quarrel. She went off with that . . .' He reached behind his head and flung the pillow away. 'They went into a room, I think; they didn't go out at all.'

'Well, then,' I asked, 'when did you hear about her being pregnant?'

He stared. 'Who said she was pregnant? She isn't pregnant. She wasn't pregnant.'

'Why *wasn't*?'

'She's dead. Drowned. She jumped off the bridge, I told you; I couldn't stop her. She wanted to marry me, or something, and I wasn't quite sure why; or what was going on. I thought it was some kind of trick. God, she hated that Lazarus.'

'I wonder why,' said Rumboldt in a quiet voice, felted with all his years of experience of refusing pills. Or usually refusing.

'Was this tonight?'

'Yes, a few hours ago. I saw her jump and the current took her towards the bank. So I ran to see if I could catch her. I don't swim. So I ran towards the bank . . . I ran . . . and I thought I saw her and tried to climb through to reach down as she came by. . . .'

'I don't believe it,' Rumboldt said very calmly; 'he hit his head on concrete, not iron. She would have been further downstream than he thinks or says. He dived into concrete; he may have thought he saw her, but it very probably was not her at all. Maybe a paper bag, or garbage.'

Lacland had begun to shake and sob, like a large shaking and sobbing machine. I thought back to the blonde that night. She would make the papers again now. For the last time. I had a feeling of being in a foreign country where the language resembled nothing I knew, and where there were no signs or conventions I could manage. . . . All this during my illness (as Venetia called it). It was too much for so short a time. Too much for an ageing, self-hallucinating creature such as myself. If Lazarus *had* taken advantage of this girl, and it was likely to be true, then he had something to answer for. And Lacland who had let her drown had something to think about. Rumboldt was already at the phone, requesting dragging and all the rest of the sorry paraphernalia which accompanies death. I wondered about Lacland in a police interview; whether they would find the girl's body.

'How did you get here?' I asked Lacland. He told me he came round, collected his wits, looked at the river again and then took a cab. It was silly enough to be true. 'What did the girl do?' He told me she drowned herself. I asked more precisely; she worked in a store, a shoe-store downtown. Her parents lived in Maryland, and were quite old. No, he had not thought of marrying her; didn't I understand, she was Lazarus's girl and had gone there that night to watch him; she said his trunks were always so tight. Then he grimaced; said she was a nice girl and might have been *his* girl. I found out later that Lacland had spent most of his money on call-girls and long taxi-rides round the city. He said he wanted to look around, and the motion of the taxis excited him physically; so he had usually taken a ride, then called a girl. It seemed a simple enough life, although the company was restricted. I checked myself for the flippant, barbed thought; the company I myself kept was no better. Judge not . . . Well, I was not judging. I was preferring, that was all.

The paper carried a brief mention next day, including an allusion to the abortive TV show in which Lacland had appeared. The river was dragged, but nothing was found. Lacland had to answer police questions. Lazarus was interviewed a long time at the local precinct but denied knowledge of any pregnancy. The girl's parents were informed. The girl did not reappear (as I for some time thought she might: what if she swam and it was all a hoax; even a Lazarus-inspired hoax?). But I soon lost that idea, and it was concluded that another unfortunate girl had taken her life while the balance of her mind was upset. I still have the clipping; it says that the girl was drowned, and it says it next to saying that in the crammed and elegant crowd at the concert hall, about five minutes into the second movement, a man had slumped finally against his jewelled wife, he being president of some chamber of commerce, dying to Mozart—his own aversion, his wife's fetish (no doubt). Last scion of a continuous managerial line, his brother now seventy-five and impotent on a bed-pan. Ridiculously, then, late in this year, an incident not altogether negligible, but nearly so, appearing next to a death in the chambers of commerce and patterned round with a meeting to decide on alimony, a false alarm about a white elephant of a prototype flying boat, and the weather (Snow tomorrow), the accidental and self-willed death of a fertile young woman. The milk of kindness would soon begin to burn.

The next thing I knew was that Lacland had taken lodgings with Lazarus, at Mrs. Pomeroy's. Gradually, at first, but soon regularly, he began coming round in the morning to get himself a soup lunch with the bums. I trained myself not to ask all the questions which buzzed in my head when I could not sleep, which was often, and I am sure that he survived only because he managed to pretend that the whole episode had never taken place. The bums were cautious of him at first— not least because he had developed a pleasant speaking voice and his vocabulary had continued to grow. But, just as slowly as his visits increased in frequency at first, so did his articu- lateness and aplomb begin to fade. By the time the scab had peeled from his forehead, he had written (at my instigation) a gentle letter to the girl's parents (who thought she was heading for a grand career in TV) and had admitted that the girl was drunk the night she jumped. He kept muttering, 'I could have saved her,' and began to take swimming lessons at the local baths. This, while putting his mind on the sad event, also gave him something physical to occupy his body. He was getting thinner, tauter, more and more muddled, until even the most destroyed of the bums could talk rings round him. All his changes occurred at upsetting speed; he was never the same person today as he was yesterday. Then the boils began, and no treatment seemed to work. He scratched and rubbed until the whole room itched. He worried, until we all felt suicidal. He vegetated so conspicuously that we all felt vital and rejuvenated. Lazarus appeared once, saw Lacland sucking up soup and went away again without a word. This was just as well. What worried me more was Lacland's reversion: how far back would he go; he had developed so quickly and I had, at that time, begun to think of him as the brilliant orphan, the foundling or changeling parked on the doorstep somewhere and only needing a firm, gentle hand. This I had not given him; I had given in to him too much. But now with the one they called my protégé waning into the shadows daily, I needed advice. This time I had to be right; there was no natural vitality to pull his life back into contour this time. He was so passive; he would arrive in his worn jeans, his torn and frayed shirt, and just sit until someone handed him soup. Liquor he would not touch. I wondered about the arrangement with Lazarus; surely if Lazarus disappeared as soon as he saw Lacland, the Pomeroy lodgings must be feeling the strain. I resolved to enlist aid and information, in this order: Mrs. Pomeroy (so deaf when she wished to annoy); Rumboldt; Venetia. Surely these three could make some sense for me as I wheezed (my breath was getting shorter) the situation out to them. They all knew something, although different somethings. I would have to try—and to keep the facts clear of hallucination. There were remedies even yet.

Some days you wake with a profound sense of being incompetent, as if the blood is gently rebelling. A few days later, as I was just managing to throw off a cold, such a day arrived for me: my pulse was rapid, but the blood felt useless, gliding on its vital journeys as if only marking time or killing time, and the top of my head felt light, detachable, as if the cranium had been replaced, painlessly, while I slept; aluminium for bone. It had been a quiet time, with the bums quietly reasserting their old and honoured habits, and slate-coloured days such as December often brings. There were no alarms, not even from the radio, and I cannot remember having heard a single police siren throbbing and twining its demented curve through the urban night. Lacland took his soup peacefully, arriving punctually at noon, although he often had to wait an hour before anyone bothered with him. I had never seen a man so passive, so annihilated with guilt or remorse. His face reminded me of a worn-out blotter due for removal from the office desk; all the doodlings and curlicues of an indifferent hand were written there and then faintly masked with a shiny outer skin. But to those who could decipher and discern, there were lines and other evidence which had no place upon a face so young. I worried and that was useless; I asked him questions, tried to get him to talk, but he just sat inconsolably there, like a furred fruit waiting to ripen or rot, and the bums finally let him be; which of course was the very thing he did not want. I had never seen a man so little anxious *to be*. Yet he at least made no move towards self-destruction. Abeyance was enough, as if he had gone to bed for a month because that was all, in his own estimation, he was fit for. And this abeyance was delicate, furtive and limp: you might say he was mentally and spiritually in bed, tucked protectively in, and his slight physical motions when among us were merely the involuntary, muscle-easing twists of the sound sleeper. He hibernated and made some of us feel as if we were sitting in the presence of an arcane spell or a hatching egg. We wondered what would come out, whether it would fade as a spell does, or whether it would soak back into itself, defeated by the toughness of the shell, as an embryo sometimes will. I once had a dog who, in late age, developed a large cyst on his anus, which deformed his entire backside and made him modify slightly all his angles of sitting, walking and squatting. It was a pitiful sight to have this once robust, lithe animal trying to turn in a circle so as to see with his own eyes the offending growth. He twisted and wrenched, but could not see it. And before he sat he would sniff the air for malign vibrations, being unsure whether the pain was following him round, but disembodied, or was actually part of his anatomy. Once he had sat down the same worried reachings of the head would tell you that he felt more haunted than afflicted, more mystified than hurt. It was the mystery that hurt him most. So too with Lacland, waiting for something worse to happen; wondering where the pain came from, and why. His daily arrivals were the same in all details: he wiped his boots at the door, entered with a diffident stoop and a semi-bow, no attempt at a smile, but in his eyes a grateful obedience. I found this change of style both moving and alarming; the graph had climbed, was now sliding down again, but who knew what further waves and troughs might follow? We were all, sober or drunk, awake or sleeping, back in school; we were being schooled in the primal and the unredeemed by someone whose very contractions of pain also contracted human history and made the future less predictable than ever. It would be too much to say the atmosphere was one of smooth dread; but there were uneasy looks among the bums, and many signs of querulousness damped down lest a fight or worse depravity ensue. Some of them knew Lacland had organized parties in the mattress-room; most had left as soon as I failed to appear. But a few had waited, just to see what would happen next; and of course nothing happened next: there was an interval, then I returned. But they talked among themselves (not to me) in their worn, attentive way, and some of them, I am sure, thought Lacland had pushed the girl off the bridge and were more disposed to exonerate Lazarus the pert midget than support Lacland the unknown, the toppled social climber and lapsing visitant.

I called on Mrs. Pomeroy, who greeted me with an offer of tea and cake, to be nibbled before a vast fire and in the presence of piston-like, shining fire-irons, none of which she could even lift. She tended her fire with a small, modern poker of unmajestic design kept discreetly out of eye's range behind the firescreen. She was short, bulging and imperfectly corseted: at least seventy-five, and faintly redolent of camphor and sal volatile. For a while we discussed geriatrics, of which she had a fine collection stacked in the kitchen alongside the equally thorough collection of spices and herbs. Neither Lazarus nor Lacland happened to be in, but they had not gone out together. Lazarus was probably at the gymnasium, Lacland just wandering. One other lodger did appear, though, and he was a jolly, well-fed, rosy English architect over on a brief visit. He and Mrs. Pomeroy chuckled with conspiratorial jollity at one another's jokes, and I wondered if she had welcomed him as a safety-measure. No one could have said that either the dwarf or Lacland was the usual type of lodger; but she found them both 'quiet young men' neither of them prey to liquor (which she preferred not to have in the house at all except for medicinal purposes) or uncouth language. Girls and young ladies (I wondered at her distinction) were not allowed in the house anyway; and she and the architect created between them an atmosphere of unimpeachable, Dickensian cheer: stifling for some, perhaps, with her rosy cheeks, coupled to a bloodthirsty chauvinism, and his russet cheeks gratulating at his own feeling of well-bred, well-heeled camaraderie. They were like two shining apples perfuming the moth-disturbed air of that house where ferns twitched still in glass cases and taxidermists' birds stared forlornly from the walls. I felt daunted, too morbid for all this rosy firelight and meat-fed exuberance; but I chewed at my cake, which was drenched in brandy, and swallowed the sweet tea. It was pointless, once you had heard Mrs. Pomeroy on 'her young men', to ask any questions: she knew what they were like; being in her house defined them for all time, and she was always sure, when she read of horrors in the papers, that *her* young men would never, never stoop to such things no matter how trying their day might have been. She excluded what did not fit her preconceptions. And I marvelled at her witness-power, against which no accusation or slur-casting inquiry could prevail. My two prize birds had an iron-clad aviary here in which sin was limited to dropping cigarette-ash on the carpet and licence to her allowing them to smoke at all, contaminating God's air and hers with burning weed. A maid did all the sordid chores of the household and Mrs. P. chortled, perspired, fussed and grew sentimental by the gentle fire as she read her romances by the light of one lamp. The wood-work was dark brown, the parchment on the lamps oxidized beyond all pattern, the dead birds had no comment or call, the black fire-grate was fresh-leaded each day and the windows were rarely opened. I soon gave up, said my thank-yous and left, my last view of her being her hunt for a magni-fying glass with the aid of which she read the romances in the small print. 'Pesky modern books,' she said, 'they got so much to say they squeeze the print until the older folk can't even see the end of a word.' She persevered, however, and I went out, past the battery of walking-sticks, cast-off galoshes, fox-furs and other aged-women's frippery on the hall-stand of bronze. The architect affably saw me out, saying she was better than she had been, having been inclined of late to worry too much about all the lights he switched on when just one would have been enough, according to her.

As I walked away, printing the thin snow, I lingered on some of the things she had said. She realized, she had said, that she and I both ran institutions of a sort; hers was selective and mine was not.

'There are some souls,' she told me, wobbling her cheeks, 'not worth saving. I wouldn't take 'em in; why should you, a man with your education and background? I knew your Maw, and she would be disappointed, I tell you.'

I answered her slowly, because this was something I despised in her, 'Does your God say *that* when the sinner arrives?'

'That is not the point. *Your* lodgers—if *that* is what I should call them—do not in any way think they are sinners. You promote them from idle hands to full stomachs; a disgrace and a waste. How can you argue about that?'

'I'm not arguing,' I said, 'I'm disagreeing. Such men are where they are because there are people who believe as you do. Or rather, do not believe.'

'Please yourself, then, but I thank God that my young men are as they are: I just wish that Mr. Lacland—John, I call him—didn't spend so much time round among those disreputable men. I have spoken to him about it but I think he has a headache these days; he didn't answer me at all. Odd, isn't it?'

I told her I didn't see anything odd at all, but she was too hostile by now to attend to anything; her face flushed and her head began to shake; her slumped billowing bosom quivered and her eyes filled with tears of righteous pique. Then, sure sign of her being disturbed, she emitted a long masculine burp, quite against her better judgment, and I knew it was time to go. Her main fear was still that she would be raped in the night by a negro; it struck me that she was in more danger of receiving this compliment from Lazarus in one of his off-key moods; but *he* was a nice young man who just was not doing too well in that dreadful wrestling; and Lacland had a headache, perhaps because he was missing his parents. No doubt he was; indeed, there was no doubt of that.

I returned and sat, suddenly overtaken with a vastation all of my own. There are times when my mind is full of death— not morbidly, but ironically. I look at the standard lamp and tell myself that if I died in the night it would allow any next person to switch it on. I would be dead; the lamp felt no fidelity. One day, of course, it might rebel and refuse to function; but such rebellion had nothing to do with the degree of moribundity of the person turning the switch. One thing was sure: no dead person would be able to test the lamp anyway. I thought of that little blonde and her accidental suicide; had she not been drunk, or had she been alone, she might have been alive even now. There was no sign, I said to myself, that the cosmos cared much one way or the other. Life was always precarious, always to be savoured while present. It was such a thought as will send a man to buy in haste all the music he has not heard, all the books he has not read—and will make him go without sleep in order to experience these things. Then he becomes a wreck anyway. No, it was no use tantalizing oneself with what could never be; all that mattered was to attend thoroughly to what was present, and to choose that carefully. If I had been able to leave my thoughts there I would have been better off. But I thought of how we cannot choose until we are old enough to choose wisely, and then it is almost too late anyway. Life was not a thing you took charge of; you let it sink into you; you coped with whatever you had, and tried to forget the dazing multiplicity of choices or the apparently desirable things already in the possession of the people around you. You fancied what they had; they fancied what you had; and the only satisfied people were those with blinkers. Mrs. P. had her blinkers (and her feeding-bag) tightly strapped on; so, in my own careless way, had I. The thought cheered me a little; I could reason myself so easily into positions I hated emotionally. I lit a small thin cigar, tasting of stale bark, and told myself I was allowing myself a luxury, even if it half-poisoned me.

It was Rumboldt who provided the necessary shock, who immersed me in affairs again. He had his feet up, having just terminated surgery, and there was a bottle on the desk. I refused the drink and was just going to ask about Lacland when he interrupted:

'Before you ask anything, let me tell you something. That girl—I don't know whose girl she was, or the girl of how many —anyway, she made blue movies. Saw some the other night at one of those police showings. Very fetching and lively too.' He studied my face for reaction, but apparently saw none. So he went on. 'Yes, she did quite a few contortions and, from what I know, invented some routines. Shed no tears for an innocent lost; that gal had a few years' start. The police got the movies in a raid, and now they're working back on her file. I guess Mr. Solly White, the promoter and man of casual wealth, will have a few questions to answer; and that Lazarus too.'

'She never turned up again,' I said, more to myself, than to Rumboldt. He slapped his wet lips, however, and answered me: 'No, she never did and never will. Trapped deep in the mud, I guess, until the next earthquake; and who'll care then anyway?'

I looked at him with the beginnings of indignation squirming at the sides of my mouth; my cheeks were twitching, but I ignored the comment. 'You know Lacland is lodging at Mrs. P.'s museum? With Lazarus.' He nodded and said he didn't think the house or the company suited Lazarus any more than he suited them. But then, he was a doctor not a social reformer.

I wrinkled my toe up and down; Doc was hard to talk to because he had so many devices to hand to prevent true feeling from hurting him. He saw too much, his routine being the other person's nightmare. I wrinkled my toes again, watching the worn, strained leather yield easily.

'I'll tell you something else. I have a theory that your Lacland was pulled out of the Chicago Cradle way back in the thirties. A bad adoption, let loose by some Hollywood family who had got him for publicity but found he was backward or something and therefore bad publicity. Maybe a divorce helped.'

'But surely,' I asked, 'there would be papers? There must have been something signed.'

'No, that's naive. These things get lost; maybe they never

were signed; I mean that just enough money was paid by some people hot for the baby racket which was flourishing at the time. They finally shunted him off, lost his name for him, and somebody took him in and then shunted him off too. I guess they kept him in all kinds of darkness; all the kinds of darkness there are.'

I surveyed the practical difficulties—the documents, the numbers, the cards, the permits—the whole cumbersome process by which modern society keeps tabs on us. It was impossible: there must surely be something. All I could think of was that Lacland had been in some kind of mental institution for a long time. Not that it mattered; he was as well off with Mrs. P. as he had ever been in his life. He might be an administrational blank but he was a human quantity. I knew that, although I couldn't prove it. Rumboldt was humming in a vaguely elated way; in the way of a creature who is comforted if someone tells him, on good authority, that you *can* measure heaven and prove it three miles long and two wide, into which there is limitless possibility of fitting souls because souls have no area. He hummed, near-crooned, in sounds pulsing and throaty, cockahoop about his discovery. I told him he should have stayed in police work, but he said something like, 'Oh, the hours,' in a sniffy, dismissory tone which I had heard him use to patients with minor complaints. It was not that we could not have hit somewhere on a documentary trail for Lacland; it was that we didn't want to hit on it as if in some chilled, gentle hysteria about the man and his present independence of his origins. What he needed, anyway, was reassurance in the present, the only trouble being that he had seen much of the worst without knowing much of the good.

I would have liked life to entice and beguile him, as if he were some child unpeeling for the first time a large flower, delving with careful but unwise fingers into the heart of a daffodil or even hurrying a bud by stripping the layers away one after another until the flower hung in daylight. Of course, the daylight had been premature for him too, for which I was to blame, or it had been too late. My timing had been off. Somewhere in the corner of my ear I heard a whole interrogation about God, conducted by a child, with the usual questions about pain, shock, heart-attack, death and heaven.

Lacland never asked these questions, which was perhaps a mark of his intermittent adulthood; he would have got only childish answers anyway. His head leaned, his chin bristle scoring his chest just above the vee of his rough shirt. His mouth had a fixed, indestructible look as if to say: destroy the rest of me; you will find no signs here. He frowned, but without the sometimes intellectual content of frowning. Instead it was a negative, frontal refusal to have any expression one might construe, or be tempted to construe. The pieces of his demeanour hung together: no give, no show; and it was plain that, whatever his intellectual capacity, he had opted out. He had shut off. There was an underivedness about him, with no comment, no opinion, no hint; he was in the dead land that lies between attitudes, and his withdrawal or indifference was like a leaden or glass spell which none dared break. Out of the dark into the dark he had come; into the lights, then, and suddenly into a darkness so bright he blinked incessantly, part nerves and part offence. He had to blink, he was so wrought-up; and he blinked as if to fend off the least attack. It was the only belligerence he could manage, but enough to deter even the rashest of the bums who, inspired with whisky and elated with the presence of an audience of familiars, was tempted to intervene, produce a slap on the back and a joke in the middle of the afternoon. But all stayed decorous and gelid; no one addressed him and he kept his words, his Rimbaud, his high-life experiences, to himself.

Edgar the Time offered to present him with his own watch —'to help him measure out the time he waits, for what it is he's waitin' for'—but prudently made the offer through me. Lacland, like a man being addressed from Mars, politely said no thank you, he had one already. Johnny Sligo of the bent back offered to play him at checkers; but I cancelled that: the strain of contest was more than Lacland could bear just now. Alan, with the duck's egg bump on his head, offered to talk to him, and Alan rarely talked to anyone; so this was like myrrh from a stevedore. Again I had to say, Another time. Even Mazzini came in still wearing his tough gloves and offered to take Lacland with him on trash-hunts. I said no to that, and began to wonder exactly what were the proportions of the sympathy, pity and curiosity which drove these

well-meaning examples of human flotsam (as Venetia called
them) to go so far out of their safe, jealously guarded ways.

Each afternoon Lacland sat, as if in state, at his own *levée*.
His nose displayed a faint armour of grey blackheads. His chin
was sharpening and his hair had quite filled the gap between
the barber's trim and the roots of his ears. His eyelashes were
often stuck together with tiny blobs of sleep. His eyes seemed
bloodshot and marinated. He sat, while the trapeze of language swung all round him at our very low level, and he said
nothing, asked nothing. His teeth we hardly ever saw, except
when he ate his soup; and he spooned it up so rapidly that
little was visible then, and in any case we tried not to stare.
The spoon flashed, was never still, and the bowl emptied or
the saucepan soon echoed with the sound of his scraping. He
was like a man between worlds, awaiting a map or a miracle.
I must not exaggerate the compassion; but there was a good
deal of it. A mild, speechless visitor from another planet would
have received similar treatment; we were glad when he took
our soup, and bewildered when he burped. His stomach must
have been registering the nervous strain or rewarding him for
the absence of breakfast. I tried to get him to accompany me
to Venetia, but he refused. And she, in turn, refused to visit
him, holding that any further meddlers in the mixture would
produce more trouble. She left him to me. After several days
of this, I wished he would only snarl and rant again, as he
used to do; or give out a flash of hyperbolical verbiage; or just
quote, or merely throw a bottle. Instead, as the afternoon
light bloomed and waned, he kept his own mind to himself,
and usually left without warning around five, floating off into
the contending buses and cars, the jostling walkers and criers,
with scarcely so much as a wave of farewell. He would look to
me, humbly yet still his own man, nodding without ever
seeming to complete a single nod, and then hurry out down
the stairs. Then the atmosphere would ease and the chatter
would increase from *sotto voce*. The bums, after the first one
or two days, regarded him as if he had been some privileged
invalid or a visiting mute; they lowered their voices and
assumed 'nice' expressions. He could not have cared less, but
studied his own inwardness and his own trance. There was a
stoical look to him now, and yet a look which contained no

trace of the stoic's mental adjustment. It was, as I said earlier, a shut-down; no aphorism, no clue, no excuse. He was vegetating, and maintaining even the spirit at its lowest.

All I could do was leave well alone. In his own way, he was coping; and, of course, he had something to cope with. If he meant to do himself harm he would do it when we were in no position to help. Having invested his own capital, he would accept the risks; he had already rejected me as most adolescents reject their sponsors, and my offendedness at this was diminishing. Fortunately this was a period free of hallucination and I thought I was clear-headed enough for what I had to do. I just had to be there. One day, for example, he arrived and I happened to be in the bathroom—for ten minutes after he arrived. All that time he stood, waiting, wondering whether or not to bolt. When I re-entered the room, he faltered a moment and then sat down on the floor, massaging his knees which seemed stiff or sore: he said nothing about them. A few days later he walked into a car at about five in the afternoon and was spun far ahead into the slush in the gutter, both legs broken. I would not have known, but one of the bums—Brownie, sitting outside—heard a screech of tyres, a woman scream, and went to see. So, once again, Lacland was in physical pain, this time in a starched ward of the hospital, with every chance of recovery but also of a limp. Rumboldt quipped, 'Now he's almost like me!' It didn't seem worth saying; but many of the things Rumboldt did say were not worth the air he gave them. It was a relief to know Lacland was safe somewhere. Mrs. Pomeroy sent flowers to him; so did the bums, at my instigation and expense; and Rumboldt kept an eye on his progress which was rapid.

He would lie there, immobile; even his face seemed cast in plaster and the nurses said he gave no trouble at all. He read nothing, said nothing and, for a time, starved himself. I would walk towards him, carrying grapes, even a book on Rimbaud (a long shot which failed), and he would nod as if awaiting execution. His legs were comfortably strapped up and he had the appearance of a double-barrelled gun, his eyes closed against the explosion of firing. But the only sounds were murmurs from the other visitors and other patients, the clink of spoon on glass and the creak of the ward-doors. He was nowhere near dying but he often looked as if he had been laid out by a fastidious mortician. There was a stunned sweetness in his posture, awkward as it might have seemed aesthetically. Warm impulses went feathering towards him and then entered the region of cold; withered to the polished brown floor. All he gave out was a crisp self-sufficiency which no nurse, efficient or brisk, no doctor, impersonal or breezy, could shift. He took all they did to him and he never flinched. Even when the ghastly physiotherapy began, when he had to try to bend the legs again and eventually try to walk, it was the phenomenally tough and tearless child we saw, his mouth in an unmoving line and his eyes on the target at the other side of the room.

It was not easy, in the middle of all this, to turn to Venetia; there was no warm trance into which I could escape. It is hard, having had, lost and re-won a mistress, to discuss new problems conventionally. We had both been overreachers: the magic box was open and the winds had long since dispersed. There were even times when we came together, affecting towards each other a humdrum civility which masked a tedium; the tedium was with ourselves but, since we had come to know each other so well, was also with each other. When two people know each other well, they realize how the thoroughly known becomes defenceless; and that is the point at which love, the white vibration, must be informed with ordinary compassion. Through revealing themselves in their love, lovers depend to an incalculable extent on compassion; and when compassion arrives and flowers in that context, then a miracle has happened; one of the few miracles we can renew daily.

I went to Venetia, finally, with my worries and my problem. She listened, crossing and uncrossing her legs, and declared the whole matter beyond her. Her impatience was obvious: that is, her attempt to conceal it was blatant, and my own self-assumed role of mundane soul-collector, stomach-filler (at least so that the two sides would not rub together for too long), struck her as gratuitous and boyish. She saw it as an attempt to evade being myself; she saw it thus because it hampered the self she wished me to be. Her care amounted to a selfish altruism: I do not say she wanted too much, but I could see deeply rooted *mores* and etiquettes asserting themselves against my slightly flea-bitten pretensions. It was a sterile, slate-cold interview over the tea-cups. I left, saying 'Nice to have been back' only to hear 'You didn't really come back at all; you passed through'. I was revisiting myself, it was true, but as I spoke, and she bowed half-mocking and half-pitying in the dimmed hallway, I thought of an image from childhood. In my first months of sleeping alone, I would call out if I awoke: to scare away the ghosts and the lurking bogey-men. I called 'Good night'; simply that, and almost without fail, although often in a too-rehearsed or sleepy voice, came the answer like manna through the darkened house and the thin ply of the almost closed door, almost like an envoi, 'Sweet dreams', and it would work. Back to sleep, bulging and reckless with confidence. I had called out to Venetia in a new darkness and there was just an echo. I didn't want to be told I was right, but only that I could still do something useful and perhaps even good. After what seemed many errors, I wanted to feel competent. But Venetia was too spiritually busy, too hectic, to see the point. In a moment of self-pity I calculated our combined ages and thought of myself as a wasted person, waiting for death and having little achievement to come. I wondered how people thought of me when they saw the shabby, life-used face hovering in the city light. I brooded on a multitude of useless minor self-expenditures and self-denials. It all added up to a quantity placed after the decimal point, with too many noughts preceding anything at all. She was sailing back to her albatross, to her Captain who was reliable and regular; regular as all vacuity is regular and reliable as all tedium is always there. She could not yet distinguish between the turbulent surface on the reliable spirit and the smooth surface on the shifting spirit. Slowly, awfully, I felt the balm of these last few years—all that we could salvage of all that had gone— flowing past me on the far side of the street; and the brambles appeared to stretch out to the very grave, where sundry soils clattered against the lid of the coffin and prayers were ungrammatical and inert.

I pardoned myself, therefore, since no one else would. I visited Lacland regularly but extracted little comment or mental mercury from him; he was too immersed in his presumed crime. I should have known what would happen, but

I have spent so many years now in losing my bearings and my sharpness. Lacland, one night, between shifts, just went away from the hospital and could not be found, odd as that may seem: a doubly lame man without a helping hand from any-one. I thought of the river again and again, but had to dismiss the thought; I felt, with some conceit, that he would have filtered an apology through to me before being so final in his own disposal. But vanish he did, and without fuss en route. At first we thought a week would be the maximum, but one week soon became several, and Christmas had gone by before my own speculations petered out, and Lacland no longer existed even as a geographical guess. The papers made little of this new incident; some men have all the news value of a flash-bulb, whereas some burn steadily for years. Lacland was a flash: once triggered, he was spent. It was a forlorn Christ-mas, as any Christmas without children and their frail, pulpy hands on the acrid, painted metal of a new toy is bound to be. The bums languished quietly through the loud season, and Venetia sent them some chicken and pudding and sent me a cigarette lighter, which was like returning to me the ship I had tried to launch and drowning all over again its resusci-tated complement. I took this on the jaw, in the stomach, deep in the peeling soul of a quickly ageing man. It was a humane killing, at least.

To her, Lacland's disappearance was a final proof; my last gamble had been a failure. I had promoted myself into ruin; had relegated her to being an onlooker while I rationalized my indolence and apathy as a humane and general devotion. It was a poor way to spend Christmas, but at least my misery was not mass-produced or even easily obtainable at any store. It was hand-made, like some fine shoe; not quite symmetrical, and therefore unique, like pot or carpet. I wore it, drank from it, wrapped it round me and shivered out of private, self-aimed eloquence into private, self-aimed indictment.

The winter days sank down like defeated animals.

One after another, one across another, legs awry.

Then they began to revive, taking longer to settle down; they began to rise early and endure for longer. I felt the sun making up its mind.

A spring in the step of the days made me feel so tired, so

spent; the vast, ingenious universe was once again considering its old habit of getting up on its feet, and somewhere the first lambs were quivering at the shock of violet light.

The lambs asked, the ewes agreed. And deep inside me the treasury of manure festered and festered, nourishing nothing but a daily routine without which I was anonymous as bracken; an old dry field that life had grown reluctantly for many futile seasons.

I prepared, seriously this time, and not with melodrama as so often in that elated, delighted youth which survived in sepia prints, bleached college pennants and mouldering letters. No; this time, quiet as candle-fat running down the stem of the candle, collecting and spilling into the holder like grief, as if spilling to give the wick and the flame room to breathe but at the same time removing the means of burning. I guttered, I was uncertain. Wan birds flew into my mind and took what straw there was; I even botched at a prayer, something said to the universe while language was still possible. Yet nothing happened: no event, but a far from negligible process in which 'Sweet dreams' echoed and chimed, then fell into the stirring earth. I became younger and more helpless than the youngest child and yet, for all that vulnerability, began to grow some strength while detained during the universe's pleasure. Breath grew shorter; walking became a feat; numbness of the extremities mostly, but sometimes of the buttocks, invaded me like damp. Time flew; it flew awkwardly and always away; I never saw it passing, but it came from where it was and it went to its destination. I remained, travelled through by systematic seconds and minutes, not broken down but breaking down, and asking no repair. No Captain intervened and told me my good behaviour had earned me a special launching into the air above the sea. I held on and life, guttering as always, clung to me as if it needed me as much as I needed it. I sat and, considering the sum total of my face, added up all the facial expressions of my lifetime, superimposing them by the thousand, factorizing, and ending up with a taut, whiskery pout. A poor synthesis, considering all the chances of happiness and the privileges of pocket. Time waterfalled, waterfell, in my head and reverberated. There was a word left, to be said to myself, to be burned home before the extinction. I resolved it should be said and prepared my vocabulary like a child waiting to be played with by his father who has not yet returned from daily work.

Old men's prayers, addressed to themselves during exhausted insomnia, grow flashy, like clothes. The colour animates the void. It reflects from the uninterrupted walls of a bare room. It creates home and calls old men worthy for their endurance at least. It populates; it lets there be light. It is the spiritual, deserted equivalent of a commotion of children who have been lying anaesthetized in parallel rows of beds in wards. Old men, wrinkled and absentminded, drool into their gruel and develop bed-sores, urinating in conscienceless liberty and doing all before and beneath them. I cannot hold; I cannot grip, even when I am concentrating hard. I try, but I slide, and when I slide I skid, and when I skid I continue skidding.

Rachel from Buchenwald came in one day with her face swathed in bandages, for the removal of hair she said and to provide a fresh start. Galatea of the mattress-room. I might see miracles yet.

Edgar the Time finally bought and showed us the self-winding watch he had saved for years to buy, thus purchasing whole years about which he had no need to bother. They ran themselves, alienated even from our winding motions. But Edgar thought he had bought off the whole of time.

Mazzini acquired a new pair of gloves, elbow-length and stoutly sewn white yielding pigskin.

Johnny Sligo began to build, light and tend the coal-fire in my bedroom. I had never before had a fire in that fireplace. There had never been fire in that place. Rachel came in and burned her old bandages in the fire which Johnny Sligo tended on the hour according to Edgar's watch, and Mazzini cleaned the hearth, carrying away the ash with delight. They absorbed me; I saw them and loved them.

Rumboldt brought cigars, pills and cheer.

Solly White received a suspended sentence.

Mrs. Pomeroy sent a cake with Lazarus, who sneered and made several vile faces to amuse me. Lazarus looked ill.

The two boys from below sent grapes, and their shared girl ventured in once a week to dust, bringing magazines and a mighty displacement of air from the sheer swinging of her breasts while dusting.

Venetia came and talked, but I could not follow her. She seemed always on the point of apology but never quite got there. Each time she came she wore shabbier clothes, deliberately, for she had wardrobes full of aromatic silk and noisy satins. She no longer caught at the light with her jewels; she seemed to be dulling herself into a mourning garb, but as I told her, there would have to be no rehearsals. Come in what you are wearing. It is the spirit that dies first, not the carcass.

Again Lazarus came, sniffing, eyeing, estimating, sizing up. Casing my joints. Behold the inheritor. Behold the eunuch appraising the dead mare whose belly is full of nitrate seeping slowly into the ground. All I was goes with me. Then Lazarus visited me only briefly and spent most of his time with the bums in conversations I heard only in snatches. He was nice to them, told them that he would soon be giving up the wrestling. Mrs. Pomeroy was very upset about Lacland, but what could an old woman do? His room would always be ready for him, and she kept the bed aired. A place was always set for him in the off-pink dining-room with the crisp, starched tablecloth and the shimmering silver. No one sat in his chair. Out there, in the mattress-room, Lazarus sat in my chair and told stories of the wrestling game. In my own room, I lay in my bed and told stories of the games I knew: trying, losing, fumbling, misinterpreting, being eloquent on slender base, being alone until the walls hummed with silence as if millions of bees had made a wall-like formation and held still.

Smoke from the fire tickled my nose. The flames coiled. The fire talked, made fugues of lapsing carbon. I dozed and woke suddenly as if to prevent myself from dying. After I went to the bathroom, which I insisted on doing, my head swam and my spine melted. One day Lazarus squinted and quipped: 'That boy won't ever come back, Papa; he's gone for good. No sense in waiting. I guess he's gone to school somewhere to learn about life!' Then he left, gibbering with wit.

It was a calm time and, what with all the rehabilitating that went on, I felt I owed them an effort. We were putting our best face to the world. Getting on our hind legs. Prancing in our lame way. I wished I could court Venetia again, and this time do it right.

But that dramatic, lovely, regal woman, for all her regular visits, still seemed behind glass. She was nice, but there was an effort to it. What she said and did was all commemorative, as if in sentimental obituary. I had only to recover and she would be herself again. I did not read. I did not speak much. I remembered, madly and fully. I went forward in time, imagining the old age of Lazarus, of Lacland, and of Rachel with her successive layers of new face.

I had intended to sleep out the afternoon. I had soup and a fried egg for lunch. But for some intangible reason (no reason is tangible in the daylight) I had been unable to drop off. I had looked up and watched the funnel of the vessel move against the blue sky and the odd, torn wisps of cloud. It made me dizzy. It was the same feeling as I had when, as a child, I had tried to stand still and upright after spinning round in some exuberant game. When I looked down, everything seemed to be moving. I looked up again. The whole ship seemed intended for the one purpose of carrying the wireless-aerials intact across the sea.

I walked in the sun, my arms being bare and sensitive to it. My legs pained from the cuts in the calves. I went a few more yards and then had to lean against the wall between two doors. I was dizzy again. I closed my eyes and felt the gentle sway of the ship, nosing across the gentle Mediterranean.

It was then that I heard music.

It was coming from the cabin on my left. I drew it after me into my semi-faint. It was cool petals and sharp skeins. My blood seemed to slow and my muscles relaxed, but the pain would not submerge. It broke surface again, dispelling the faint and the sickness in my lungs. I looked at the door, which seemed to make the music fainter.

I tapped on the door and waited. I lurched off the wall as the ship moved. The door opened. My lips were stuck dryly together, and my first word wrenched them apart:

'I was just passing, just listening.' I said this more shyly than I had spoken for years; it was the sight in the slightly opened doorway: all bandages, with three slits and hardly any bulge of a nose.

'It's Respighi. Would you care to come in?' He spoke awkwardly, diffidently; but the awkwardness was also that of someone speaking a foreign language. I said thank you and went in, past his arm. The room was heavy with the smell of antiseptic. The music came from a gramophone on a chair. The record scratched badly. The man motioned me to another chair, and we listened, remote as gulls. Again I found my mind among cool petals—slightly wind-blown and idle, wandering, like lost hands. For the next quarter of an hour or ten minutes, neither of us spoke nor looked at the other. The man rose to turn the record over, and his movement was a conspiracy with peace. I hardly saw him. There was a silence, then a violent scraping followed by a trickling theme which swelled. Sun-dry palms swept against an ebony floor; rice, dry and crackling, was poured in a white cascade, spilling everywhere. Girls were gliding over the shining black floor, wincing as their soles felt the hard rice; soft-footed across the black mirror. Then it broke. The needle scraped round the centre of the record for some time; the man moved across and checked the machine. 'The Pines of Rome,' he said musingly.

He motioned at nothing with a pale, strong hand. Then he started the machine again, having wound it and inverted the record. He told me to smoke if I wished. Then the music began again; I began to see cypresses, smashed columns in the sun, then an imperial procession. It was over quickly; it had seemed much shorter this time. He had begun to rise when I checked the machine myself. He wore a suit of dark blue battledress. We began to talk, over-carefully at first, and then at mutual ease.

He began: 'I myself was very lucky. Then, one day, they came. I was placed in a pleasant courtyard in a bright cell. I was there for two days—an odd interval for someone from the Resistance. Half my cell was bright, the other half dim. About mid-afternoon on the second day I heard marching in the courtyard. They stood my ten-year-old son Mario against a wall. I saw him spit. After the shots he fell, very small, dead in the sun.'

And then he was in a room, with the torture shovelling momentum into itself and going no closer to any end, with

nothing in the room audible save the questions and the no's
and the cumulative acts. Until at one refusal, far on in the
interrogation, the child by now decorously ruined behind the
curtains (behind which he could not actually see his daughter),
and the wife unhonoured with curtains but her ivory back
skinned and the skin slit down to the lumbar section, there
reached him the first inflow of levity, countering that petu-
lance, that despair of theirs in their wasted ingenuity of
blackmail. Until they incarcerated him again, thrice-mourn-
ing man, jailing his secrets with him, in walls which said this
man has been found to flourish in a new category of something beyond coaxable reluctance. Having quelled the last
effort of the minotaur with one tremendous shake of his head
which cost the firing of his soul, he sat still. Later he looked
at the old fatuous photographs of the family martyrs, cancelled and invalid now, and pressed them to his forehead.

So he was like a storm perpetually gathering off land and
falling into the sea: miniscule, feeble, innocuous through surviving. I remembered once that I had gone looking for a man
in a mist when we were fighting in the woods. I had taken a
torch, a powerful one. The beam cut through the mist and
struck against the gnarled trunks of the trees. But when I left
the wood and walked off the fringe into the edge of a small
meadow, the ray cut forty yards or so into the mist and no
further. I just stood looking at the clear end of the tapering
beam and watched the mist swirling towards me. I wondered
at the point where the beam died; somewhere beyond it the
wounded, delirious man had gone; and I never did find him.

'They put swastikas on my face,' he said wryly, 'and I do
not want those on my face.' I nodded and waited.

'Have you,' he asked, 'ever held a fire-hose? The water
pushes blindly along the tube. It kicks under your hands.
Sometimes it even breaks loose and the water drenches people,
and they curse you. All you can do is hold the hose and try
to tame it.' Death, I thought, is very vague; but suffering is
always precise. We spoke gently for some time and then he
began to tire. I closed the door evenly behind me with an
acute sense of deprivation. On deck a muffled horn blew. I
limped up the stairs and then, as I came up out from the well
of the stairs, a wet ghost seemed to brush past my face. Just

spray. The ship ran through a patch of mist, or seemed to; and then we were in sunlight again.

That night I went to a film-show—a musical set in Hawaii —and later lay in bed more cheerful and feeling refreshed. When I met the man later in England, his pale hooked nose sliced across the horizontal wrinkles in his painfully sore, pink face. The eyes were old, shining as split coal. And we walked, went pike-fishing in the local dams in the North, visited the galleries and sampled the cinemas. He smoked a curly cherry-wood pipe and wore a sloppy-brimmed trilby of grey. Just before Christmas, one Christmas, we stayed four days on the moors, in the mist, and sat by blazing fires in the cottages and inns, drinking warm black stout. Walking on the moors made us feel like perambulating gods, and we carried flasks of brandy and mutton sandwiches wrapped in cellophane. It was a good, tame time of no greatly original conversation, and as I lay in bed I kept recurring to it, having finally lost touch with this man and his new-made face, but powerfully re-minded of him by young Rachel and her bandages. Why she was not in hospital I could not imagine; I looked forward to *her* new face.

I noticed that Lazarus now visited the bums with increasing frequency. They enjoyed his stories of the wrestling ring, and I began to wonder when he went to the gymnasium. I soon found out: he went there hardly at all, having decided to begin to quit wrestling—not immediately, but to work up to that over the next few months. He was even talking of a fare-well bout. Then something slight but significant began; whereas my door into the mattress-room had almost always been left open so that I could hear the talk and the laughing, the door now seemed always to be shut. Some visitor, whoever he was, had taken to closing it behind him as he went out, and I wasn't quite strong enough to open it again myself. It may have been two or three of them, for many came to spend a quarter of an hour talking; and it might have been out of considerateness, but it did seem closed more often than usual. And it was worrying; I thought about Beethoven going deaf and about that day when, in thorough deafness, he sat com-posing and pressing the keys without making any sound at all. No hammer quite reached the wires, but he himself could hear it all. I seemed to be living my life in the same way: playing it by ear and wondering if I looked foolish to those who watched. It gave an odd feeling of premature burial, with no one attending for much of the time and, when people did come, not even noticing I was in the coffin at all: as if good taste or good tact forbade the mention.

The world, or at least the inside reflection of the one outside, ceased to filter in, and all I could see was the sky, an occasional bird, usually a pigeon, sailing in calm spirals, and a small never-opened window opposite. Somewhere, no doubt, cuckoos were calling across the frost and spring was gathering for its onset. I breathed carefully as if I were in one of those big libraries (usually with a large glass dome) which echo the slightest sound—a page turned, a word erased, a nose blown. No one could hear me, but I did not want to hear myself. The meals became less regular, I think, and the callers fewer. I stopped the little green alarm-clock from ticking; it was an insane, coercive noise, a death-watch beetle lodged in a green leatherette shell. In intense quietness I counted my days; counted my pulse, the sounds of other doors being banged, the distant whistles which began a day or announced midday or end of work. After the news bulletins I even turned off the small radio; I could not stand the rambling, deliberate informalities of the disc jockeys. Slowly the world contracted as if I were the last tree in the copse, and they, the other trees, had somehow shrunk into my own diameter.

My senses sharpened. I began to compile my account of what went on next door. There seemed to be more noise: either because my hearing had become acuter or simply because the bums were becoming free and easy in my absence. Venetia hardly came near in two weeks, and when she did she looked strained, sly almost, and spoke hectically from a tight mouth. She was not telling me all she knew, and I suppose I was taciturn. We did not part on very affable terms.

Then the bumps began, making the floor in my bedroom quiver briefly. It might have been Lazarus doing gymnastics to impress and amuse the bums.

Guffaws began to arrive, and then the higher pitch of semi-hysterical laughter. I heard a squeal or two.

The house continued to creak; it had always creaked, but

it seemed to be undergoing some brutal perturbation of the spirit. All the sounds, percussive or stealthy, faded into the sub-silence again, like snow falling on open sea, and always only the waves were left, which I had heard as long as I lived there and which I had even cherished during long spells of insomnia. And they *were* spells too. I tried to relax, but the silence built tension; I could hear my drying muscles crack when I turned about in bed. A humming noise, like a tiny fly or hummingbird trapped in the inner ear, would blur everything for a second or two, and then would stop.

I concentrated on the guffaws and the bumps, which both became more numerous. Sometimes there was music, distorted by doors and walls, and usually of a frantic type. It was like listening to tape-recordings of several parties, or several jubilant funerals. I felt my face settling into a perpetual frown and when I tried to smile for the exercise the skin resisted like the leather of shoes left in the cupboard for a whole season during which they were not needed.

So I took to deliberate, callisthenic grinning in private—in case I would need it again. One day the snow arrived again, tossing and swirling against the window, pillowing me in and muffling the noises.

Shortly after that there was a day when, about two or three in the afternoon—some hours after Edgar had brought my bowl of soup and a cheese sandwich—there came noises of people. Bumps and shouts filled each minute. It was rowdy and I began to wonder. I made as if to get up but my head swam and my knees turned to water; so I slipped back, and soon fell asleep in spite of the noise.

A fiendish racket woke me as the light was failing. I stirred again, this time resolved to investigate. But something held me back: a rope—in fact a child's skipping rope which someone had tied round me and the bed while I was sleeping. It went across my chest and then beneath the bed at either side. It was a shock; I took twenty minutes or so to wriggle free, and the effort exhausted me. I slid off the bed, setting aside the warm blanket. Then I stumbled quietly to the closed door; it was locked, and beyond it the noise was wild. I looked into the keyhole and saw the key. So I recalled my boyhood, staggered back towards the bed, rested there a while, and then tore a sheet from the days-old newspaper. My breath was bucketing out and in, and my temples were pounding. I slid the paper under the door (there was a gap at least half an inch high) and pushed at the key with my only writing implement, a ball-point refill which I used without a holder. The key resisted, refused to budge. I was trying to be delicate, but eventually forced it as hard as I could. Obviously it was at an angle. So I began to scrape and scratch at it, trying to turn it back again.

It was tedious work. I cannot say how long it took to right the key, but I did it finally, and then pushed. I was amazed that no one had noticed my efforts, although of course the noise was heavy. Bumps and yells, vague commotions of bodies and cries of triumph suggested not so much fighting as a party. I retrieved the key after it had fallen and drew it towards me. It was a small, iron key, shiny with hand moisture. I cleared my throat and unlocked the door, then opened it slightly, peered out across the small hall and into the mattress-room. My mind was like a twig on a high tree during a snowy day: no snow stuck on the top but, on the underside, and equidistant from one another, there were small drops of water. I was all memories and could keep no new facts. It was in such a condition that I listened, wondering at what I saw.

Only a quarter of the room was visible. Edgar the Time walked slowly and vaguely across the visible part, his face red and shining. He was carrying a sheet, or what looked like a sheet. The sounds were those of high, advanced intoxication. Then I saw Rachel without her bandages, her face no different, but smiling giddily at someone and her arms flung forwards as if she were going to take off and fly. Then there was a rush of bodies, jostling and colliding with hysterical laughs. I could see Mazzini, and his hands were bare, a vivid white. I leaned out further and saw more of the room.

It was like sorting out light with a prism, although a cloudy prism. I thought what I saw was a hoedown. In the centre of an admiring ring (all of whom had bottles) was Lazarus, naked but for a jockstrap, with a dumb-bell in each hand. He was doing acrobatics, flinging the bells up and catching them again during the end of a double somersault. At each catch, the bums cheered raggedly and drunkenly. I saw Edgar the

Time with a peasant-style scarf wrapped round his head (he had changed since I first saw him; his attire was different altogether). He had an unbuttoned tartan shirt around his shoulders and white canvas shoes on his feet. As Lazarus jumped high, Edgar jumped low, bouncing with glee and more animation than I had ever seen. He seemed to have a loin-cloth which flapped about before him as he jumped. It was a towel from the kitchen.

Phlegmy cheers greeted each gyration from Lazarus. He posed then flung the one bell he now held into the air, and quickly flipped himself upside down, this time catching the bell in the small of his back. He was hairy and drenched with sweat. Again he vaulted upwards, this time flinging the dumb-bell clear away, expecting one of the bums to catch it but also, I thought, to frighten them. It sped upwards and landed in the far corner with a sullen clatter. They were too busy watching him to catch anything. Once again he jumped, this time twisting, landing and, almost at once, jumping again, high enough to land on Edgar the Time's shoulders, where he landed untidily and stayed until Edgar collapsed, laughing. A surge of bodies enthusiastically slapping Lazarus obscured my view.

Then into the picture came Mazzini, wearing only a shirt and his briefs. His right hand was in a sling and seemed to be wrapped in several newspapers, in parody of plaster. He joined in the scramble, but maintained something of his own —a solemn, clumsy back-and-forwards step during which his naked belly wobbled and his head appeared to work loose. He glowered seriously at his feet, trundling his heavy body to what could be heard of a rhythm from the radio. Pushed and jostled, he held to his step, at the same time trying to keep his right arm to his chest. Lazarus had begun to squeal, like a small boy with all the overtones of a man's voice. I could not see him, and was looking for him when Mazzini stumbled and fell. He roared from the floor until someone sat on him; it was Johnny Sligo, whose head was concealed in a sack tied round his neck. I could tell it was Johnny because he was bent double; so what sat on Mazzini seemed like a two-layer man or a folded horse with his head well into the feed-bag. Mazzini snuffled and struggled. But Johnny Sligo, who all this time appeared to be shouting his head off from inside the sack, stayed put, gripping at Mazzini's supposedly broken arm and also sinking a firm grip into the loose fat on the belly.

Lazarus cheered and shouted something like 'Let's go!' At once Rachel came into view, writhing her way along the wall with only her violently working face visible; the rest of her was shrouded in a faded sheet, so that she looked like a nun or a bride. She flung an arm upwards and part of the sheet followed the motion, then fell away, revealing a bouncing breast. Her hand clawed at the wallpaper and her mouth twisted as if she were in pain or religious ecstasy. Then she began to snarl, and they all began to snarl back, Lazarus's disproportionately vast voice leading. She writhed and twisted as if magnetized to the wall, at once pushing the wall away and allowing it to pull her back. She made three-yard sorties, back and forth, snarling into the middle-distance; and as the vehemence of the snarls from the bums increased, so did that of her own, and her sorties became faster and more contorted. 'Devil!' she shrieked, and they all took up the cry.

Lazarus leapt into view, bellowing: 'I am the devil! Escape me if you can!' Rachel broke away from the wall and ran across the room, the sheet spilling away from her as she disappeared from my view. They all ran, cursing and mouthing, and then she returned into view, this time minus the sheet, and clad only in panties and a brassière through which her nipples protruded as she ran. Lazarus pursued, then vaulted like a young lion or a puma on to her back, and she went down under his weight. The rest followed, scrambling and fighting to touch the girl, who now screamed in short bursts, almost dog-like. I wiped my hand across my forehead; I was sweating.

A game of follow-my-leader ensued, with the wildly flapping Rachel in the lead and Lazarus immediately behind her, now equipped with a large camera which he brandished like a bomb. Then Rachel fell over the first chair she reached, giggling sharply. Lazarus reached behind him and pulled Johnny Sligo from the line, deftly thrust him forward into Rachel and took their picture with scarcely a pause. Rachel's legs were in the air, propped against the wall, and Johnny was bent double between them. It looked obscene. Everyone cheered and clapped. Almost at once Lazarus removed the picture from the camera, brandished the photo on high and tantalized the girl with it, offering it and then snatching it away as she reached. She organized her big pulpy limbs and went after him, sniggering and breathing hard. They surged across the room, out of sight, and then she reappeared with the photograph in her hand, looking at it hastily and laughing incessantly, in long high barks. She laughed as she drew breath in and then expelled it in an even louder sound. The wooden floor trembled at the tumbling about. I caught sight of the two boys from downstairs and then of their girl-in-common, in a white sweater and leotards. She was feinting with her two males, pretending to box and parry as they tried to tickle her. I was thinking of the drowned little blonde when successive cries of 'Yes!' broke out, and I saw Lazarus, now with the sack on his head, charging like a bull while Edgar the Time played the matador with a kitchen towel. Lazarus would pause, pawing the ground; then he would charge, blindly, I think, and to cheers Edgar swung the towel round in an elegant billow. Lazarus went crashing on into their legs. He repeated this several times until he missed their legs and went headfirst into the wall. How they cheered at that! He rebounded and sat still, tugging at the sack.

I went back to the bedroom for the skipping rope; as I walked in I noticed a spider descending from the ceiling at great speed towards the bed. I watched him travel down, manufacturing thread as fast as he could go. Then I blew at him just as he was preparing to land, and up towards the ceiling he went in a panic. I picked up the skipping rope, hauled on my trousers and made sure I had the key. Then I went out again and straight into the mattress-room.

They were quieter now, but animated beyond the usual. The air stank of various liquors, mostly whisky. As I entered Rachel let out a whinnying scream: 'Look!' She was the first to see me.

I dangled the skipping rope at them and almost hypno-tized them with it, standing there in my unshaven and untidy state, not fresh from bed but tired from bed, and looking (I think) like a dragon at them, with the fire of anger burning outwards. 'Well?' That was all I said. I repeated it, but I could see there would be no explanation. They were all too excited, and I noticed several bottles of some colourless liquid. It smelled and tasted like pure alcohol.

As I bent to pick up one of the bottles, Lazarus pushed forward and snatched the skipping rope, saying viciously, 'That's mine!' He wrapped the rope round his neck and then crossed the cords so that the gaily painted handles dangled in front of his groin. He then crouched and shouted: 'Watch me, Papa! I'll show you how to milk the cow!' He pulled and squeezed at the handles, calling for a bucket, and finally over-balanced, the handles clattering to the floor. I closed my eyes and stood there in silent self-discipline. I noticed then, as I had often noticed before, that when my eyes were closed I could see slight, swimming organisms always moving north-west across the thin film of blood. When I blinked, they would snap back into position and then begin their jerky course again, always in the same direction. It was a calming experi-ence, like studying the intimacies of your own corpuscles. Then I opened my eyes again and saw Lazarus still on the floor, puffing out his cheeks and snorting with trying to suppress a laugh. The others were self-consciously plucking at their undress.

'A nice party, this, Pap,' said Lazarus, tugging at his dirty-looking beard. I told him that it looked it, just that. A nice party. 'We were just getting to the games,' he said.

'So I noticed.'

Then he offered me a drink; I refused, but then as formally as I could I greeted, in this order, Rachel, Mazzini, Edgar, Johnny Sligo, Brownie (who seemed totally drunk), and the others, some of whom I had never seen before. They had all 'dressed up' for the occasion: in weird underwear (thank goodness for the furnace, I thought, for their sakes), in paper hats, most of which had fallen to the floor, a dressing-gown or two, towels, sheets, one top hat and several rubber masks, one of which had the eyeball suspended on the cheek. Lazarus asked me to join in a game. I told him I wanted no violent games, but he said this would be quiet. You forgot my birthday, he said, and I admitted it.

'You sit there,' he said to me, 'and you, Rachel, cover him with a sheet.' She did so, and I smelled her sweat from the fabric: an oily, dank odour. She seemed in a trance and little concerned about her near-nudity. I sat and waited.

'This is a trial game,' announced Lazarus to the others. I didn't like the sound of that; it was ambiguous anyway. Then Lazarus took several of them into a huddle and whispered furiously.

'This old man is on trial for losing his best friend John Lacland, and we the State will try him for that offence.' I shook my head at him, but thought things would quieten down if I only sat still.

'First question: do you admit you have lost our friend Mr. Lacland?'

'No. He has lost himself,' I answered. Mazzini laughed but soon stopped at a glance from Lazarus.

'Do you admit, then, that he is lost?'

'It would seem to be so. Yes.'

'Was it you who found him?'

'I and some others.'

'So it must have been you who lost him!' They all cheered at this sally, and Lazarus beamed at the applause. He suggested they have more drinks, as refreshment; this was a recess.

Then he went on, his eyes dancing crazily: 'So you lost him. And you failed to find him.'

'You are,' I said, 'making a fool of yourself; and you are also making a mistake.'

'No mistake; Lacland is gone; lost. Right? Of course. You are guilty. Is he guilty?' They all shouted yes, although some of them looked uneasy by now and wondered what was in his mind.

'I have your sentence in my pocket,' he sang in an almost operatic voice. From his pocket he fumbled out what I think is politely called a French hip skirt: that is, a band of black crêpe with a fringe of tassels.

'That's mine!' Rachel yelled at him, her hair over her eyes. 'Give it back!'

Lazarus raised one hand to silence her; then he resumed by opening the thing and slipping it like an academic hood round my shoulders. It drooped forward and the smell was rancid. I twitched my nose and tried to rise, but my legs were stiff. I sat back for a moment, asking him if he was through. 'Hold him down!' he shrilled as I partly rose, and two of them gently detained me by my shoulders. Rachel was plucking at her garment, if such it could be called. 'Our sentence is that you never take it off. You will be buried in that.' I told him that the possibilities were highly unlikely, but he swept the remark aside; he was trying to whip them up again into some kind of frenzy. How reluctant they were. He stomped, ranted, raved. He walked round the room at vicious speed, tapping them on the front or back as he passed them. Then he opened his mouth wide and began a noise like a muted trumpet at which all flinched. In fact Rachel and Johnny Sligo sat down, a sign of a broken spell.

Then he began a series of rhetorical questions.

'Who brought the skipping rope? Who milked the skipping rope? *You* thought of that, or anything good as that? Who milked the milk-rope? You milked it? You milked it? Who milked it? I milked it. You bums.' Those who showed any expression at all just smiled and nodded.

He went on: 'We got to jail this guy. Take him down to that cellar where he lost Lacland. Put him in that crate and lock him up. Feed him on bread and water. Yeah, let him starve like that poor guy.'

Edgar came up, hand in pocket. 'Is that true, Papa?'

I told him it wasn't. He sat down, hand still in pocket. 'We ought,' he said, 'to buy you sumpn; some kinda present. Hey, we oughta buy him sumpn; sumpn he ain't got.' There was the usual murmur; they were all drinking quietly again.

Lazarus flung up his arms. 'Buy *him* sumpn! He'd lose it, just like he lost Lacland. Got no memory!' Then he caught the hip skirt and pulled it back, so that it now hung down my back. 'Let me hug you, Papa,' he said, putting his arms carefully round me. An odour of acrid vomit came from his bare, hairy arms. He stayed like that a moment; all I could hear was a clicking noise and then a scream from Rachel. I turned, but she was pointing past me, so I turned again and saw nothing. I was wondering when I felt a sharp pain at my neck and reached round hurriedly; it was flames, and I tore the burning thing over my head and threw it down. Johnny Sligo catapulted to his feet and trod on it. The clicking sound had come from Lazarus's lighter. I told him to go home and also to hold his parties elsewhere. 'You guilty!' he screamed as Mazzini advanced towards him (Mazzini now with his arm-length gloves on). 'You condemned!' he threw at me as he went through the door, still in his brave nudity.

Johnny Sligo crossed the room, picked up a shirt and some other things and took them out. I suppose he threw them down the stairs. Then someone muttered, 'We better dress,' and they moved vaguely about, cursing and picking up this or that. Rachel wrapped the sheet around her and looked woefully at her burned girdle. Then someone brought me a glass of rye, and I accepted it.

We were settling down to a quiet drink when everyone stopped talking and moving; Venetia had appeared at the door, just looking with sharp narrow eyes. She swung her umbrella in ostentatious impatience, noting the persons present like a teacher who is calling the class-roll mentally.

'I see you are up,' she said calmly. 'I am glad you are well; and your friends. I ran into that dwarf as I entered, and he seemed to be—dressing himself as he went.'

'Probably so,' I answered. 'He can hardly walk the streets almost naked.'

She smirked, 'Quite.' I saw someone behind her, a male figure in an expensive-looking coat, crouching, as if his head grew from beneath his shoulders.

Then, just as abruptly, she took her leave, trailing her hand graciously as she moved through the doorway. I felt my stomach becoming agitated; my heart began to race. I gulped at the drink and it burned in my throat. Then I made my way to bed again, assisted by Edgar and Brownie. I felt ill and needed sleep; but I would not be able to sleep because I thought I had heard a door closing in my life, just before my death.

I returned to a region I carry within me. Grey hills enlarge into grey mountains. The sea has an olive look; the land is alluvial, and the rest is bare rocks, agonized shrubs, small moss, and the fog coiling round. The earth creaks as if with rheumatism. Grotesque icebergs go planing by the low islands, like swans carving a track through floating leaves. Images of canoes and boats and icebergs come soaring out of nowhere to stand, stranded and upside-down, in the thin sky. It is a zone

of no emotion, never responded to, just known of. I saw myself
on an ice-flow, saying goodbye to Venetia, having swapped
ecstasy for contentment, now swapping contentment for self-
sufficiency and not very pleased about the pawnbroking involved. It was like being a boy all over again, trying to be
yourself and yet wishing too to be 'one of them', and therefore
modifying your footwear, your hair-cut, your way of speaking
and even your style of making water. Saying, there is some
line I cannot cross: I cannot chalk it or point to where someone has already drawn it, but I know if I cross I have begun
to lose myself to other people: I could not say what I am, not
exactly, but what I am not is clearer. And so we go, relying on
some vague sense of who we are, hoping to engage in things
which will prevent us from being what we are not. It is all too
neat. I seem more of a process than of a person; so do we all,
and that is why we wrap ourselves up in routines and catch-
words, lest we develop so clear an idea of ourselves that we
are paralysed from the start. It is like being a boy on Sundays,
arranged into clothes which smelled of tailors' shops and were
given away as soon as they smelled familiar. The boy, polished
and awkward, walks along in the sunlight beside or behind
his parents and gleans from the air a willed solemnity which
dries the spit in his mouth and sets his normally broad throat
tightening with suspicion of every word. 'Occasions' do that.
And then he marches through the church-door into the nose-
itch-making taint of mouldering wood and mothballs from the
dark, stern clothes of the worshipping parents. Small children
howl at the touch of holy water; are they howling because
they do not wish to be named? Older people kneel on arrival
as if they have been shot or told to prepare for execution,
burying their faces in their hands; will-power alone could not
keep the mind on its theme while the eyes rested on the
stirring world within the pews. Outside, where no one is as
solemn, bulging birds twist their necks as they angle worms
from the carefully provided ground. Cars run by with a splash
of gravel at the corner. People out for a Sunday drive in their
Sunday-best convertibles go cruising by, their talk cutting into
and across the disciplined periods and chants of the service,
while, in the high distance, an aeroplane drones, nibbling its
way across limitless nothing while the children point and say

it's not silver really; that's just the sun catching it. And when the sun catches us, do we shine in the same way? Or do we lack a mirror-quality which aluminium or steel has; or which any colour or surface-texture, if flying high enough—near enough to the sun—momentarily acquires? In the gutters the steel residue of a shower catches the sun too and 'shuntles' as they say some kinds of raincoat are supposed to do, turning from grey to green at the fold of an arm. When I used to go out, and when the sun shone on me, I used to feel it rebuked me: I was walking too slowly, holding my head down, guarding my eyes from the glare.

Again and again Venetia returned me to my boyhood, as if she were saying: Take note, you are going backwards and the general motion is not seemly or elegant. Take care; you have only yourself to blame, like the man who introduces people to 'his wife' as if she had no name, and speaks of her to his friends as his wife, as if he did not wish to localize her too much or reveal something private such as first names; or the man who, with an impersonal egoism all of his own, introduces her as Mrs. Myself, thus establishing the lonely power of the surname. Those names we are given under Christ are the ones which fade out; the other stays, as much as to show that blood and lineage come before faith, the faith being the more personal, the more intimate of the two.

My daydreamings ran feebly now. Nothing wild or compensatory reared up, making the daily seem pale and helpless. The opposite happened: the day's dimness and torpor dwarfed what my memory and imagination could do, just as the bums' tricks and capers gave them something to look back upon, as upon a circus or a jamboree conducted by themselves at their own instigation and to fit their own needs. I ran down, being intransitive in every sense. My only transitive was to run myself down, which merged into the other process and took me deeper into self-dispraise than I had ever been, making the most of fragments and scrapings, refusing to cut loose, refusing to be Napoleonic. Just vegetating in that small, too-familiar room well below my income. Looking back on the way I had lived was again like being a child who arrives in, muddy-shoed and hungry, groping for Coke or cookie, and in the act stumbling into the parlour which, on this day, is not

the silent kingdom of mahogany but the scene of adult dispute, which rises and falls like the tide in the cavern where
the boy has been playing, and mounts until he erupts into
the shiny, uncomfortable room and all invective stills at the
footnote, 'Not before the child!' at which he is bundled out
and the door slams shut like a train's last truck being sucked
into a tunnel. Again those doors kept shutting, leaving only a
blank panel with a number and, sometimes, through frosted
glass, a suggestion of what lay beyond, when you were not
locked out. It is being locked out that terrifies; being locked
in keeps you near the nerve-centre, and it is perhaps easier to
be heard if you howl inside the house than if you howl at the
front door. A memory came: towards midnight, across the
street from where I was convalescing, a door slammed and a
woman's voice came loudly: 'Stay out. I hope that'll teach you
a lesson!' This was followed by a robust, adolescent's voice
raised in defiance: 'I'll pack up and move out!' Then I saw
him peering in at the window, knocking at the glass, the light
going on in the dark room, then just as suddenly being shut
off, by which time the boy was ringing the doorbell again.
Half an hour later he was let in. Soon afterwards I heard the
same male voice calling something gaily as it left for an
evening out, probably having made its point quietly by the
fire, and dismissing the fuss with one imperative, kindly
intended 'Don't wait up!'

The world gradually changed. Lazarus came back to collect
the camera he had left behind. The hip-skirt had been an
augury; he had decided to go into business in the line of
provocative underwear. He told the bums that much of his
business was done with men, and by mail. Solly White was
underwriting the venture. It was the old story all over again
of the pupa and the butterfly, and Lazarus would survive. In
one way I hoped he would because I could never forget the
natural trick that had been played upon him through his
body, just as he himself could never forget how people—those
unsure who he was—would classify him under 'dwarf' as
under, say, 'curiosa'. He was just the sort to plant a skin-
disease in the underwear, but I hoped he would not go as far
as that. I hardly ever saw him, but he occasionally visited the
bums and had struck up some kind of friendship with the two

boys below, and their girl, having met them at the *auto-da-fé*
in the mattress-room. I believe he was offering the girl some
wild underwear which the boys would pay for out of their
tuition fees. After all, someone said, a new stimulus must be
needed down there and Lazarus was just the man to supply
the black silk and the goads, the fringed hip-skirts 'allowing
maximum freedom of action' to the wearer. One day I received one of his mail folders which became more intimate
the more you unfolded it. Rachel was posing for him, I could
tell. What I had seen of her on that frisky day made me aware
of that fact. I noticed that his milder models (I mean styles,
of course, but perhaps the girls who posed for these) were soon
discontinued: his folders became more and more erotic. I
thought of Lazarus, quietly and comfortably sitting with
Mrs. P., working out names for his latest creations: such names
as 'Dare He?', 'Blood-rush', 'Left Bank' and 'Attention!' Old
as I was, I allowed my mind to dwell for a day or two on the
images in his folders of slit-side panties, nipple thimbles,
uplift pads, foam pads, underwear-for-girls-who-like-action,
peek-through nylon mesh, glove-fit from ankle to toe and
black bridles. But then I grew up and down again, deciding
that Lazarus merited such a career, and the profits from it.

Now and then someone mentioned Lacland, but only in
passing. He had come as a ghost, and as a ghost had gone
away. Virtue's fig had choked him. I telephoned Venetia
several times but she failed to answer. I tried to stop my mind
from dwelling on the male figure I had seen behind her that
day, and I hoped she had not. . . . But when I called her
before her breakfast-time and very late at night, and still had
no response, I could not help feeling deserted. No doubt of it,
she felt rebuffed and slighted: she had exerted herself to get
me well and here I was relapsing into undignified company
all over again. I thought how few people there were to whom
I was not some kind of disappointment: to Venetia an habitual
slummer, a vegetable Samaritan; to Lazarus a species of soft-
languaged *Herrenvolk*: to Lacland a malign warder and Nosy
Parker; to Edgar the Time time-obsessed; to Mazzini a
rubbish-maker; to Rachel a prude and a lie-abed; to Mrs.
Devine from Bonavista a hopeless night-owl; to Rumboldt a
sentimentalist and a self-deceiver; and to that little blonde

who drowned herself no help at all when I might have been. Then I stopped: I could not be mother and father to everyone, nor could they behave as children to me. Life was more cheerful, more accidental than that. I therefore cheered up, pretended I was more accidental.

The bums were quiet while I lay in my bed; it was only at night when they thought I was asleep that they became rowdy. But I persuaded myself I was asleep, so the noise did not trouble me after that. Great fresh-washed slabs of sky came sailing past the window; it was new sky, had never before slid across that gap, and I marvelled at the universe's relentless processes which included all of us and all that sky. I thought of Solly White who, in his day, had been a drinker: he had told how, to get him home without his driving the car himself, his wife had arranged to have him knocked out by a garage mechanic each night for two dollars a knock-out. When, after several weeks of safe driving home, being driven by his wife, he found out, he gave up drink. Lazarus was his new intoxication, weirder than the last one; but he managed to discern Lazarus's market value, which was more than I had ever managed to do. I fretted and debated. I could not read or even listen to the radio. The newspapers seemed no more than crass compilations of irrelevance: the world had always been thus and it would not change, even though the names of the war-mongers, the chairmen and the premiers did. I felt as alone as the egg in its shell, remembering that the embryo has a small air-sac for its convenience. My breathing was still irregular; Rumboldt kept saying 'heart' and warning me to be careful. I must not exert myself at all; but I am sure I did myself more harm by being in bed, worrying and working up a bed-sweat, than I would have done stumbling around making soup for the bums and seeing that they curbed themselves on the whisky.

If Lazarus ever held that final bout of his, I never heard about it. He and his partner almost certainly lost. One day I even sent out for the sports pages in order to read about the professional ratings and the scheduled bouts; but there was no mention of Lazarus, although I did see the names of Gulliver and Tomahawk. I sat there with the sheets strewn over the top blanket and held the relevant portion close to my eyes. I was reading like that when I saw several of the bums hovering in the doorway, as if waiting to ask a question or a favour. They looked embarrassed and tearful, almost. What was wrong was unusually wrong: they had never congregated in this manner before. I waved at them to come in, but they hung back. Finally it was Edgar the Time who advanced towards the bed, one hand obstinately in his pocket (it was where he kept his watch). In his other hand he had a piece of the paper—one of the pieces which had come with the sports pages I was reading. When he handed it to me, the others went away suddenly and Edgar himself began to drift towards the door. Then he too was gone.

It was, of course, something about Lacland. He had been arrested in a supermarket, carrying a shot-gun. With this, he said, when interrogated, he was going to cleanse the world of its innocents. He meant that he was going to do away with the helpless and vulnerable; it was such a bad world. He would have to be tried, and I could see him being put away for a long time: not in jail but in some genial, well-meaning institution. Fortunately he had not shot anyone. After a few days I arranged to visit him in his cell, with Rumboldt accompanying, and we managed to concoct some kind of defence. I remember that in the ordinary way, much as I remember it is this month. What I cannot remember in that easy, resigned way is Lacland's face, lined and scored, pale as milk and seemingly paralysed. He had lost all faculty of assuming an expression, but his demeanour was gentle and submissive. I construed his shot-gun threats as mere metaphors, a means of drawing attention to himself. The gun had not been loaded and he had not been carrying any shells. Finally after some money had been spent on lawyers and Rumboldt and I had testified (I in my best suit and on my best behaviour, with all my education behind me), he was bound over with a severe warning, none of which he needed or seemed to care about. I remember him as he stood there, shifting from one foot to the other, studying the ceiling and the back of his hands. He was lucky not to have been hauled away for the psychiatrists to play with as a world-sadness man or a case of acute melancholia verging on astute sanity.

He had gone rather bow-legged, and as he walked he

seemed to have always too much weight for either leg. Consequently he reeled round and forward with each step.

His face was scaled with dry skin and several of the whisker-points had become infected, resulting in many pimples. His whiskers appeared to be growing backwards into his skin. He scratched non-stop.

His ears and nose had become red and coarse, and his hair had gone dry and lank. He looked as if he had been immersed in stiff white paint and had not wiped it all off. He was going grey all round: sideburns, forelock and top. But it made him look less 'distinguished' than faded. He was a pathetic sight in his tattered blue suit and frayed shirt; so pathetic that we did not have to argue as forcefully as we otherwise might have needed to.

Rumboldt then gave a testimonial for me, which was singularly embarrassing, especially if you can appreciate the oily but cynical nature of Rumboldt's vocabulary. I, the lesser wretch, with my means, would tend to Lacland, the less pardonable wretch, and, I got the impression, I would thus enable them to catch both of us as disreputables and put us both away safely somewhere. Eventually Lacland was given over to me, on a bond. There have been easier assignments in this world, and I was too ill-feeling by then to know whether or not I could qualify as a mentor. I decided to try.

When we got back I took Lacland straight into the mattress-room. All the bums stood up, nodding their heads and trying to smile. It looked well, but Lacland did not notice. In fact he sat down on the floor, eased off his shoes without untying the laces, and then slumped into what looked like a coma. I left him there and went to my bedroom. I picked up my books, my picture of Venetia (written on romantically many years before), and carried them to the bathroom. We then took Lacland in and undressed him for bed, noting the caked scum on his feet and the ragged state of his nails. He was still unshaven. His hair had bits of fluff distributed upon and within it, as if he had recently been snowed upon. He slept deeply through these procedures, and even began to talk in his sleep when we laid him down. I couldn't tell what he said, but it sounded frightened and like a child's gibberish. Then we left him partly covered by the grey blanket which was too small to reach his chin. I went back briefly and pulled down the shade; I myself had never used this shade, it being too transparent to help someone as sleepless as I was. He began to snore.

I arranged my clothes and books in the bathroom and went down to the basement for the camp-bed that I had used before. It was damp so I brought it up, puffing mightily with the effort, and stood it against the radiator in the outside hall. As I went by the boys' apartment I thought I saw a face, oddly like Lazarus's and at his height, peering out from the darkened room. If it were Lazarus, he would easily be able to guess what had happened.

Then I went to sit with the bums, who were very quiet and depressed; it was as if they feared Lacland for something he had done or said to them. I might have installed a reprieved murderer in the next room; instead I had installed a reprieved innocent, which is perhaps what they feared most. They themselves were far from innocent, but they were harmless.

Time, from then onwards, with my back to a new canvas surface, and my insomnia in a new setting (the bathroom), became a blight. Images of primroses would filter into my mind, as if I were craving for the spring. No news came from Venetia, and I didn't bother to phone. My chest pained now and then, and my water became strong. I brushed my teeth twice as often but found, although I was in the bathroom much more than usual, I was neglecting to bathe, being content to lie down and take the weight off my legs. Breath became hard to get now and then, and my pulse beat madly some days and could not be found (by me) on others. When I spoke to the bums I noticed how many passive constructions I used. I didn't bother to tie my shoes and when I took soup I began to forget to pour water in the saucepan after use, even though I did intend to wash it later. I developed the habit of sitting with my hands crossed, and one foot on top of the other, as if I were afraid that the vital current would escape. By linking hand to hand and leg to leg I felt that I could keep all the juice in my own circuit to myself.

I cast around for things to do. I began to smoke more and more of those thin cigars and even sent away some package tops to buy holders for myself and a few of the bums. I enclosed a dollar bill to cover the supplementary costs. Noticing

an advertisement on a book of matches, I sent away for a free
sample of an asthma cure and forgot even to try it when it
came. It would have helped my breathing, perhaps, but I put
the packet somewhere and could not seem to find it when I
looked, and when I thought I knew where it was I could not
seem to want to get up and try it. It was as if I were cached
under the arm of some itinerant giant, choked with the hair
in the armpit and yet held too firmly to fall to his feet and
thus be left behind as he advanced. When I spoke to myself
the bathroom gave massive reverberations. When I slept I
woke with a cruel ache in the small of my back, and my eyes
were rheumed over like a baby's.

I tried one reckless thing; I telephoned the flower-shop and
ordered daffodils, a dozen dozen, and stuck them round the
mattress-room while the bums behaved as if they were being
prepared in a funeral-parlour. The scent filled the whole
floor, at once sickening and heartening, and to walk from the
bathroom into the other room was like going into the country-
side. I put none in Lacland's room because the scent would
probably trouble his sleeping; he did little but sleep or pretend
to, and he merited as much rest as he could gain.

It is thus with the old, caught between elaborating their
memories and minimizing the aches. The world filmed over
like disused water, and I worked my own private spell, my
pre-death, in the aroma of small cigars and decaying daffodils.
When the flowers grew crisp and pale I left them there, not
minding what the bums thought because I was sure they had
fed the flowers on whisky. If you feed a daffodil on whisky it
will get up and dance and those daffodils were worn out with
dancing in the nights. Serve them right: you feed daffodils on
water, water on daffodils, and old men on next to nothing.

Lacland slept, hibernated, in quintessence of peace and
certainty of food. In the bathroom now, to shave, I first of
all flick the pink mat to the right, towards the toilet pedestal,
and turn on the hot. I cannot shave in bare feet or even socks
in case I skid or slip, and the hot water takes a century to
come upstairs. I no longer inspect my face, so that shaving
becomes just as hazardous as if I am standing in bare or
stockinged feet: I do it by feel, not by sight, and when the
cuts have congealed, I rub the crust away with my thumb.

We have no toilet-roll dispenser but keep the roll on the radiator; the sheets are warm to the anus. It is a perverse, unintended luxury, without which I would be lost and homeless by now. The washstand is strewn with hairs and the inside of the basin is pitted with the tiny speckle of cut-off beard. The speckle has worked its way into the cracks by now and gives the surface an appearance of minor stucco. I am losing buttons. I collect them up and mean to sew them on one day, but that day will never come.

A faint dung-smell from my cigar that day; it was like being returned to elemental earth during voluptuary joy.

Lacland, once again, for the eleventh day, took soup at two in the afternoon and went straight to sleep. He will have to be washed.

Mail arrived for Lacland, looking familiar: I took the liberty of being his secretary and opened it. As I thought: 'Provoking Designs in Intimate Apparel', fresh from the hand of Pee Wee Lazarus, now dignified as Daring Productions. I threw it in the waste. It is no use adding the lingerie of stimulus to the shortening flame of a sleeping young lion. Lazarus was making good use of his camera; use, anyway.

The sun is stirring us now, blazing an arc-light on the selves we had forgotten. In this heat, even to shrivel up is to move in one way or another. I ask no more; this is the last cosmic imperative, bidding me respond, forcing me to shift.

The bums are singing now; what song I cannot tell; it is several songs, no doubt celebrating the world for what it is worth. It could be Annie Laurie. I could be Annie Laurie. Annie Laurie could be anyone. Why try to establish such correspondences? We try too hard. I am wondering about Venetia, her new man, and her attitude to me. So much has gone, so many trysts and trusts have washed away. A vigorous wealthy woman can hardly be expected to perturb herself endlessly with a man who devotes himself to something like the parish mission, founded on whisky and consolidated with sputum. Where the wrecks founder, there found me. Where the wrecks wander, there I wander. I go nowhere, I spend nothing. I add this day to yesterday, wondering at the reprieve. The house will be here when I have gone. It will follow me in what is left of my racing mind. *They* will come and decay until the money has gone or that lawyer bungles. But I cannot see a lawyer running all this: as well to ask a priest to see that the call-girls are better organized. Set them all gently in the quiet riot of my head; give them all a home in my vacant brain where the springs of nothingness are rechristened.

I want to haul Lacland from his bed and train him in these tutelary arts. But he is a goldfish, snoozing in his pool again.

I want to tell the police that Venetia is a missing person; has been abducted and subverted.

The flies have come out again, small and frail, but they sting the face with their feet and cluster round the lights as if seeking maternal embrace.

Soon the city will blister us with its pavements. All the heat in the world will funnel into these streets and drive the mind untidy with longing for the cool sluice. Odd, I have money to live all my remaining days in sudden luxury, but I shall not go. I shall not go. That is where Venetia is now, as is her habit; she has gone to visit luxury in the south, and she will stay there even when the sun rises high because down there they are equipped for luxury. Here we snuffle and sweat through, pushing the vast stone uphill with our itching noses.

I consider Lacland, newly elected flotsam, from whom there is now no cry, no roar, no foul-mouthed assertiveness and not even the slop-bucket for emptying. He has come a long way. And I, I shall travel to the end of the ages in my shabby clothes, victim of my even shabbier calling: the preservation of the least qualified. Sing no sad songs; drown cats and blind puppies; I am the hut on the hen's legs, and I have chosen my epitaph. It appeared to me, as in a vision, on a bottle of whisky: 'Federal Law forbids sale or re-use of this bottle'. It had better.

A day came when the telephone rang and it was Rumboldt asking if I had seen the paper. I had not. He sounded awkward. I asked him if he was well. Yes, he was, but he wondered how I was. I told him I could still take bad news if that is what he meant. Venetia had been in a bad accident, with a male friend, in Florida, in a rented car. A collision. She was dead. She was killed on impact. So were her accompanist (as Rumboldt tactfully put it) and three other people. It was in the paper, about the ex-movie star and actress who had suddenly quit the movie world and taken to the quiet life which she owed her daughters. In the paper, he said, there was a picture of her from many years earlier and a short list of her movies. I told him I would cherish the clipping if he sent it. He said he would bring it round during the evening and have a look at Lacland as well. That sounded as if the bird would kill two stones. I agreed and said I would not visit the opera that night, or dine out, or be holding any kind of party for which he would have to dress. Baffled, he hung up.

So she had gone, in a flash, the lovely tall quick talker. I went to the basin and washed my face. Without even an agreement or amnesty made between us, she had been squashed like a fly or a May-beetle and there was only the twisted metal left. Had I made some efforts she would not have been there at all, and certainly not in *that* company. Perhaps, with me, she would have been in no company at all. Coy, wry, trombones humdrummed in my ears until a violin cut them down. To us all, without warning: no letter in the box saying 'Shall be back late' or 'Shall not be back at all', but just arrested and knocked. Once again the human universe had caught me on one leg, the hut on the hen's leg. Can you cry when you know there has come an end of the misery you were making? Can you revile or rave, fume or shout? You can do something, and what I did, abruptly as a child, I did into the pedestal in my bathroom, wondering at the processes of this accidental globe.

I had visions of dead repose, studying the exquisite curve of her jaw, the shells of her prominent ears, the smooth bulge of her much photographed and much kissed mouth. But, as I heard it, there was no face left worth rearranging for view. Two days later I appeared in Saint Petersburg among her disapproving relatives who seemed to think I had driven the other car. I never saw her. Earth clanked on the wood and the photographers massed at the gate. I dropped a small package of my own, some letters and a tooth she once pulled out and gave me.

It was a white hearse on white-walled wheels with the matt black casket inside under a mass of wilting flowers in all the pastel colours, like dismembered macaws dusted with poinciana. She rolled slowly over the sun-hot streets, followed by half a dozen cream convertibles with curtains of ivory beads inside the front windows. It was like looking through a garlic slicer. I stood under the trees, just short of the ochre-coloured hotel with the high white bell-tower whose icing never melted, and I watched the motorcade interrupt the other drivers in that city of the aged where, each second or in adjacent splits of a second, a varicose leg gingerly tests the road for quicksand or stumbles against an uneven piece of terra-cotta sidewalk as if a whole pyramid had loomed out of the downtrodden afternoon. The aged perambulate endlessly. Each day is ticked off on the calendar, each reprieve making tomorrow more dangerous.

A dry wind bullied the tops of the palms and drilled the tricolour flags. I knew how the white hearse appalled streetfuls of the retired as they prospected among the stores for guava- and papaya-marmalades, read the sullen plaques at cut-rate, whispering with oblivious reverence the holy quotes—'Jacob *was* wrestling with heaven', wondering if the italics implied that Jacob might sometimes have *not* been or that, in case the beholder doubted, Jacob really *was* doing that. The seagulls evicted the pigeons from the quay when the hearse came into their sector. The sea went on patting the hulls of the yachts and dinghies. Not many yards away the sand endured the calloused feet of retired colonels marching at a brisk clip from one end of the beach to the other, by numbers, touching a fist at each end on the concrete wall to prove they were still in the world, and then off again to scatter flimsy shells and sand-showers over the sun-bathers on lodging-house towels.

Everyone knew. Each day the dead were quietly filed in the cemeteries and their diamonds went into shallow trays in the locked, barred windows of little shops. It was a funeral surrounded in time by hot gospel from the microphone on the bandstand in the city square, percussed at by nocturnal fireworks and breakfast-time bands, and patrolled over by sardine-silver jets keeping an eye on the nearby enemy. Time came and went, a small time, a funeral's time, while senior citizens transferred their savings into the mammoth skyscraping banks at four per cent and purchased antiques, conned the day's necrology, leaned on their tubular walking-rests as the red lights flicked on at intersections and walked gently through the pared quiet of the parks.

I stayed on, of course. I was eligible and appropriate. At
night I saw an occasional buck negro lounging in white
tuxedo at a street corner; a Charon figure with his boat round
the corner behind the seventy-cent fat-free lunch. Derelicts
offered one another peanuts under the trees or sipped root-
beers in cool uncomfortable alleyways roofed over. The
withered and life-tired piloted long-bodied cars at ten miles
an hour along the sea-front as if stealing up on salvation itself,
with the chrome epitaphs—Catalina, Impala, Monterey,
Fairlane, Skychief, Valiant, Metrocruiser—stamped irre-
vocably on flank, front or rear. Occasionally one of these
cream catafalques outwitted the arthritic fingers and exploded
into a roadside eating-house at sixty unintended miles an
hour, launching the heart-attacked driver into a mess of egg-
and-bacon, smashed plates, furious urns of coffee and broken
one-handed eaters. You were always watching.

Bacon on the beach: or so I thought. Back on the beach, as
women bent for shells in ankle-deep water, whole epics
tumbled into view. Where life had forced its way out many
decades ago, there were now only blanches of scar, the
maternity wrinkles like knitting, legs varicose with congre-
gating blue snails, ankles like plumber's joints and, everywhere, tired hams aching with salt of the sea. And the
wrestled-at, depleted bosoms, like twin mare's bellies, weighed
on the midriffs and tried to breathe the air. At ten the whole
city breathed its last and some senior citizens cowered before
the last halitosis commercial they would ever see. At ten the
whole city *does* breathe, *is* breathing, its last; and we are all
cowering because we remember.

At three in the afternoon they buried her with my package
and I wondered what had become of the Chevrolet she drove
with such consistent inaccuracy, and if anyone had ever
ironed out the dimples from her numerous minor collisions.
Six wrecked ladies from some local Chapter stood erect at
the graveside bearing small green flags. One wore high heels,
and she tripped badly over a plank when she turned away.

Since one o'clock that day I had been sucking at a fragment
of meat caught between two molars. As earth hit the black
casket the meat floated free like a small soul, and I knew then
how it felt to die. Before I assess a character I like to have

nothing stuck in my teeth; and before I appraise a soul I like
to be able to do a discreet whistle between my teeth. The
spaces, after all, are my own. I can still take a small pride
in that.

After the funeral I bought a five-cent cigarillo and went to
sit in the park. A youth in jeans and sweatshirt harangued the
passive audience for ten minutes or so ('Jesus finds even those
who do not look for Him. Life is made new in Jesus'). That
sort of profanity. Then there was a straggling attempt at an
awful hymn about a mountain and a light, and the youth
disappeared after aiming his ciné-camera at the dumb-
founded ancientry. I puffed at the butt of my cigarillo and
noted a drunk blundering against the seats as he negotiated
the aisle and made for the opposite side of the park where
afternoon shoppers in mink stoles in eighty-degree heat were
obstructing the arrogant young arriving from school by bus
with irregular columns of books before them like bits of rift
valley or cliff.

The old faltered home, clutching small brownpaper bags
which held just enough victuals to reach this hour tomorrow.
And I thought of the solitary egg in the efficiency-apartment
saucepan, the fluid white stiffening into pulp to nourish a
decaying frame and later to slip unrecognizably out between
the unpretty hams into civic water, down the equally civic
pipe and eventually out into shallow sea by the motel sign at
Edgewater. I thought of civic water and civet water. The
minnows below the fall pipe from the sewer are deft. *Their*
combustion is truly internal; and death—death is at its most
when there is, for the first few moments, only you yourself
who, if you could know, do know that you have died. It is
that first non-knowledge or possible knowledge that counts;
it is the loneliest moment in history. Or, as a small unterrified
boy once said, death is when you don't look in your schoolbag
any more. Or when the Automat opens its door, amputates your
hand and serves it back to you, curried, further down the line.

I sat there, brooding, for two hours. My mood was, I
believe, acrid, as if I had inhaled the ash of my cigarillo. I
snorted ash when a group of ardent brothers through blood
or sect mounted the platform and found Jesus again. They
sang and vowed. The microphones carried their message right

across the park to the bus-station where a small male child
was making surreptitious water against a low-placed pictorial
ad. Then, blessed interval, a vacuous young animal in a
Hawaii-type shirt began to prepare a small red car for take-
off, and the engine-noise, as of a constipated elephant blurting
seriatim into a sol-fa series of metal trash-cans, shattered the
evening, and I merely saw: on the platform, nylon short-
sleeved shirts and wide bow-ties; a few brass wind instruments
funnel down and one bald-headed man declaiming. It was
such a mime as you expect only a cigarette's time before the
end of the world, and the self-damned are queuing up to
change their cosmic policies. Then the red car shot off, sput-
tering and choking, and I heard the roll of faith's artillery
again. The quintet were singing now, without instruments,
their only competition being the correct toots of the pigeons,
the wheezes of departing buses and the sussurus of heels as
people hurried home to that underwater TV programme.
'Jesus will be good to thee; For He was goo-ood to me!' I
appreciated the good news, wondering if, on this evening, He
would stop that waitress from sweeping the sweat from her
left arm with her right. This is what she always did as I drank
my chowder where I always ate, I having insufficient interest
or initiative to change my dining habits. Each night her
sweat-sweep speckled my person and soup with faint brilliants,
and I got accustomed to both the tepid shower and the tiny
extra flavour. So, just to see what would happen, I sang
sharply on that occasion, canting my head so far back that I
heard a slight click from my neck: 'He was goo-ood to-o-o
me-e!' All the people around me were suddenly nodding and
confiding to one another, and I had to nod back at them, just
like the aghast boy who has been told his fly is open and nods
bemusedly before he musters the audacity to look down.

I walked past the quay, pausing only to expectorate at a
squirrel (minus its tail it's a rat), and then sat on the sea-wall
scowling at the water. By my side, oh joy, I rested my small
brownpaper bag of goodies: one half-bottle of cheap champagne; one nasal spray; a phial of eye drops ('instant cleansing
relief') and a package of cigarettes ('Don't look for premiums
or coupons as the cost of the tobaccos blended in these
cigarettes prohibits the use of them'). I always avoid coupons

and green stamps if I can. I noted the misuse of *prohibit*. Oh yes, I had a small ten-cent French pastry too, containing, besides ordinary ingredients, mono-diglycerides, algin leavening, lecithin and sodium propionate, the last 'used as a preservative' (where and on whom? I wondered). I stopped grumbling to myself. My lady-friend had been neatly buried. My cares would trouble her no more; and, surely, with sodium whateveritwas to preserve *me*, and in the absence of coupons or premiums, I could gain an instant cleansing relief when *my* time came. 'Sir, the clean deceased is in now.' Thanks to mono-diglycerides we have the mono-human.

I unpacked the nasal spray and squirted the filth deep into my head cavity. It was bliss, and I knew then that Jesus *would* be good to me if, quietly and without fuss, in front of the ochre-walled hotel whose bell-tower's icing resisted the wild sun, I slid my purchases into the dark water as emissaries and temperature-takers, floated my Matador paper-bag after them, and then slipped in myself, following the Taylor Champagne's hollow bottom with my own hollow bottom and my two-dollar short-sleeved shirt. But not tonight.

As I walked on to deposit my goodies and change my socks before going out to eat, I sniffed the evening air deeply in and knew, just as deeply, that someone would be good to me. Doing my best not to seem pigeon-toed among the pigeons, I sang out of sheer exuberance a modern lyric of my own devising. It went like this:

> 'He will be good to me, in all my sin.
> Oh, *who* will?
> Sodium propionate, and thrill-
>   ing lecithin!
>
> They will be good to me,
> I *know* they will;
> But none so good as these
> Di-gly-cer-ides!'

I intoned the last line with a rattle of post-nasal drip which accidentally erupted into an almost operatic viscous fortissimo. A few young men, lolling over the sides of stationary convertibles as if they had been at sea without water for weeks, seemed to stare. I gave them my ferret-smile in which I bare both floors of teeth and then try to point them outwards while squinting my eyes. They winced and turned away.

When I reached my 'efficiency apartment' I slid my diglycerides, etc., into the miniature fridge which purred into life as if overjoyed at having something to cool. Just like the clay over where Venetia was buried. I decided to stay in town a little longer, just to give the lecithin, the sea, the funeral homes and whatever else a fair opportunity.

The days passed. The sun in its tedious way did its usual thing. I strolled the streets and watched the human flow; but there was more life in the birds and automobiles. I knew by now that something was growing upon me: not the city or the climate, but something foolish. There were some birds I am tempted to call bluebirds, which they were not. Their tails spread into a minor fan just as glossy and brocaded, in light blue on royal blue, as the most elaborate male vests. I thought up rich fantasies about riverboat gamblers and city bankers. Even the palm trees looked human: their trunks were single bandaged legs, swelling slightly where the bulk of the bandage came and slightly concave where the edge of one bandage met the edge of the next. It was as if the trunks were varicose and bound in elastic. Other trees, with their upper branches and all their foliage sawn off, looked like many-fingered agonizing hands planted to the wrist in rich Florida earth. Other trees still had irrelevant plumes or ferns sprouting from their tops as if a passing child, for a prank, had planted a few fairground feathers in the soft centre of the trunk.

Such were the humanities I made of the unhuman scene. I had to, confronted almost everywhere during my walks with appalling, discreet store-windows recommending burial above ground at less than the cost of interment, and extolling the secular and metaphysical dignity of above-ground chambers in spacious halls designed to last. The roof alone, I read, called for 25 tons of steel and 150 tons of concrete. Not only that: there was sufficient area to ensure permanence, which was a relief of sorts. I explored the throbbing streets, thought of Venetia in her trench, and allowed my mind to play on the formulas I had absorbed: 'The grave is no divider; it is the key to a new beginning.' The grave was a protractor, then. I thought of lovely golden maggots and twenty-one-year-old worms, the latter unrolling their body-saddles to make their own kind of love in Venetia's mouth. 'We have a variety of space to accommodate any desire,' I read; as if a baseball ground's acres of humus (or of prestressed mausoleum concrete) could rehabilitate the defunct hedonist. I dreamed of ardent widowers leaping to their ardent widows just because there was enough space to play in, and of TV cables or antennas being let into coffins just because there was enough sky above enough land.

Then I checked myself. They intended nothing like that at all, but some concept consonant with the air-conditioned chamber and the superiority over bronze, wood, stone and marble of prestressed concrete casks, proof against many röntgens. I could see a point, but began to miss it again when I reached belfry music, urn gardens, free pick-up, niches 'clean, dry, ventilated' (as if the niche were an aperture in the slimy body), and budget or de luxe burials. After thought, I resolved on a Pet Burial, not a human one. It was better all round. The earth would be mounded to ensure dry graves, I was told, and there would be a casket display during the belfry music. So I filled out the coupon on the Best Friend's Folder and entered myself as an old dog gone in the teeth, predominantly mastiff but some wolverine (an accident while picnicking), so please could I have two caskets and could the carcass be cut exactly in half, the forelegs in the concrete and the rear in the ivory. Each to be three feet in length with a slot for mail and a TV antenna disguised as a congeries of hyacinths.

I received an answer assuring me that my somewhat unusual request had, here, found a sympathetic ear and that predilections or forebodings bizarre to the busy, workaday world would find maximum co-operation when the day came. Death was no divider. . . . In short, I could rely on BF Happy Hunting Grounds: Weekdays, would I please note, were 8 to 5.30; Sundays by appointment. I thought of Venetia in the clay, in the trench.

Two days later I caught the northward jet, smoked all five of the free cigarettes provided, and arrived in the city during cool sunlight about four in the afternoon. I felt, all the way, as if her body was in the cargo compartment of the plane, waiting only until we landed to get up and stretch before preparing to dine together hand-in-hand, like two lovers, in the half-light at Michelle-and-Pierre's. But that was many centuries ago and hosts of 'sensible decisions', on which ruin and disaster are always based, had been made. Again, I noted my passive construction and I longed violently just to hear her use again an old endearment, 'Angel-Pangel' or exclaim, as she often used to, 'Right!' in a kind of champagne-thrilled assent to something I had said. At least, I consoled myself, *guilt* has not destroyed her as it did so many women, especially those nurtured by the church-fearing. No: Venetia had died from an escapade, just as I had; she suddenly; I at insufferable length.

I have learned a simple fact: as you get older, a negative personality begins to grow inside you which has much in common with everyone else who is ageing but refers to yourself hardly at all. That is why I now excel in transposition, one day becoming a Florida pelican (the 'Flying Suitcase') or a vermilion poinciana, the one with my long grey scabbard beak at rest on my well-combed chest feathers, and the other tossing in the suave Gulf winds like tree-trapped confetti. I sing to myself luxuriously, 'He snags the whiskers of his chin, The branches hold his beard.' And all the time the macaws in my head dispute the price of Anheuser Busch when I am anxious only that they should sing the joys of being gaudy and much photographed.

Another funeral had begun it: I mean it began what is so obviously wrong with me. I knew a man, Harry, who retired from teaching to settle in Saint Petersburg with his mongrel puppy and all the books he had accumulated but had never read. All he had to do was wipe up after the puppy and catch up on his reading: a neat, directed life with, for me, an almost liturgical flavour, demanding slogan or heraldic motto. But when he died suddenly, without pain, someone had to go and wipe up after the puppy until it was sold, keep turning the pages of the books until they too were sold, and of course see Harry buried, which his long-dead wife still alive in a mental home in California and his revulsed daughter, long since married to a real-estate man in Idaho, would never do. The wife would pray firmly for his agnosticism for fifteen minutes during the mental bagatelle of her institutional day (as she had done for the past fifteen years, according to Harry), and the daughter did pay for the last rite.

That night I asked for worms to take me too, for wood over my head and enclosing what was left of my breathing. I prepared myself for a prayer, but the words refused to recall themselves and I had no substitutes. Instead I sat up and put on the light, reached for the Bible and scanned it. As always, when looking for the last word, I hit on Revelation: 'Blessed are those who wash their robes, that they may have the right to the tree of life and that they may enter the city by the gates.' Keep clean; the cameramen are down at the gates. 'Outside are the dogs and sorcerers and fornicators and murderers and idolaters, and every one who loves and practises falsehood.' They always are; who will take them in? How shall I say farewell to her in scripture? These threatenings came from those who had not lived here below. But I found John's third letter, and the funeral came alive again.

'Beloved, I pray that all may go well with you and that you may be in health,' as the nostrils blew apart and the noble head returned to aboriginal pulp, in necessary transformation. 'I know that it is well with your soul'—knowing that it always was and that I will lie about anything to discover what you now know. I just could not imagine how it felt, or how it would feel if I were to arrive and find there is no communication after having lived through the life we have. Have had. 'For I greatly rejoiced when some of the brethren arrived and testified to the truth of your life,' meaning the bums who all, it seemed, had pictures of her from her famous days, clipped from magazines in their very distant past, and perhaps the only thing they had kept without ever showing it. I had never seen the bums weeping, but I had now, interspersing their shakes with hacking coughs and strange, childlike flicks of the hands. Miss you, now, having been lacking. The truth of your life by which you made up your agile mind, congealing it therefore, so that perhaps *it* was not hurt when you were banged out of this world in which the bums and I guard your kind. 'Beloved, it is a loyal thing you do when you render any service to the brethren, especially to strangers. . . .' Can you hear me, Venetia, because this is my excuse and your eternal reminder; I am too old to be fooled by my own perversions of religious metaphors, but I know that you are loyal although critical, and we did have all those times. My own, newly lost, these lines are vacuous tricks I play with prophets' runes. They twist, as does life. I have daffodils in mind, but it should be hyacinths: to intimates, as to strangers, for there is no dividing love. 'For they have set out for his sake and have accepted nothing from the heathen. So we ought to support such men, that we may be fellow workers in the truth.' They have accepted a few sardines and cans of soup, and to the truth are powerfully reconciled, as I am not. In helping them to swallow it, I hope myself to learn the angle of drinking. Miss you, have no food for you, had no food for you; am spent. Please forward my love to yourself. How they all stood, as if your coffin were in the room, among their whisky-fed flowers and empty cans. They lament, they have your picture in their indescribably filthy pockets. *I have written something to the church*, it says, but I have written about flowers and these will be eloquent for long after we are together. *So if I come, I will bring up what he is doing, prattling against me with evil words.* He is in the lingerie business now. Remember that special negligée we saved for years? Cerement. *And not content with that, he refuses to welcome the brethren, and also stops those who want to welcome them. . . .* I have little control, of men as of grief; spare me another of those long, deep, searching, agate, acute, longing, critical, sweeping, futile, magnificent looks. *I had much to write to you, but I would rather not write with pen and ink; I hope to see you soon, and we will talk together face to face.* Surely we have earned that, even if we have never earned anything else or even taken what we did not deserve. Miss you. Wish you had not been hurt.

I closed the book then, fast, as if to capture lightning. It was a long time since I had written a letter to her; I had never written a letter of that sort; I had never said out like that or found the text for a letter I could not mail. No amount of excess postage would carry that to where it ought to go. There should be some provision for such emergencies—the last mail —but there is none, and you have to fall back on praying; fall

back while praying. Good night, I am curbing myself and
resolving that I must not now abdicate from the thing which
I clung to while you were in despair of our living—good night,
I will discharge this obstinate burden and then discuss it all
in a peaceful rain-shelter, where the wind hits our hips while
we stand at awkward, affectionate old and middle age, like
lovers in deep, mouse-loud corn.

I went into the mattress-room and picked up a bottle from
the side of one of the divans. Daybeds, nightbeds, all-time
repose. To meet in paradise, with all flags out, with the wind
whipping them and the sun renewing the very marrow—that
is worth the soldiering through down here, among these
rotting anemones. Give me time and I will leap through them,
like a boy racing through the house with the filling and
bulging hose, anxious to reach the garden before the spurt
begins. Oh, she said, I wish you would be more careful, look!
the hose! It's ruining the carpet! We walk on carpets, anyway.

Edgar came to me, his shirt open and his bulk seeming
colossal in the reflected street-lights in the room.

'You want a drink, Papa? You take this.'

'I have one; just picked it up,' and I was whispering.

'You should get your sleep. You can't go without sleep,' as
if he had heard this somewhere, but didn't quite believe in it.

'I'll sleep, later; don't you worry,' I told him. 'I just felt I
needed a drink. It's been'—my stomach and throat contracted—'a day, a real day.'

Then he said it. 'We should give you sumpn. Sumpn you
could keep with you, so you wouldn't have to go lookin'.'

Had he, all along, meant a bottle? A flask? Or a death? I
said good night and returned to the bathroom, in which the
first of the sphincter-driven bums would arrive to make water
very quietly about seven or seven-thirty. I sat in bed and drank
what I had, a putrid-tasting rye. Then I lay there willing
myself to sleep, trying the superhuman effort of wriggling all
my toes, and then of counting sheep or lambs or bums. I had
no success until I tried, deep in my rumble of a faded voice,
the refrain of 'Frère Jacques, dormez-vous?' thinking of all the
children I had never had, would never have, contracted in the
almost impossible tenderness of an old, lamenting man on the
edge of bright discovery. Forgive me, I know hardly what I

do, not realizing even if the French song is a question or an imperative, and far from knowing the rest of it, hoping that this, like the cat-wash a child gives his ears, will suffice to attain the desired result. But no, go back upstairs and wash yourself properly, and behind the ears too! But I do not know, not just now, the rest of the song; it is precisely the *rest* in the song that I am seeking. Then I am walking along concrete alleyways with long skeins of cord trailing behind me, and as I walk I feel them clutched at, and there are forms holding on as I forge forwards, my eye on some violet light at the end of the canyon, my eyes set firm against Babylon into which I am trailing all my skeins and all the attached. We flow, like a wrecked fan or a wind-ripped umbrella, into the main street all blazing with neon, clanking with trucks and buses and the buzz of colliding men. The skeins are shaking and I have all I can do to negotiate the green lights, what with being tugged back by some and hurled forward by those who have panicked at the noise and have run across in disregard of the traffic. I tell them to calm down; I have given my life for them and I can hardly withdraw it now, having come this far and having offered this much.

Down below, a car-horn has jammed, and the continuous bray fractures the night, stimulating cats to copy. I have no all-comprehending boot to throw at horns and cats, but I have a small curse, such as: 'Let all the megaphonic stop.' It goes on, of course, and I reverse the small pillow. It is no use. I should not, of all nights, sleep on this one. Venetia is still, much below me now; but, being so vital, her aura has not dimmed yet and we are to keep watch, cat-eyed, for the last flicker of her vitality. I watch, and the only flickers I see are those from the neon signs. Venetia, you were better than that; it was not your flint or your fuel, it was the striker.

Over the days I came to terms; at least I came to terms with coming to terms, tearing up another of Lazarus's mail advertisements—the same one, riotous in black and white with exposed bosoms and painfully uncrossed legs. I too knew of sopping silk and the fury with a reluctant fastener. It was not so long ago, and there was no way of forgetting. I took my thoughts and drilled them; always gave them the eyes left, so that I should not think or see or remember. And the screaming

in the night became a part of my local nightmare; I called it
nightmare, weakening it with the very word. Sails of gleaming
turquoise bloomed against the sunsets; whole acres of silk,
warm and wet, ballooned over me like relics from some
gorgeous, rent balloon, with no basket visible, all in the
colossal casualness of life's order. Buttocks butted me, gently,
out of nowhere; pink sand filled the corners of my eyes; dark
earth made its way into my underwear; lipstick poured from
my nose; perfume floated up at me from the washbasin and
the stair-well; a long arm, downed and feathered, snaked
through space to encircle me, but never to hold me; ears
opened like flowers but seemed deaf; mouths opened, some
pink and others vaginal, but said nothing. I spoke back, in
uncouth vowels and stuttering consonants, but always into a
vast wall of zinc which sent my utterances carefully, accurately, back to me as I stood waiting over a vermouth or a
coffee for my reply. I said, 'Without love there is no contentment'; it came back, 'There is no contentment without love.'
'So what?' I cried. 'Make up your mind!'

Edgar the Time's hands were on my shoulders, shaking me;
no, I was shaking his hands, and he was strong as a wrestler.
I came to, shook my head and asked him for a drink. He let
go, as if expecting to be attacked, all this by moonlight, and
brought me water in the toothglass. 'Tell you something,' he
said, 'the cigar-holders came; we should hold a cigar party.'
I think he said that; it made sense; I *had* sent for those things,
and they were bound to come. It would be a luxury in that
room, to act and smell like bank directors for a few hours, and
I resolved to buy cigars by the hundred. They came in boxes
with the lid held down by a nail. I clung to the box of small
cigars; as to a talisman. Edgar fetched more water, and
switched on the light. I saw his rugged, used face attentive to
the flow and the angle of the glass; he let the water run until
it was truly cool. I drank again, gulping, clutching at the
blanket and wondering, suddenly, if Lacland was all right.
Edgar reassured me that Lacland was still sleeping, or seeming
to sleep; he had not left the bedroom since he arrived that
day. He was eating and he was visiting the bathroom during
the evening. (I wondered that I had never seen him; and then
I realized that each evening I had gone to play cards with the

bums.) I eventually sent Edgar away, hoping he would not say good night with his usual exhortation to no one in particular to buy me something. I need not have worried; he tip-toed out, closing the door and, from the sounds, checking on Lacland just in case. Then there was absolute silence and I tried to be with Venetia; I anatomized her, reached at myself (the rare virility of it) and abruptly snatched my hand away, she being dead and these being merely myths of memories; a cheat. It was not easy to look at the hand which had held, to feel the palm, and then to realize that one experience in a thousand simply could not be any more. I began to choke again, feeling sharp-teethed with error, and her voice did not sound. Not even the phantom of her face, or the presence of her far from exhausted electricity. Nothing but the rumble of the central heating and the fainter sounds from the street. Thank God, I thought, there is no window to this room. The dawn was misering itself out there, with snatched bits of land to reflect on, and bribed birds to sing hallelujah because an old planet had managed to survive again. In sleep, I died, unprotesting.

Lazarus

PAPA NICKO is getting old, not old in the way that you'd recognize him in the street as an old man, but very different from what he used to be. He was always full of wild ideas, sure enough, and this Lacland showed Pap at his worst. He dreams himself into situations which don't exist, and you have to tell lies in order to keep your own sanity while trying to be of use. Papa is like God: he has his own ways, and they do not bend. He held Lacland back instead of helping him forward. He tripped him up when he should have put out a hand to steady him. So do you wonder I grow dishonest? But I am not one to talk, not now, not after the way Lacland wrecked my wrestling career and tried to steal my girl; I am not too young myself, but I helped that man as best I knew how. I never bothered him and I never asked him a favour or anything. It was me, not Papa, who helped him to move up in society, gave him the books and the radio and even stole things from Papa to give to him. I got no thanks, anyway, because you never do, and you can squeal till the sun turns green but you won't get thanks, from old men or old bums, or young bums or God Himself. You try and you get your hand slapped back so fast it might have leprosy on it. So, after a while, you stop trying; you get on with your own business and leave the Laclands to their own cleverness. Those bums up there, they're no use to man or beast, and that Papa, well he is dying quietly, they say, and Lacland is living quietly. You can try only so hard to keep in contact with your friends, or your acquaintances, and then you lose your pride. You feel

you are committing a major crime if you hold up your head
or show your face, and so, because you have moved into a new
business, the sort of business which should interest any genuine
man, you mail them something just to show you haven't forgotten them, and they tear up what you send because I found
the pieces in the garbage when I was round there one day
photographing that broad with the jellies. She wouldn't take
money, she said, the broad, but she would take me; so now I
am a partner, a third share, in another occupation, you see,
and there is no telling where we shall stop—in business
success, I mean. But there is too much competition in this
game, and I can hardly be like Annie Eventuality and model
my own product. It is not easy, you see, and I have still been
trying to do my good share. But the harder you try the more
they hand you off. And those treacherous bums, you can buy
them liquor by the barrel and tell them things the sports
writers would give their eye-teeth for, and they just turn
about one day as if you have the disease of smallness, are too
small for their big company. You can't trust them, none of
them. Fickle as women, they cringe if you give them soup or
liquor, and then rip you to pieces once your back is turned.
I go to see the girl now, and photograph her, but I no longer
go upstairs where I am not wanted. You would think I was
a hound from hell, judging by the frosts I get. Or, rather, got,
for as I said I go there no longer. I could be of use, seeing how
frail Papa is and seeing how useless that Lacland is. But they
won't let a man be himself up there; enter in, and you too
are a bum. Well, I am no bum and I am no good shepherd
either; nor do I snore all day like Lacland. I do my best at the
business and if that is not enough for one small man, I don't
know what is. And that Venetia, that dead broad, stinking of
perfume and flashing her jewels, the rich pampered bitch, she
was the worst of them, turning them all against me on account
of my height, and look where she ended up, smashed to pieces
with some fast-talking executive on a dirty weekend. They
cannot fool me. I have just about had enough, what with
Mrs. P. moaning all day about that poor Mr. Lacland and
his bed still kept warm for him. You can go so far, and then,
when they ignore you, well, you just move off to where you
are appreciated. Solly White is just about the only man

around here with any drive, and he is too fond of the bottle, I think. All the same, you can talk to him and not be afraid he is going to grow moral or refined on you as you talk. Some bums they all are, I must say; some flock. One of these days I am going to fill some whisky bottles with pee and leave them around that room of theirs; one by the bed that Lacland took from Papa; one in Papa's bathroom, for good measure, and a few by the mattresses in the big room. And then I am going to wait with my camera and get some instant pictures of the fools as they spit out what they have never tasted before. In remembrance, from me.

It is a sad thing to see Papa going like that; he has been a good man in his time, and there are those who will miss him. He still tries, as you might imagine, but he is always wrong. What these bums need is a kick in the backside twice a day, and then they will know who their friends really are. I mean those who kick them in the backside. And that Rachel, well, she needs a good man and should stop hanging around those dives, selling all she has for whatever she can get. I recall she took up with some quack doctor who said he would give her a new face and even got her to bandage herself for treatments. Some bum treatment which makes her face that much hairier, in which she has a good start anyway. These bums. You never know what they will do next, except that it will be stupid and mean, and even dirty. I am the only one who earns his living, and that is the one fact they cannot stomach, it being a world of work away from them, and the sort of nightmare they have prayed never to have.

Last week I saw Papa and Lacland out in the street, just going out for a walk. It was quite warm but these two were wrapped up in overcoats and scarves, with rubbers on their feet in case it rained. Papa's face was white and thin, and you could see he hadn't had a haircut for months; the strands hung down on his coat collar and they looked none too clean. He shuffled like some zombie and his eyes were running. There was a button missing from his coat and his rubbers had broken so that they flapped away from his shoes as he walked. Lacland had on Papa's best coat and he walked like something back from the dead, with his shoulders round and his head bare, the hair uncombed and his face unshaven. There they were, like two old woman from one of the homes, sniffing at the air as if it would poison them, and flinching at the traffic which is never heavy on that street. They peered up and down wondering which way to go, which way was safest. And then they turned left, Lacland holding the old man's arm, at a very slow pace, as if they thought there were holes in the ground and might fall right through into hell. I very nearly whistled at them but decided not to; they weren't interested in me, and the shock might make them jump under some passing car. Off they went, weaving and wobbling, sometimes with their heads close together in talk and sometimes with their heads so far apart you would think each was trying to pretend he wasn't with the other, the shabbier one. It was as if the wind was blowing them down the street, not as if they were walking with their own legs and their own wills. Wherever they got to, they would get there by accident.

I was still there when they came back, and they looked tired out, with rings under their eyes and their faces like pastry. Very slow, slower than before, they moved up the street towards the brownstone, and glancing anxiously at the road as a car went by. Lacland still held Papa's arm and they came towards the door like crippled scouts in Indian country, looking around as if they expected arrows in the back, and pausing every now and then to consult each other about the weather or the wind or the air or the last thirty yards. They were like two slow-motion scarecrows, the sort of thing Mazzini would have cleaned up in a minute dead. If they had fallen into the gutter you would not have looked at them twice, but would have decided some bum had thrown his very old jacket and pants in there out of shame. So, on they come, their mouths open, gasping for air although they have not been very far and almost certainly have done nothing while there. That Lacland needs a good root at a girl; a change of oil. And Papa needs a good nurse he can tell his troubles to. I myself have heard enough of these, and I cannot say I ever believed half of them: he just liked a bit of attention. So they pause at the steps, and I am looking down on them from the window with this juicy bit from the boys' room plucking at my trousers to come in and talk to the boys; what, she says, can I find in the street that I can't find inside? She giggles then and tweaks my privates, the broad. Looking down at Papa's bald head is like looking down on somebody's bare kneecap with hair growing straggly at the sides of it. Lacland is going grey, and fast. They are still standing there with their hands in their pockets, stubbing their toes on the steps as if they think the steps are made of quicksand and might not let them through to death by suffocation. Then Lacland motions to Papa to go in first, but Papa refuses and motions to Lacland to go first. They both stand there motioning at each other, and there is no action whatsoever. This could go on for hours, I suppose, but suddenly Lacland links his arm into Papa's, and they start to enter together, side by side, and the last I see of them is them smiling mildly at each other, like two old women deciding who shall pour the tea.

I hear them go by, shuffling and talking slowly; Lacland in his strong voice, but running on reduced power, so that there is something very like a squeak, such as you get from a boy whose voice is breaking. Then Papa, in a voice that sounds like tissue paper being torn, with no body in it at all, as if he is being stifled by something he cannot see. Their footsteps come nearer, then stop; they have dropped something although I did not think they were carrying any parcel or bag. I heard a crash of something soft and papery on the floor outside this apartment, and then a sort of groan as if one of them, probably Lacland, was picking something up. Then a small chuckle and a wheezing laugh which is surely Papa's, and the footsteps—or rather the foot-shuffles, go away from me and I know they have begun to climb those stairs. I wonder what they dropped; it would have been one of those cheeses or cans of soup, I suppose. The way some people live, without any more hope or push than a slug under a stone. The bums are worried because they think Papa is ready to die, and they are probably right. But, then, he might last for years yet to keep them in their usual idleness and Lacland need not worry about losing his bed. One of these days I shall go up there again to see how things are, and to hell with the insults and the combined frosts of them all. A man has a right to see his fellow creatures, and there are still a few jokes I can tell, a few entertainments I can arrange without trying too hard. I would like to photograph them with my instant camera and just show them how lousy they all look in their filthy clothes in that filthy room. I might even take up a stack of the lingerie handouts, just to give the bums a kick. I will certainly slip a few bottles of pee to their bedsides one night and have the boys ask about the whisky the next day. Life can be so dull if you don't work something out to break the monotony. There is just one thing. All I would need would be a kind word, a sign of appreciation, and I would go up there, where they say I am not needed, and tell them exactly what I think of them. But you know how people are. If you speak the truth, being a friend, then you become their enemy. If you don't speak the truth, then you are their enemy anyway. One day I might try, but only on a day when I feel they will listen to me and not throw me out, as they did last time, before I have had a chance to dress or before I had said my piece. When you try too hard, they hate you; and when you try gently, they blame you for being half-hearted. A man as small as I am cannot win; but he can get some strong holds on their weak areas. And, as Papa said to me once, when you are walking alone in the dark you don't care what you stumble against if you have been walking alone for long enough. One night, then, they might stumble on me, or against me, and give me a decent chance by taking me back up to that room, with their foul breath being breathed at me, and their shaking arms helping me to struggle up the stairs, like Lacland from the basement, while their legs shuffle them forward, and the rest of the world looks on and says somebody should give them a home. They will stumble, sooner or later, against me or some dead cat, whether they are coming in or going out in the dark or in the daylight, whether they are coming in out of the rain or, as they seem to do quite often now, going out into the rain for the freshness of it. I shall bide my time and give them their own time. When they stumble against me they will find that house all the warmer to return to, or the rain the freshest and softest they have ever chosen to walk into.

AFTERWORD

Heretical Signs of Authorial Grace

Stylists are the heretics of the American literary world, where the density of the imagination is a weight not easily borne or tolerated. Underneath our ingrained mistrust of cerebral difficulty, there is a paranoid fear of artifice summed up by E.M. Cioran: "Every idolatry of style starts from the belief that reality is even more hollow than its verbal figuration, that the accent of the idea is worth more than the idea, a well-turned excuse more than a conviction, a skillful image more than an unconsidered explosion." Word spinners are sophistical solipsists, sinister magicians who saw reality—rather than language —in half. Deep down we suspect that stylists murder the universe: for the strut of a peacock paragraph they'd gleefully stab the world in the back.

Paul West is a high priest of style who doesn't profane the universe—he pays it sacral homage by expanding and deepening, rather than shrinking, its reaches. Relishing existence's kaleidoscopic highs and miasmic lows, his redemptive fictions embody the communal ideals of an anguished moral sensibility. West posits an indifferent cosmos, but rather than lapsing into surly gloom he launches into ecstasies: sensual epiphanies and infamies are fattened, rather than trimmed, by art's resurrections. As West states in the final chapter ("An Ist Among the Isms") of his 1965 literary study *The Wine of Absurdity*, existential and fantastical worlds need not collide:

> "...we have to remember that what we create through imagination is something we invent which exists independently of the world around us. Certainly it bears some resemblances to that world, but it is parallel without being identical."

In the same year, West published in England what he considers to be his first novel, *Tenement of Clay* (the writer rightly disowns his derivative rookie effort, *The Quality of Mercy*). The book's oneiric intensity and ethical earnestness more than match the thirty-five-year-old writer's convictions about the mysterious connections between mind, community, and the imagination. Drawing on strands from Joyce, Proust, and Céline, West uses a highly wrought language to mirror the baroque complexities of human consciousness, its poignant desire for wholeness, its dark flight toward fragmentation.

In *Tenement of Clay* the fledgling author plays patty-cake with the primal, transforming the tortured voices of New Babylon into music sensual and grotesque, sullen and graceful. As raucous (and plaintive) as a one-man band, *Tenement of Clay* strikes notes that run through the rest of the author's work—its prose poetry sounds the obscure depths of the unconscious. West said in a recent interview that his streams of dreams "...which appear to be the voices of those characters, are their covert, clandestine, underground, interior voices, not the voices they use to talk to people with." Yet this writer isn't your garden-variety romantic with metaphysical designs of grandeur, nor is he an absurdist who flattens the world for sadistic fun. The passionately Manichaean force of his imagination (while never less than heretical) is human rather than hierarchical, jumping from the dangerous and the voluptuous to the regenerative. West delights, without judging, in everything that *is*, because the ultimate reason for its existence is incomprehensible. The mystique of the imagination promotes a reverence for life, a catharsis attained by confrontation with what *The Wine of Absurdity* calls "life's tragic magic."

A meditation on modern urban life narrated by a midget wrestler, Pee Wee Lazarus, and a flophouse keeper, Papa Nick, *Tenement of Clay* hoists on West's "trapeze of language" his perennial themes—the fluidity of identity, the ambiguity of charity, the dangers of dreaming, the indifference of existence. The wordless innocent, Lacland, changes from a Rimbaud-quoting barbarian and savior of midget wrestling into a defender of innocence. Eventually he becomes a suicidal mummy under the yin/yang tutelage of Lazarus and Nick. The former is a fleshy imp of the perverse ("a trash-can of lust, a moral litter-bin, and anthropomorphic sink"), the latter an ineffectual intellectual do-gooder ("a turkeycock sublime") sinking into a fantasy world. Nick's exchange of a life of riches and learning for a life of charity (hosting a brownstone filled with "minor monsters") propels him into a permanent crisis of conscience, a muddle of bad faith. Papa Nick curses himself as a chameleonic freak: ringmaster and Doctor Frankenstein, paternal clown and would-be saint, nurse and satanic demiurge. He's the first of West's protean self-describers, a mind shooting out tangled skeins of irrational images and rational arguments.

While Lazarus seeks to destroy his mentor (like many of West's second-bananas, he plots against his benefactor), Nick fends off physical and spiritual decay with increasingly lush, though unmoored, imaginings. Death not only concentrates the mind in West's novels, it occasions gloriously unhinged song: "The grave was a protractor, then. I thought of lovely golden maggots and twenty-one-year-old worms, the latter unrolling their body-saddles to make their own kind of love in Venetia's mouth." Given the author's celebration of interiority, it's a mistake to see the novel as a satiric send-up of Casper Hauser, or a Horatio Alger story gone demented. As flummoxed then, as now, with West's chorus of being, admiring critics in 1965 didn't know what to make of a narrative about mangy down-and-outers as piteous and mythic as an Elizabethan black comedy, let alone its hallucinogenic prose— skipping from ripe surrealism to back alley deadpan—reminiscent of Samuel Beckett spiked with dashes of Damon Runyon. But seen from the perspective of West's later novels, *Tenement of Clay* becomes a tragicomedy about the metamorphosis of the imagination in the face of life's intractability, though West's fictions are not so much supreme as agonizingly provisional.

Papa Nick, Lazarus, and Lacland have been hurt into being — they're obsessed with self-invention to the point of excluding (though yearning for) connection. Pint-sized imperialists of the spirit, their egotism links West's vision of the unfettered but still imprisoning imagination with those of nineteenth-century American romancers and modern European fabulists, from Poe to Goytisolo. Thus, West's sympathy for the downtrodden and maimed springs not only from social conscience,* but from an artistic empathy with those who risk obliteration and madness, images of which, from Papa Nick's mine field and Lacland's embrace of

---

* "It is not communication with God that will save us," writes West in *The Wine of Absurdity*, "but communication—on levels of love, friendship, shared interest, principles stood by communally—with one another."

oblivion to Lazarus's dream of being a trapped buzz-fly, crowd *Tenement of Clay*.

Underlying West's complex vision of creation is a necessary link between art and the abyss—the muse as rattled divinity leading us out of nothingness. Papa Nick sees his nurturing of the hoboes as a kind of artistic Darwinism:

> "I was making the organic fit to withstand the inorganic; the sturdy buzz-fly able to fly confidently against the glass of any window, to rehearse and rehearse until one day the glass would be lowered and out he would sail into the corrupt ether. The creative will understand it was like watching the granite take shape under your hands or the paint develop lucid configurations on the canvas… Call it fidelity to the God-given; I am reluctant to dignify too much what I did."

Delusion and genius, hubris and inspiration, morality and self-indulgence are intertwined in a heterodox sacrament, a slapstick parody of art as evolution.

Tenement of Clay presents, in embryonic form, West's ongoing meditation on this mandala of creativity, madness, and stoic heroism. For West, inspiration consists in resisting the onslaught of experience, and *Tenement of Clay* is a keystone in his project of developing a conscience in the twentieth century. This is a quest whose meld of self-abnegation, art, and intimations of empathy is shared by writers whom we usually identify with oppressive conditions, for whom the very act of imagination is a sign of bravery. As the Russian poet Marina Tsevetaeva writes in her essay "Art in the Light of Conscience":

> "To let oneself be annihilated right down to the last atom, from the survival (resistance) of which will grow a world. For in this, this, this atom of resistance (resistivity) is the whole of mankind's chance of genius. Without it there is no genius—there is the crushed man who (it's the same man!) bursts the walls not only of Bedlam and Charentons but of the most well-ordered households too."

Those who are crushed (such as the bums in Papa Nick's care) are labeled "mad" or "depressed" or "lost." But those who survive, opposing what Tsevetaeva calls a "single unit of will, like a one in a row of zeros," are the geniuses, though their visions are redolent of apparent insanity, see-sawing between exhilaration and anomie, insight and ignominy. Lazarus's melancholic doodling in the bar ("And I just sat quietly, making circles in the spilled beer on the booth table, and quietly speeding up as if I were writing a long letter of letter "O"s to someone who would never read it. I rubbed my

finger faster and faster like a whirlpool right through the table…")
is replaced by Nick's rough-hewn drawing of a human being. An
imagined humanity resists the pull of a universal vacuum—an act
of irrational rebellion.

In this literary revolution, style is a dark sacrament, a heretical
sign of authorial grace. West's phantasmagoric sentences— seeth-
ing with speculation, metaphor, and emotion—school us in the
primal, the unredeemed, the enigmatic. *Tenement of Clay* proffers
brilliant set pieces (Nick's coffin-burning dream, Lazarus's buzz-
fly fantasy) that make it worth wading through the occasional
sermonette. The novelist has remarked that his early books were
too wrapped up in realism, in a documentary quality that later gave
way to the purely hallucinogenic. Ironically, *Tenement of Clay* isn't
freighted with an excess of realism so much as with an overload of
religious symbolism, an allegorical structure that sometimes viti-
ates its dadaesque delights and its theology of linguistic wizardry.
As an operatic tale of evolving comradeship as well as consciousness, *Tenement of Clay* proves that West's surrealistic conjuring
thrives on tension, a fruitful encounter with the external that has
made his recent experiments with the historical novel, such as
Rat Man of Paris and *The Women of Whitechapel and Jack the
Ripper*, indispensable examples of realism redeemed—reality
prestidigitated through a discovery of the subterranean links
between history and creativity, companionship and nihilism.

Tenement of Clay is West's first go at the imagination as an amoral
paradox, demonic as well as angelic. The lusty freedom of his art,
bounding over all that would limit humanity to dogma and slogans,
expresses a moral hunger for communication, for a sustaining
passion. At the beginning of his career, West provides an image of
love that, for all of its erotic panache, also seems gentle: "Through
revealing themselves in their love, lovers depend to an incalculable
extent on compassion; and when compassion arrives and flowers
in that context, then a miracle has happened; one of the few
miracles we can renew daily." The dank and evil earth out of which
West fashioned *Tenement of Clay's* urban hell has been reshaped
over the years: into the horrific statuary of *Alley Jaggers*, the rabid
ravings of *Caliban's Filibuster*, the dehumanizing squalor of *Rat Man
of Paris*, the diabolical empiricism of Victorian London in *The
Women of Whitechapel and Jack the Ripper*. Yet West's benedictive
architectonic—the metaphysical and emotional blueprint of a
master builder—remains the same, from the flophouse frame of

Tenement of Clay to the cathedral walls of his latest novel, *Love's Mansion.* Into these domiciles Paul West lovingly swooshes the mad breath of imaginative life.

BILL MARX
Cambridge, Mass.